FLORIDA SUNBURN

A Factual Fictional Journey of Redemption in The Sunshine State

Michael W. Newman

www.mwnlegacy.com

First Edition

ISBN: 978-1686644115

Dedication

This book would not have been possible without the patience and long-suffering of my lovely wife, Julia ("Pequeña"), my beautiful daughter, Emmannuela ("Marshmallow"), and my awesomely cool son, Mikey ("Fireplug"). They came back to the house when I quit screeching "Hey hey! I wrote a funny!" Picture my son also, coming in all sweaty and gassed from his martial arts class, giving me "that look" as I giggle uncontrollably hunched over behind the laptop screen. You know it - it's like "that look" from the Uber dude when you drank too much Peach Schnapps and threw up the powdered donuts in his backseat. Or "that look" from your homie when you get caught sneaking his last buffalo wing onto your plate on Super Bowl Sunday. I also get "that look" from my family when I say we are going to Kentucky instead of Miami for Spring Break. As Marshmallow says, "That look is cringeworthy!"

To my family… I so totally, totally, totally take back all those times when I was an incompetent husband and father to you three.

Please note, though, my dears, that nothing stinks more than the feeling I get when during a heated argument with one (or all) of you, I suddenly realize that I am wrong.

Okay, there is one thing worse than that. Whenever I smile and wave at another parent in your school parking lot during pick-up, only to realize that the other person is smiling and waving to the parent behind me. Big time bummer, I tell ya.

Introduction

Woo-oo-wee! Hot damn that church band can kick ass with "God's Not Dead"! Ain't it so, people? What's that, Reverend Mansfield? My language? Oh, shee-yit. My bad, my bad. Yeah, my language. What up with that anyway? My mother always said I shoulda never be let out in public. Hehehe... uhhh... *ahem* Egads. Tough crowd. I guess I picked the wrong weekend to start goin' to AA.... So. So! So, you may be wondering, why is this tan, hairy dude up here in front of the pulpit? Isn't it time for coffee and donuts? I gotta check Facebook! Personally I'd rather be at the gym on a Sunday mornin' punching a rhythm on the speedbag, but what're ya gonna do? My wife's been pushin' her take on me hard to tell you this cool testimony. Goin' against her take makes for a real nasty scene, right honey? Mmm-hmm. Okayyy. What I'm about to tell y'all is an incredible story of redemption. It will blow you away! Bigly! Manalive, it's a serious power-trip to be up on stage. My adrenaline is on carbonation. No, the story ain't mine. Jude Layden is my first cousin. One of many authentic Irish-American men in history. He's hard and scrappy with an Instagram-worthy bod. In the octagon, the man is wicked fast and impossible to predict. Outside a honky-tonk, he'll kick your sorry ass just for grins! And he ain't stupid. Jude knows what's what. Or, at least he thought he did. You know well what happens to that hard pride. It's a shuck, ya know it. Just like it always happens, the devil done showed up like no time ever before in Jude's life and sifted him like wheat. What I'm gonna tell ya is his side of the hot mess in Florida he got sucked into. And his then coming to the Lord Jesus, with the personal wounds and sins and all the crap in his life he effed up bad. I tell you what! The best part is, Jude got hisself right with Jesus. He stepped into the Presence of Glory, and got put into his

New Jerusalem. Hallelujah! Blessed be The Lord! I hope Jude's story impresses you, the members of this good congregation, just as it impressed me and my homies in Pastor Clemon's men's group. Shall you listen? Okay! Let's begin.

It was the hot summer of 2014. The hottest summer on NOAA record. And Baltimore's Big 100.3 played the hottest records all summer. The U.S. of A. was mourning the deaths of Michael Brown, Eric Garner, and my idol, Robin Williams. *shake my head* On the international scene Russia was fighting deep in the Ukraine, and ISIS was ramping up. I don't recall the exact date, but Obama was seen on the telly scouting the fourth hole with Tiger Woods at Pebble Beach. The bubble-headed bleach blonde newscaster noted the President's skilled expertise in multitasking his red-faced Presidential outrage with rapid-fire postings to Twitter on an iPhone in one hand while grabbing a five-iron off the golf cart with his other. Jude, pissed at God and all humanity that America's final move toward total oblivion would happen long before he was able to collect his due Social Security, took a seat by the telly in his mechanic's garage looking at the blood trickling from his finger. An injury which would have kept a regular guy from stepping into the cage for five rounds. Jude just laughed it off. He got serious and swore to hisself that the people made a dang big mistake with those last two Presidential elections. Facing Obama's image along with his captioned words on the telly and cursing all that is a good and right, Jude murmured a fair warning that if nothing was gonna change, then hells-a-poppin' that dank and broken Baltimore neighborhood around him was soon gonna be like the hot summer movie blockbuster, *The Purge....*

1 Hope and Change

Despite growing up to be a hard-boiled and hard-headed man without a devil's care, there were four things Jude Layden had learned from his boring and impulsive childhood. One, that a boy cannot play Scrabble with his family without at some point during the game getting slapped by his offended grandmother. Two, if he wanted his perpetually angry, dementia-crazed grandmother to curse out loud, all he had to do was suddenly yell, "BINGO!" Three, his family was so poor that when his single mother and three younger brothers and two sisters played Monopoly and passed *Go*, they collected food stamps. And finally, four, as evidenced by the dried blood and SpongeBob bandage on his right index finger, there is no way to fix a kid's bicycle without getting yourself seriously hurt.

Now, as he sat there in his custom car garage with a short stack of crinkled yellow collections notices on the desk crushed underneath his taut and muscular arms, he pulled the colorful prepaid *Jay Z* credit card out of his wallet, flicked it a couple of times, and glanced over at his daughter's still broken five-speed bike. The bike looked back at Jude, like a metal menace out of the Transformers movie in the corner of his shop office among the scattered loose car parts and greasy tools. Jude's daughter's birthday was just two days away, and being otherwise broke, he had promised Chloe to fix the bicycle as her present. With no money in his bank account, all he had was some loose change in the desk drawer and this Visa prepaid card he had found in the park by the swings, which he wanted to use to get Chloe a small grocery-store-made birthday cake and a few bottles of Mountain Dew soda.

Gingerly, but with concern, Jude randomly picked up a few collection notices.

Classics Auto Parts Supply – two months past due - $769.84

Toney's Oil & Fluids – ninety days past due - $588.64

Manila's Best Parts – one hundred twenty days past due - $456.29

Those were the yellow notices from people he was at least friends within the custom car business, the bills he could hope-to-God keep postponing almost indefinitely with just a friendly phone call explaining he was "onto his next trick-car job and the money would be coming in soon". But Jude knew better. Times were tough for him and his garage. He shook his head. It was all he could do right now to keep from crumpling up and throwing the yellow slips in the round basket in the corner and calling it a day.

Crows cawed annoyingly on the rooftop edges of the garage, their droppings leaving a slick mess in front of the building entrance no one bothered to clean up. A short, greasy Latina, as wide as she was tall, lumbered by the garage window with the forearm of a skinny four-year-old girl in her right hand and a foot-tall soda cup and straw in her left hand. The little girl was singing and tried to keep up but was repeatedly scolded by the puffing woman. A heavy designer leather purse dangled from the woman's shoulder and banged against the girl's head with each step. Jude became incensed at the poor little girl's misfortune, and he wanted to yell a belligerent crack at her mom out the window. But he hesitated, choosing instead to talk to himself in his mind.

Look at this horizontally-challenged chola. An amorphous blob of unidentifiable, unwanted species of gastropod. She is raising her daughter to be the same as her. It's a nonstop generational disaster. America is the bigger loser since abandoning its way in the 1950s. That human bowling ball there sees nothing wrong with the way she spends her food stamps on junk. The poor little girl has no father in her life. But she will have twelve play-daddies before she hits eighteen years. Her real daddy is wearing barrel-earrings and three hundred dollar Nike kicks.

Still living in his momma's basement. Unless he's in jail. Fat men don't go and marry women convicts. Just shows how screwed women are in the head. Some late-model women in America go through soy-boys like shoes and purses. Whose fault is it? Can a man live but with a woman? Better to walk away and save the assets. Or risk splitting it on a bad wager of the heart. It was Eve who was deceived first in the Garden of Eden. Here I am, millennia later, choking on the apple.

Nobody knew cars like Jude. In the Baltimore car circuits everyone called him the best mechanic to go for help with their classics and sports cars and tricked-out four-wheel drives. Creditors in the classic and muscle car trades liked him for his skilled craftsmanship and genuine personality. They gave him the money breaks he needed to keep the garage open during the what would-be, short-lived Obama recession that hit his Fells Point shop harder than a left turn in Baltimore rush hour traffic.

The bigger cash outflow that kept him awake at night and had him hanging over the financial edge was the bank loan on the high-value classic Italian restorations he couldn't seem to get completed. And then there was the garage's massive mortgage. All together that added up to an almost four grand outflow this and every month, with the bank's loan payment on the Italians already overdue a week and a half. Mr. Wright at the M&T Bank had already extended Jude's loan payments three times over the past year. Jude doubted Mr. Wright would be willing to allow another late payment. If the payment did not come into the bank soon, the Italian classics would most likely be repossessed. But that didn't faze Jude, for what does a Baltimore banker know about a classic Italian automobile? What could a beta-male banker do with a repossessed Italian jobbie?

If nothing else, Jude had his own well-known mechanic's expertise which he had learned in his grandfather's garage on his side. His winning smile and soft personality, too, got him out of tight jams. The postponement game he played with the bankers he had done before many times, and most times he had lost and paid the penalties on the loans. But for now, as he looked at all the potential work in his shop, he put it to himself he was going to be able to manage. He would make a go of it all weekend long, even if it took away time from his marriage and his daughter. Something he often swore he would never do, because his own father did it to him. *Dad knew struggle and secret battles with demons. He knew suffering. He lost himself - wasn't able to lift himself out of the depths. It was just too much for his weak soul. Du-u-ude. Revere him as one of the great men you learned about in-*

The cellphone in Jude's pocket buzzed. *Sweet Home Alabama* rang out.

"Oh shyte. It's the misses." He pulled the phone from his shirt pocket and looked at it. "Nope, it's worse. It's her mom. Do I answer it?"

>Ring<

"Do I answer it?"

>Ring<

>Ring<

>Ring<

"Oh heck… *Hola!* Gaylord's Mortuary, you stab 'em, we slab 'em."

"Wha'? Wha' you sayin' Jude? That no good. You are doing it again. When you gonna treat my daughter and Chloe right? Huh, when? Be a man."

"I guess you are not calling me for a hug and to sing Kumbaya, Mama Chela."

"Wha? *Carajo miercoles!*"

"Sorry, I don't speak taco," Jude deadpanned.

"Wha? You are overdrawn at the bank again. That what Margarita tell me. She have no money."

"It's all good, Mama Chela. Chloe has her birthday party this weekend and—"

"You need to get on it. Julio say you gotta put new lawn down. The lawn is died. The city gonna fine you lotta money."

"Hey, like my chest, grass doesn't grow on a playground," Jude laughed.

"Wha? What ev's. My daughter need money. I not gonna give it to her this time. You unnerstand that? You gotta present for

Chloe or do I need to get one for you? When you gonna be a man?"

"Can you stick with one complaint at a time? I am a man. Men can't verbally multitask like women. A present? We bought a new garbage disposal in June. I'm very proud of that."

"That no good. I tell you Julio—"

"Mama Chela, how are you really? Are you still struggling with depression?"

"I don't struggle with my depression. I have it down. Julio is no happy with you right now."

"Why should today be any different? Where is your husband? Hiding under the bedroom furniture?"

"Stop to talk and listen me now! It's the same with all you people! *Carajo!* Margarita never should—"

"All you people? Are you ashamed of my White Man's History? And there you have it, my people: racist minorities are convinced by the libs that minorities can't be racist."

"And you sexist! You no good for Margarita and Chloe!"

Jude sighed. "Racist and sexist have lost all meaning in lib America."

"I show you, you sexist. All *gringo* mens like you is sexist!"

"That's fartable."

"You *gringo* mens so bad! I no need to say it to Margarita or anybody! She and anybody know! She know all about you and that *chiquita* at the gym!"

"It doesn't matter anymore to keep bringing up a hoax. Once it gets said, a certain percentage of the uneducated will always believe it."

"Jude, I don't wanna get into with you, but you pissi—" she flatlined.

"Watch what you say! The limp vegans will pass a law to take away the heterosexuals' enumerated right to a cell phone. Then how will you shrew at me?"

"Dammit! I not giving her any money this time! Take care of your marriage, I tell you! Or the real man who replaces you will! *Carajo miercoles!*"

"Tsk tsk. Listen to that language. Are you a Catholic?" Jude stood up from his seat to take a better look at a classic red and white Corvette convertible passing slowly by the garage window. "What are you?"

"I angry, Jude! You no—!"

"Angry? Go to Mass and pray the Rosary for me, Mama Chela. Mary has nothing better to do today anyway. Ask her Son for more water into wine. That could be a good use of Jesus' time. Better than asking Him for the Raven's kicker to make a forty-three—"

>Click<

The red car kept going. Jude sunk back into his chair. *Good. The fattie hung up on me. So I won't get blamed for it this time.* He exhaled loudly and shook his head. *That woman is a luxury travel agent for guilt trips. The problem started when we gave them the right to vote.* He looked at his closed hand on the table. *Mother always said, a closed fist and a closed heart hold the same thing: darkness.* His sweaty palm slowly opened up. *Focus, my brother.*

With uncertainty about delivery in his mind, the master mechanic scanned the scattered works in progress in his garage. Three cars other than the Italians were in his shop that day for work. A 2005 Jeep Wrangler Sahara that was getting a custom lift kit for super swampers and a snorkel, to be finished with a zebra-style enamel paint job that would be completed by his business partner, Filiberto. An easy three grand and change to earn. The Jeep's owner was a high profiled asbestos claims lawyer and a regular with the garage. Jude assured the wealthy gentleman the Jeep would be ready before Monday, earning Jude the hefty profit to go straight into the business' bank account to cover the checks he would in a moment write for the shop's utilities. *The customer said he would pay me cash on Monday,* Jude thought to himself. *I can get the clams into the account immediately then before the checks clear. What is the risk of an overdraft? Actually pretty bad.* First, to be clear, Filiberto had to get the job on the Jeep done in time, and he had yet to show up that day in the garage. Even so, Jude had a strong faith in his partner to get the work on the Jeep done in time that weekend.

Next to the Jeep was a finished '69 Camaro V-8 that had needed its engine rebuilt with all new pistons, rings, and valves, and a new custom white top put on. That cool car, too, was of a wealthy gentleman, and it, too, would bring in some nice coin for all the work Jude himself put into it. Problem was, the customer said he was going to be late with the payment as his recently ex-wife just gave birth to their first newborn son out of town, but that when he would finally show up, it would be "with cold cash in hand". Four grand and change right there.

A third car dropped off by another customer was, as is known in vintage car restoration, 'a basket case' consisting of a re-welded frame from a '64 Land Rover holding a just rebuilt engine, axles, panels, two doors and only three windshields, with next to it a sundry of other parts in boxes that Jude wasn't even sure would be useful. A new clutch and transmission for it was on back order from the auto parts supplier waiting for it to arrive by boat from England. With the wait for that and other correct parts, that truck was many weeks, if not several months, away from being completed. The profits from this project would be a long time from coming as its owner, who was currently residing in Paris, France, had merely left the vehicle at the garage one evening with a hastily written note explaining his imminent departure across the pond at the arrival of sudden newfound fortune: the Maryland Lottery's newest millionaire. *Man,* thought Jude. *Why can't I ever win the lottery? I guess it is because I'm not stupid enough to waste my money on a ticket with a one in over forty-six million chance to win. Margarita wastes money on tickets. My wife. I wish she wouldn't do that.* The mechanic smacked his forehead. *Focus, brother.* He wondered if it was even a good idea to complete the Rover rather than just scrap it for parts and walk away with what profit he could split with the owner. That would probably be the best way to deal with the basket case.

Those three cars were as given palatable projects. The real potential money makers were the three classic Italian jobbies he borrowed for on his personal credit to rebuild and sell for big coin. Those, he was sure, would provide more than two years' mortgage payments and still leave enough over to take his lady, Margarita, and their Chloe down to Jost Van Dyke Island in the Caribbean for a few weeks. Jude had not been back to that formidable island in too many years. When he last set foot there he was just out of college, living in the Caribbean with an island girl from St.Thomas whose father owned a good-sized Tyannis sailing yacht. They sailed in to Jost for Foxy's New Year's Eve festivities. One of the best of the planet's many End of the Year celebrations.

Clearly cars were a passion for Jude, thanks to growing up in his father's and grandfather's garages in Milwaukee. But his heart was always wandering. After completing a degree in Econometrics at Beloit College, he travelled western civilization, stopping in Paris and Rome and London. Coming back to tour Mexico and Belize, and then The Virgin Islands – there the longest of his travels while on the St. Thomas hottie's yacht. When his tuition loans ran out, he found himself shacking up in Baltimore with another girl he met in the islands: a rich, waifish blonde with bright green eyes from Spain studying art history at Johns Hopkins. *Paloma!* He smiled to himself. She eventually left him for a John Hopkins lacrosse star headed to medical school when his lusts took him elsewhere and he wouldn't cough up a ring. Broke and for the moment tired of the travels, Jude crashed in Fells Point, first bartending at John Steven's and then opening the garage with Filiberto, a regular at the bar John Steven's and knew cars well.

Now, Jude lived with his lovely wife, Margarita, after a shot-gun wedding, and their lovely daughter, Chloe. Always, it seemed, there was never enough money to pay the bills at home on time. Even at the worst of financial straits, Jude came through and provided for his family by going back to bartending nights at John Steven's. Free boiled mussels and steamed shrimp with french fries to take home from the neighborhood dive fed his family well.

At the moment when Jude was staring off into space, thinking about the island of Jost, in walked a strange young fellow with curly short hair, a few brown pimples, and a scraggly beard with sideburns. He handed Jude an envelope with three hundred dollars cash in it, saying he would bring his Hemi 'Cuda to him for an oil and filter change in the next day or so, depending on his schedule which he didn't define clearly. The transaction was fast, and Jude wasn't paying attention to all the strange man said. It wasn't until the young man left when Jude realized who the young man reminded him of: Mr. Tumnus from *The Lion, The Witch, and The Wardrobe*, by C.S.Lewis. He scratched his head a moment in confusion but didn't think much of the situation. He was just happy to have the quick easy work and the cash in hand. The sealed envelope was placed in a drawer of his desk and left it there. *Focus, my brother.*

A few minutes later, in walked Hector. Tall, gaunt, and wiry, with a smarmy mustache and slicked back hair. Half black, half Latino, he had a simple past without education. Days of cheap weed and nights of dark rum in the barrios of Old San Juan, Puerto Rico until his mother sent him stateside to live with an uncle in East St. Louis who soon tired of his laziness and kicked his butt out of the house. A judge ran him out of town to Baltimore less than three months later. Jude met Hector by chance watching a bar fight erupt on North Street. Both men were anxious to jump in for the grins, but the police broke it up soon enough.

Though not a mechanic, Hector knew garages and their tools, and Jude needed a man like that in his shop for sundry gigs. For two months he sorted tools, swept and mopped, and picked out spare parts from large bins for reuse or resale. Then Hector got himself arrested for a minor drug possession charge. He only received one hundred and twenty dollars in gate money and a bus ticket, which he hocked, when he was let out of Maryland State Prison. Thinking Jude wouldn't take him back, he answered a Craigslist ad for a part-time job in a competitor's garage. Accused by the owner of stealing from the vending machine and hitting on the married blonde receptionist, Hector was summarily fired. He shamefully returned to Jude's garage begging to be taken back, which Jude did without a hassle. A friendly rumor gave Hector another side gig at Jack's Corned Beef restaurant down the street, both jobs paying just at the minimum wage of seven twenty-five an hour.

"Hey, Judes, mah main man. Wake up! Gots some work for me heah?" Hector asked. "I be needing some green before I gets me locked up, agin."

Jude ignored him, hands behind his head, dreaming more of Jost Van Dyke.

"Hey, you listenin'? I sez I gots a toaster that after only twelve slices done started burning mah bread. She ain't listenin' to me none neither."

"Don't worry. In prison your sex problems will be rectified. Pun intended."

"Wha dat?"

"Are you dense? It's an analogy. Pun intended."

"Where be Filiberto?"

"It's not my turn to watch him."

"That jack owes me eight bucks! I may pop him one!" Hector took himself to a fight stance, lifted his fists by his face and tucked his chin down. He led with his left foot fast steps. Forward. Back. Shimmying side to side.

"Please don't pop Berto. His face is too good looking to the ladies. I see that bruise under your eye hasn't healed."

"Hehehe. Riiight. I din't see yas at da studio last night. What up wit' dat? You not trainin' now?"

"Had no time. I changed the valves on the Bel Air."

"Maaan. I wuz watching that tight little scrapper, Vivek Nakarmi, sparrin' last night. The dude totally busted up this other guy with some serious hits," Hector kept shifting. "Totally busted up that guy. Rocked his world." With a step forward on his left foot, Hector kept his back straight and let loose a jab, "Pow!", then a cross, "Pow!" He paused a moment and relaxed his body and hands. "Nakarmi finished the sparrin' with no damages. With more trainin', Ima gonna be as tough and tight as him. He is gonna be on a card soon."

"I hear he is from Nepal. He learned to roll as a kid to protect himself from the bullies at school. It's why we fight. To save ourselves and save the world."

"Maybe Nakarmi be green, but he don't live his life by fear and wishes. You can see it in how he carries hisself sparring and around da mats. No deceit in his fight or his life. Hehehe... You know. I wuz thinkin'—"

"Careful. Don't hurt yourself."

"You know dat guy I be sharin' in his big apartment with?"

"The elderly homosexual fella from Bertha's Mussels? The guy who allows you to stay with him for free because you are good eye candy to his homo friends? That guy?"

"You knows I don't allow no gay old man to touch me. But dat don't stop da man from spying on me in the shower! If he do it agin, man, I gonna cancel his subscription to Life magazine!"

The shower voyeur was not Hector's only problem in life. His probation terms had so many trip wires attached hitting one could make a prison cell his next home for a long, long stretch. He was told to get a cell phone so the probation department could keep in touch. The parole officer mandated that he keep his phone on at all hours for 'spot checks', even if his employer at Jack's Corned Beef did not allow cell phones behind the cooks' line.

Then there were the random drug tests. Hector would get called and have four hours to make it to the test site downtown. But every test cost thirty-two dollars, plus four-fifty for the bus fare. And if he is called at work, he must leave work immediately. If he does not have the thirty-two dollars when he shows up for the test, they declare him a no-show. The tipping point for him was getting called three times that one week for tests and the demand that he pay his monthly court fine adjustment (forty-seven dollars) on the spot or be put back in prison. His employer at Jack's was already talking about firing him. With the time taken off work for the tests, his paycheck did not cover the drug tests and fine. Hector finally told his probation officer that he was dang tired of it, and just wanted to go back to prison to get his time done inside. His parole officer thus scheduled him to report back to prison one week from the following Monday.

"Dangit, Jude," said Hector, shaking his head and grabbing a broom. "I jes cannot catch me a break! I be heading for prison agin. Nuttin I cans do about it neither. Can't even shower in mah own home." Hector was forever sweaty and smelly due to the hot humid Baltimore summer.

"Go take a shower and change up and I'll give you some work to do. Yes, mon. Wonderful system we have here," Jude commented. "You're a convict with an EBT card. Tough life for you, *amigo,* but no sympathy from me. Stop breaking the law and looking for society to step up for you, Money."

"Hey! I ain't no regular criminal! I be a 'justice-challenged individual'! Aiiight? Know I be sayin'?"

"No, I don't know. I don't have the problems you have because I don't do stupid things that get me locked up. Lucky to be in Baltimore where the judge doesn't see your dark skin as a threat to society. Even though you're an accelerating burden to society that ain't gonna stop any time soon.

"I only gots three priors. None for distribution. I ain't no threat to nobody," Hector upturned his cheek. "The system's no fair to people of color. You is lucky cuz you is white."

"Used to be a Habitual Offender law down south. Black, white, magenta, color is whatever. Your multiple rap sheet priors for simple possession would have had you getting' straight up life with no parole. Now there's this teen kid in Baltimore who gets busted a fifth time shoplifting a bottle of Mad Dog from Circle-K. He's released by the liberal judge! Claiming the kid's crimes were done as 'an economic necessity'! That's American cultural norms today. Crime now pays. Prison pays. You're using my tax dollars to get three hots and a cot in prison. And you have the balls to whine about your sorry-assed life in this predominantly white society? Go look in a mirror to find the problem."

"A mirror, *eh*? My muthah told me all da time afore she died that all the Laws of Our Good God wuz a mirror. The Laws of

God done given are how's you sees your sinful self. But like a mirror, Laws only shows that you be dirty and can't clean ya none. The Laws of God can't even make ya clean in spirit none, neither."

"Yeah, yeah, so the televangelists tell me. You reek. For eff's sake, please take a dang shower before I have to open up another air freshener. Then go ahead and clean up the shop good, *comprende*? There is a heavy oil spill under the Jeep and a filled anti-freeze pan that need to be dealt with by the Camaro. And clean the dang bathroom, will ya, finally? Sheesh, man. Like you, it reeks to high heaven!"

"Watchin' Barrett-Jackson on *Speed* channel last night. When 'mericans gonna build good cars again, Judes?"

Jude pulled back the bandage on his finger. A spot of blood dripped down onto the desk. "Deep cut. Won't heal quickly. When we get right with the unions, activists, quotas, rules, regulations, taxes, licenses and the bloated U.S. government. While they are at it, they should do something about all the Latinos here. They are nothing but a drain. Can't even speak English with most o' them. Press two for English? Mexicans, Guatemalans, Salvadorians, Freakin' Ricans."

"Ohhh, that's mighty white of you!" Hector stared hard straight at Jude and nodded slowly. "Corn flake cracker!" He threw the broom down.

"Hey, Money, what did you say to me?! You need a bag of Cheetos and some purple drank? Here's some change. Run across the street to Smitty's convenience store and get me an orange soda out of the machine. Get yerself something, too."

Hector smugly grabbed the coins and sprinted across the empty street. From the window, Jude watched him. Hector checked that no one was looking and reached up the machine's chute to pull down two grape sodas. He smiled and wave at a cute chick going into Smitty's as he strutted boldly back across the street, with Jude's spare change jingling in his pocket.

Hector opened both soda cans and handed one to Jude.

Jude took a swig. "Where'd you learn to walk as a kid? Chickens in your backyard?"

"Mmm, aaah! Drury at the gym tells me I strut likes the only rooster in a hen house. So yeah."

"Drury knows how to fight good on his feet, but he can't take down nobody. He TKO'd Daniels in the ring two Fridays ago with a right hook to the temple. His classic strike. Daniels never saw it coming. He was gassed. Tried to take down Drury in the third with a wrestling move and let his hands drop. Open side left and BAM! Only one shot to the head. Daniels went down like a bag of sand. You missed a good fight. Daniels is tough. Drury is tougher. I've taken both down hard." Jude grinned and leaned forward. "Both of them could beat your ass under the clock. Maybe you and I should get in the cage sometime?"

"Mmm. I don't wanna hurt ya none. Hehehe. What's on TV?"

"A Hillary Clinton rally. Ain't she cute in her pastels? We're trying to have a civilization here," Jude threw up a hand in frustration. "And 'Cankles' there is blaming a right-wing conspiracy for her fat thighs.""

"Respect. Hillary Clinton gonna be our next president. No joke. Dat's a sure bet," Hector looked at the papers on Jude's desk. "You is sweatin' da bills agin."

"President Hillary Clinton. Can anything good come from Arkansas? Do you have any plans for the future if this garage goes belly up?"

"When I gets me out of mah times in prison, I wanna buy a used one-ton truck with money from mah uncle and starts haulin' junk from basements and garages. What should I gets for a truck?"

"Listen up: crack kills."

"No, seriously! Mah uncle in St. Louis is gonna sport me a truck. We gonna goes inta bidness."

"Best bet for what you need is a Ford F350 longbed. Otherwise, it's a Toyota I would recommend. Though it's quite a bit smaller. Best built and best customer service out there for losers like you. They always follow up on recalls on my wife's

Celica, and they do the repairs for free. That kind of commitment to their product buys a lot of customer loyalty. I've been to Barrett-Jackson twice, by the way."

Hector picked up a broom. "Yeah, so you done told me afore, but you e'er been to Pebble Beach Concourse?"

"Not my place to go. Nothing but rich little wankers who ride in limousines and fly in on G6's. All those dudes are driving up the cost of classics, which only fill their garages and never get driven. To buy one of the world's best road machines for storage and never drive it is lame to the rest of us car enthusiasts. Like marrying a hot showcase nymphomaniac and sleeping in separate bedrooms behind locked doors. Investment or not, it's just wrong. Cars are meant to be driven and enjoyed and to bring out your emotions, carbonate your arteries, create memories."

Jude turned the flat-screen television around to show Hector the *Speed* Channel show of *Top Gear*. It wasn't often that he allowed himself a free moment to watch the show, but today the show had on the Pagani Huayra, one of his favorite exotic cars. The Silicon Valley dealer on the show rented it out on a local track for five grand a thrill.

"Man, I would trade my left nut for just a ten-minute drive in that beauty. Look at that hapless loser in a helmet and racing seatbelts. He's got money, but that is all he's got. And dude is chilling slow at 125 miles an hour around that track. The dang Pagani can hit over 203 flat. That's hot. Too hot. He is probably ripping a hole in the seat with his puckered up butt cheeks."

"I agrees with ya. Dat car is da ballz, homie! Wowza."

"Most of 'em end up in the Middle East. World class supercars always end up in the Middle East. That's where the exotic-car money is. Saudi Arabia, Dubai, Qatar. If we could give up our addiction to their oil, they'd be screwed. Unless other countries start buying sand or eating dates in bulk. Let's build the Keystone Pipeline, and they'll be back riding on camels. It's sad, I say. Enzo Ferrari would never have built a car for clientele who treat their vehicles better than their women. Both are treated like property. But the women are prohibited from voting, owning real estate, divorcing, driving. Impotent incels in white robes and covered heads crossing the desert in top level hypercars. What a waste."

"Oil. Dat's why USA be fightin' all the time over there. We should make the peace wit' dem. But if not, they cans fights they own fights with each other."

"I heard on Fox News that Saudi Arabia may be going into Yemen any day now. I hope we don't get involved."

"You don't see no good news much about the world no more. Like nothing be happenin'."

"'Course used to be the news reported what happened and the people made an opinion. Now the news gives us their opinion and we have to decide if it happened. Let the Middle East countries start paying for the all the wars instead of us, and then maybe we can afford to buy fancy cars too."

"They payin' for the wars? Dream on, boss."

It's all a dream to me, Jude mumbled in his mind. I'm stuck in a bad marriage. Drowning in large bills. Earning small profits. And there's no upside to tomorrow. There is nothing in the shop but the Italian jobbies that will bring me enough coin to set me up. And those are months away. Where is Filiberto anyway? He should be painting the Jeep and working on the dang Italians. Five grand for a 200 miles per hour thrill around a track in my favorite car? Never happen for me. This garage could be foreclosed on any day now. What prospects would I have if it does? None. Master mechanics are out there all across America changing spare tires on the sides of highways for chump change. Every guy I know in blue-collar industry is on the edge of being unemployed. This Obama recession is killing my jam. Obama must intentionally be ruining the U.S. economy step by careful step. Are we 400 A.D. Rome? Bread and Circus has been replaced by SNAP and the Kardashians. Welcome to the new economy. Foreclosed houses are being bought by investors, and turned into Section 8 housing for 'single' mothers who get WIC and SNAP. Their criminal boyfriends like Hector here get Social Security Disability, and work under the table for cash. All that while us poor shmucks work legit jobs and get taxed to heck to pay for it.

"You know something? The last guy in America with a job better be making fourteen trillion dollars a year or we are seriously boned. What am I going to do about these dang bills. Hey, Money, I can't pay ya today, sorry. My wallet is ripped empty. And my bank account has gone out for therapy on post-traumatic stress disorder. It's like I'm permanently overdrawn. The bank has a picture of me behind the teller cage with a huge lemon on top of my head. I have to pay these bills in front of me somehow. Just can't cover you right now. This is so effed up. It's like I dropped acid at Beloit College, and I'm still waiting to come down."

At the crescendo of Jude's rant, his partner, Filiberto came waltzing in and slammed the side metal door with a loud thud. He was dressed sweetly in Versace pleated khaki pants and a sharp blue Brooks Brothers oxford with a leather belt and matching wing-tip shoes. In his arms he had two grocery sacks, one with a six-pack of Coronas and limes, and the other with beef jerky, Doritoes and corn nuts – 'man snacks', he called them.

"Phew! What stinks?" Berto whiffed.

"Hector. As usual."

"You working on your Bel Air's valves today? Need my help?"

"Not in those clothes, you can't help. But no longer necessary. I replaced the valve covers yesterday, no thanks to you. Took me all day. Where were you anyway? Off on some sexual reverie again? I thought you'd be in yesterday and today. We gotta get the Jeep done up this weekend."

"You watching *Top Gear*?" Filiberto demurred, handing Jude a Corona and a beef jerky. "It has the Pagani on today."

"Thanks, I needed that. Seeing it now. I'm wondering which oil sheikh is going to be the high bidder for the black one they are testing out today. That car screeches around the track like it has wings."

"Rich oil sheikhs? Again? Those guys have the coin."

"You know, 'Berto, we are due Monday on the garage's mortgage. And the Italian jobbies' loan is going to be two weeks late on Wednesday."

"Mmmhmm. No problem. Hector can cover it for us easily. Cantcha, Hector?" Filiberto smiled.

"Wha? Me? You be owing me eight bucks!" said Hector angrily heading towards the bathroom. "And Judes done told me he can't pay me none today, neither!"

"You want a tissue for your issue?" quirked Jude.

Hector turned around and took himself to bouncing a fight stance again. "Wanna see what Master Sugi done taught me? I be tight and rippin' you apart. Come on. Come at me. Pow!... Pow!"

"Got good news for you, cupcake," said Filiberto ripping open a pack of corn nuts.

"Indulge me then," Jude was not amused. "Let's blow it up for once, you and me, without a breakout fist-fight."

"Got someone who wants to take a good long look at the Bel Air if—"

"THE BEL AIR? Are you screwed?! No way! I'm not selling it! It belonged to my grandfather and then my father. They both loved that car more than life itself. I lost my virginity in that car!"

"So you've told me before. Found the girl while trolling the roller-skate rink during your high school years, didn't ya. You want to pay the bills you are yapping about? For this month, and surely the next six months. Until we get the Italians done up and sold. Think about selling the Bel Air. And anyways, the guy promises to sell it back to you if you want at a later time. Funny, the dude only wants it for sure for a short period of time," Filiberto winked.

"I am s'posed to believe that? Who is this miracle-money guy? Another friend of yours from Little Italy? The last guy who sold us a rehab car from Little Italy didn't tell us about the oily stains on the headrests."

"Funny, yo. Every man likes a little ass. No man likes a smart ass."

Jude bared his teeth to Filiberto.

"Not exactly a problem this time," said Filiberto "The miracle-money guy's name is Paco. He lives in Florida. South Beach and Sanibel Island. Next week is car week in South Beach. Then it will be car week in Fort Myers. Think about driving it down and entering it in the two classics' contests. If Paco likes it, you'll be so money. You have nothing to lose. Except a coupla weeks stuck on vacation in Flo-ree-da." He munched on some corn nuts.

"Except the car itself. This isn't a good weekend. Chloe's birthday is Sunday. Margarita will castrate me if I miss it. You know well we are already on rocky ground in our marriage as it is. Plus I'm busted and can't afford a vacation. Hector had to steal a soda for me. By the way, Hector, I HATE grape soda."

"Don' be hatin'" said Hector coming back from his shower with blue shop clothes on.

"Chillax," said Filiberto. "I'll cover all your vacation costs. Paco says you can stay with him. He has a chill house on the beach on Sanibel and a penthouse in South Beach. The Sanibel house is ten thousand square feet."

"Ten thousand? I lose my wife in thirteen-hundred. I'd spend all my time looking for things. Like doors. To get out."

"She's hiding in the bathroom like all women do. Twerking in South Beach party havens. Good bar scene at Doc Ford's on Sanibel. Jimmy Buffett on the jukebox and rum punch till you pass out. All on me."

"What? Heck, you cover the costs? Brah, you don't have any money! None at all! You prolly shoplifted them clothes you got on. I'll take what you're saying with a truckload of salt."

"I got money now," Filiberto grinned widely. "I have a new lady, and she is divorced with a huge alimony and says she will make me her kept man."

"Really? Where do you know this broad from?"

"You don't need to know about my sweets right now. Paco wants to see the car before the South Beach Rally on Tuesday. So you better leave sometime this weekend, if not tonight. Here's my girl's credit card."

"I'll prob'ly get pinched with this card being stolen."

"Trust me, it's all good. Here's a grand in twenties, too." He dropped an envelope on the desk in front of Jude.

"Holy Adam and Moses!" exclaimed Jude.

"Can I goes, too?" asked Hector enthusiastically.

"You're supposed to report to prison in a couple Mondays, if I recall correctly," said Filiberto.

"Don't really wanna go back inside. I'ma thinkin' to slips me out of the country to see my next chapter of days in Puerto Rico agin anyways. Much closer to get to there from Florida than here. I can't drive, though. My license gots revoked. Only can hitch a ride down witcha to Miami. From there I can makes mah own ways to gets to mah homeland."

"A grand in twenties," Jude flipped through the envelope in his left hand as he fumbled his cell phone out of a desk drawer. "If the dude only needs the car for a while, then why not? I'll just rent it to him."

"No dice. He wants to buy it, cupcake. There's more fun money if I keep sleeping with this toasty broad," smiled Filiberto. "She says I turn her on cuz I'm half-Latino, half-Italian."

Jude dialed his wife, Margarita, with one hand as he put together a gym bag with his cell phone charger and a few work shorts and t-shirts from the garage wardrobe with his other hand. She answered coldly. Little worked out of Jude's mouth to soften her up.

"Your honey, Megan, from the MMA studio called," she snapped. "Your credit card payment was declined. Again. She says you can't train until it's settled. Again. My mother says she spoke to you about the grass. Now you tell me you are off for Florida for no good reason? *Cerdo!*"

"I'm not a pig. I gotta do it, hon. Filiberto says there is a hot lead to buy my Bel Air. It will solve all our financial problems for a long time. Trust me, hon'. Put Chloe on, Rita."

"Hi daddy! How are you?"

"Chloe, sweetie, daddy is leaving for a week. I won't make it to your party, but when I get back I will buy you an iPod like you want. Okay?"

"You will! Really! An iPod! Mommy says they are too expensive! Really, an iPod? Did you fix my bicycle?"

"Uh, no, I didn't, baby. Not yet."

"Ohhh. It's okay, daddy. You can fix it when you come back. Mommy wants to talk with you. By the way, I had a blood test in school today. And guess what! I got an A-positive! That's like an A-plus, right daddy? I had to fill out an emergency form for the blood test. The paper said 'In emergency, please notify:'. So I put down 'please notify: doctor, my mommy would be no help'. Here's mommy again."

"I take it Chloe and I will have to go to my mother's for the week until you get back, since we have no money and no food in the house," Margarita spoke somberly into Jude's ear. "It seems we have this situation all the time, Jude. You running away from your problems. And me and Chloe stuck home alone with them. When the heck you gonna make it up to us?"

"This is why I stay single," said Berto.

"I heard dat," added Hector.

"Yeah, I know," Jude turned away. "Okay… Okay hon'… Your mother will take care of you just fine. She always does. Good woman she is. No, I didn't mean to insult her. Why does she think that? Pick up the *Jay Z* prepaid card here at the shop to get Chloe a cake. I'll leave it in the office desk drawer, top right side. There's still a good balance on it. And there's three hundred in cash in an envelope in the lower drawer—"

"Hey! You says you can't pay me none!" Hector groused.

Jude winked at Hector and pointed his index finger under up at his jaw, "Chin up, princess. No not you, hon'. Hector is here. I said I didn't mean you. Don't worry. I'll be back in no more than a week or two max and I will make it up to you and Chloe good. I promise." Margarita hung up on him coldly with no more words.

"Chillax, Jude," said Berto as he crunched on some more corn nuts. "It'll go smooth. Plus I'll paint the Jeep before Monday."

"Some weird pimply guy – except for the facial hair, I'm not too sure it was a guy, might be gender neutral - came in earlier to tell me he is bringing his Hemi to us for an oil and filter change tomorrow. So I expect you to be here all day working on the Jeep for when he shows. Got it?"

"Aces, *hombre*. My Italian mother has facial hair; you got something to say about that?"

"Nothing," Jude was dismayed.

"According to biology, each of us has a gender. Or maybe science only applies to global warming. Are you sure the pimply guy was a human being? Maybe he was species-less."

"More like Dr. Seuss - thing-one and thing-two. We can let McDonald's decide with the right gender Happy Meal toy."

Jude went to the Bel Air with his sack of clothes and turned on the Motorola AM radio. While he sat back waiting for Hector to join him, Bruce Springsteen plucking his guitar rang out loud and clear:

"Got a wife and kid in Baltimore, Jack.
I went out for a ride, and I never went back.
Like a river that don't know where it's flowin'.
I took a wrong turn and I just kept going.
Everybody's got a hungry heart.
Everybody's got a hungry heart.
Lay down your money and you play your part.
Everybody's got a hu-hu-hungry heart..."

Jude turned off the radio.

"You okay, Boss?" Hector consoled.

Jude lowered his head speaking softly, "It's the damndest shuck. A man can but see with his heart."

2 Driver's Seat

Jude and Hector hit the road in the Bel Air with the top down, the wind blowing through their hair, the all-AM radio switched onto WMAL to get the news. The mobile vagabonds watched the hot afternoon sun go down as they made their way south in the heavy traffic of first the Baltimore-Washington Parkway and then Highway I-95. High-speed congestion hit fast, with cars near bumper to bumper cruising along at 65 miles per hour and up. Not until past Richmond, Virginia still on I-95, did the traffic lighten. Only then did Jude take off his gold Ray Bans. Hector slipped into a nap for a while when they crossed into North Carolina, where the AM radio stations started playing only Jesus-tunes or baseball highlights.

Jude could drive a long, long time without rest, especially with the car's top down, but the Bel Air guzzled gasoline like a Key West fisherman drinks rum. At the many gas stops along I-95, through North Carolina, past the tacky *South of the Border* resort and its overpriced tourist garbage, and on into South Carolina and Georgia, the credit card from Filiberto's broad was working fine each time as they filled up the Bel Air with gasoline. None of the station attendants or cashiers bothered to question Jude about the name on the card, which read, "G. Alber, Esquire". Filiberto had told him the woman's home zip code and that was all that was needed each time to ring up a sale. *Berto knew what he was talking about. This card is a gem.* Jude thought each time. *Whoever G. Alber is.*

At one stop in a 7-eleven gas station convenience store on the Georgia-Florida border several hours past their departure time and on into the night to the wee hours of the next morning, Hector got hungry and tried to shoplift some man-snacks in his pants' pocket. Jude halted him briskly at the door and made him put them back.

"Look. There's a po-po car across the street. You wanna get us both locked up here in nowheresville? Be smart, man. Bubba in the big house would really like the candy-cane you got."

"But, Ima hungered," countered Hector.

"Then I'll buy you a sandwich. No crime on this trip. None. Understood?"

"Naw. Fogget it. Don' want no sandwich. These here Twinkies?"

"Those Twinkies have been on that shelf since you were swimming around in your daddy. Put 'em back. I'll get you a sandwich."

"I said I don' want no sandwich!"

"Then you'll get nothing and like it!"

Hector slumped his shoulders and walked back to the food aisle to dump his stolen stash.

While they were heading back to the Bel Air sitting at the gas pump, a pimple-faced but well-tanned upper-teenaged boy in crisp Religion jeans and a red Nautica shirt and flip-flops ambled alongside and asked where they were going.

"Miami," said Jude, opening the long door wide to get in the car. "South Beach."

"Miami? That rocks! They got good coke down there. That's why yer going, isn't it? For the coke, right? Ummm, you guys need some coke right now?"

"Diet or cherry?" asked Jude as he fired up the Bel Air.

"I got some pills if you want for your drive!" yelled the kid over the din of the engine. "Quality stuff! Adderal cheap!'

Jude waved the kid off casually. Then Jude watched the banger flip him off in frustration in the rear-view mirror. The Bel Air screeched away from the pump area and out to the pot-holed street headed back to I-95 South.

"Yo, you shouldn't oughta done that, homie," said Hector. "Back where I's from they be blowin' ya head off for dat jokin'." He held up his hand like a gun and pointed it at Jude. "POOM!"

"Everybody likes a little ass. Nobody likes a smart ass. So says Berto all the time. I get it. Sometimes I can't help myself," Jude laughed.

"You gonna be stone cold dead one day, big mon. Yo life right outta yo hands," Hector replied as he rolled up leaf tobacco into a ZigZag. "You *gringos* don't get it, does ya. It's called respectin' the gangbanger. Or dis him and you be dead."

Jude jerked the Bel Air abruptly over to the side of the road in front of several fast driving cars whose drivers blared their horns and swore at him.

"Get out. No, seriously, get the eff out of the dang car. Go back to your own God-forsaken land Puerto-wherever which I am sure is full of law-abiding citizens who don't participate in underage prostitution or drug runnings and gun cartels. Send me a postcard if you do make it there, pussycat."

"It's okay, boss," Hector recoiled. "I dint mean nothin'. It's all good."

"Dontcha see what's wrong with America?" Jude sighed as he pulled away from the edge of the road back into the rapid traffic. "That kid is popping Adderal to make himself feel better. All he read before he dropped out of high school was that book '*Heather Has Two Mommies*'. No discipline ever in his childhood. No chance he could cut it flipping burgers at Mickey D's or stocking shelves at Wally-world for minimum scratch. So he's selling cocaine and pharmaceuticals at a grungy gas station instead of working a steady job to pay for his high end designer-label clothes. He's thinking he's Puff Daddy or Kanye or somebody hot like that. Instead, in a few short years he'll be in jail. Or dead from a heroin overdose. It's happening all the time, all over America. This country is going down the sewer, I tell ya. I don't know what it will be like when Chloe gets older, and it scares me."

"Least Chloe gots a good daddy. Somethin' I never done had," said Hector sadly. "My parents were sep'rated and my daddy died on me. My mama done says over and over it was an accident at his job, but I don' know. I think it was murdah. My daddy done owed lotsa bad people money. Last time I saw daddy I was seven, wearin' a suit that dint fit me none. He was bein' carried out of the Cathedral in San Juan in a closed box by his bruthas from the countryside of Puerto Rico. One of ma daddy's bruthas slapped me when I asked if one of them was gonna live with me and my mutha now. Never saw them bruthas of my daddy again. And I never let a man set me straight again after dat. Mama did up cookin' for the neighbors during the day and strange men after dat at night to support all us. So don't accuse me none 'bout prostitution again! 'Kay, boss? Sore subject!"

Jude turned to look at Hector and nodded in quiet solemn agreement.

"But mama always said her and her family would serve da Lord. And I believe in dat."

"As for me, a Pastafarian," chided Jude. "I, too, will serve. As in serve the dinner piping hot and saucy. Our noodles, who art in colander, angel-hair be thy name. Thy pasta come, thy tomato sauce be yum. On top some freshly grated mozzarella and parmesan. Give us this day our garlic and cheesy bread. And forgive us our pepperonis, as we forgive those who go meatless. And lead us not into veganism, but deliver us some Papa John's pizza. For mine is the vermicelli, the meatball, and the marinara sauce, forever and ever. Ramen."

"Uncool, bro," scowled Hector with his arms folded. "You be dissin' our Lord."

"What are you thinking about?"

"How comes Wile E. Coyote never got the Road Runner? Not even once. C'mon man! He failed every time? And never gave up. That's some determination. We could learn from dat."

"Hect, bro, if you had a brain, you'd be dangerous."

Nothing more was said between the two men during the remaining time they drove the most perfect drive on the Eastern Seaboard: A1A down the length of mid-Florida to Miami. The AM radio picked up and held onto the strong signal from a local Latino station. Hector mumbled the words to some songs that he pretended to know.

With no food in the car and the two of them not having eaten since leaving Baltimore, Jude and Hector's stomachs rumbled. It was more important for Jude that he save the grand in twenties that Filiberto had given him just in case they caught trouble somehow during the trip. Jude knew well that long road trips such as this one inevitably catch dickens along the way from some rogue cop. Florida's cops did not mess around. If they did happen to get stopped and asked for I.D.'s, Hector would be tightened up quick and shoved into the back of a squad car with final destination unknown. This flip of cash from Filiberto he had was his only bargaining chip in case of that juggernaut. Jude was hoping that when they would for sure meet Paco in Miami as Filiberto promised, the dude would treat the two of them to a good meal in South Beach. He didn't let Hector know that, though. Hector complained often about having no food or drink. Jude only wanted to get to Miami before the sun started to set, and stopping for food now would take too much time.

It was six in the evening on a hot Saturday when they rolled into the hopping neon section of South Beach. They parked the Bel Air in front of the Delano Hotel, the one Madonna owns part of, on Collins Avenue and went inside to 'tap a kidney' and wash their hands and faces with cold water in the gilded bathroom. Finally Hector took the grip and asked Jude if he was going to get them some food.

"Nah," said Jude. "We ain't got time to eat. We gotta find this Paco dude first. Go outside and pull my phone from the glove compartment. Battery's probably dead by now. We'll have to find a place in this here Delano Hotel to charge it up and call Filiberto for the next step."

Jude plugged the phone into an outlet at the small Art Deco bar near the front door. Giving a heavy sigh at Hector's incessant pleading for food, Jude allowed him to order up some kind of quick appetizers, along with two Coronas with limes. After the Jamaican-jerk chicken wings came served at the bar for them, Jude laid a twenty on the counter while the barkeeper was flirting with a young Brazilian hottie wearing a pink thong and a mint green Juicy tanktop.

"Dang. Thas nize." scorched Hector as he gazed at the well-tanned girl.

Jude sidled up to the bar. "Whazyer name, tar-bender?"

"Ned'dog! If youz mah friend, then it's DogFamBam!"

"Cool. Tell me DogFamBam. You ever heard of a guy named Paco Roman here in South Beach?"

"Do you read the bible, man?!" asked the Jamaican. The hottie next to him batted her eyelashes slowly.

"No. Definitely not."

"Then you ain't mah friend! I will only answer to Ned'dog! Or 'your honor'!"

"Ah. Ok, 'your honor'. Ever met this guy Paco Roman?"

Ned'dog spoke low. "You wanna know?"

"Uh, yeah."

Ned'dog leaned over the bar. "You really wanna know?"

"Dang it, yes!"

"Gonna cost you twenty bucks." He held out his open palm to Jude.

"Forget it, jack. I might leave a good tip if you hang with me and tell me what I need to here."

"Z'okay with me." Ned'dog grabbed a dishrag and stepped away back to the girl. "I do' know nothing anyway. I is just a barman. Don't tell no secrets. Don't believe no lies."

In a few minutes the phone was partially charged. Jude called Filiberto to get Paco's number. With the number now written hastily on a moist hotel napkin, Jude called Paco. An answering machine picked up the line. The machine's message was in Spanish, English, and French, telling the caller not to leave a message or number but to call back. Jude left an impatient response anyway saying that he and Hector were seated at the bar by the front door at the Delano Hotel and wished to be called back as soon as possible.

"Dude's not answering. I left him a short message about where we are. Let's kick it a while out back of this hotel until I ring him again in a few minutes."

Jude and Hector took their Coronas and plate of Jamaican-jerk wings out through the open backdoor entrance, smiling when they saw the swimming pool with a metal floral-themed table and chair standing in the shallow end. In short order, they were stopped by a big Haitian orderly in a short-sleeved yellow polo shirt and khaki pants with a blue-tooth in his ear, who asked them if they were staying in the hotel.

"No, we aren't," Jude responded. "We just want to kick it some and take our shoes off to dip ankle-deep in the pool."

"Sorry," said the burly orderly in a heavy Creole accent. "Past these steps down is for guests of the hotel only. You'll have to go back to the bar."

Shaking their heads the two men with their beers and wings headed back to the bar.

"At least it's air-conditioned inside," quipped Jude. "The dang sun is about to set and it's still dang hot as blazes out."

They stepped back into the bar, and the Jamaican bartender swung around and said, "There you is! The bill's thirty-two dollahs and sixty-eight cents. What the 'nads, people!? You only left me a twinny!"

"Thirty-three bucks for two bottled imports and a paltry wing appetizer?" Jude was aghast.

"Yes, mon! Don' like it, don' be ordering it. But don't be horking me on the bill!"

"Dang, Hector, we shoulda gone low-rent. Can't imagine what Madonna sees in this place anyways. Art Deco is good and all, I guess. Dang overpriced though. So not worth it. Wonder how much the rooms rent for. Do I have to sacrifice my first-born son to get a room here?" he sarcastically joked as he dropped another twenty in a bar-puddle on the zinc counter in front of the barman.

"Fo'get it. You can't afford it, slice," said the bartender. He picked up the wet twenty and flung it onto the back counter.

Hector grabbed a stool at the bar to show he wasn't leaving until he finished eating his wings. Jude sheepishly took the stool next to him. The harsh silence between them was strong enough to send the barkeeper shuffling down to the end of the bar again to talk with the Brazilian babe. Not a minute later, Jude's phone rang.

"Layden here."

"You the guy with the Bel Air?" chirped the other end of the line.

"Yes. Yes, I am. You Paco? We're in South Beach."

"No, I'm Antoine. Antoine Fairy. As in Tinkerbell. You're in So-Be. So I heard. You're at the Delano. I will be there in twenty to thirty minutes. Say hello to DogFamBam at the bar for me. T.T.F.N."

>Click<

Jude looked up at Hector and then at the bartender. He shook his head in massive confusion.

"T.T.F.N. Ta-ta-for-now, says Tigger. Antoine will be here in twenty to thirty minutes," said Jude loud enough for the barkeeper to hear.

"An-twannne? Swell. The poof owes me two hundred fitty dollars. He better pay up when I see him," said the barkeep.

"Wha' for?" asked Hector with jerk sauce dripping down his chin.

"None yo' business!" replied the corn-rowed barman as he went back to his conversation with the Brazilian toast.

"Whassa poof anyways?"

"A homo, got it?!"

"The dude definitely is gay," said Jude to Hector. "Wonder what he has going on with our man, Paco. Filiberto says Paco is rich as all get out. Is Antoine the valet. Or a toy?"

Hector wiped wing sauce off his mouth and held up two fingers to the bartender who pretended not to see him.

"You don' mind if I has another plate, does ya, Jude?"

"No, heck, why not. We may be waiting here a while until the gay guy gets here. Man, I can't deal with gay men. Why women like gay men for best friends, I don't get. It's like they exchange clothes and secrets about having sex with men."

And wait the two men did! For the next three painful hours, Jude and Hector sat at the bar drinking Coronas. They complained and moaned loudly to one another about the long, blazingly hot ride down leaving them sweaty and smelly, the wait they were suffering now, and the problems both of them had left back in Baltimore. Beer round after beer round, they watched lovely young ladies dressed in skimpy bathing suits come in to talk to the bartender. Jude wondered where he and Hector were going to stay that night. Filiberto said Paco had a house on Sanibel and a South Beach pad. But according to Jude's GPS, the Sanibel fantasy island was hours away by car if Paco rejected them staying with him in South Beach. And for sure they couldn't leave the Bel Air outside in the Miami streets, Jude exclaimed with a furrowed brow to all who were within range. No way, he shouted out. Or it would certainly get jacked. For sure.

"Last call!" yelled the barkeeper even though Hector and Jude were the only remaining patrons in the bar at the end of the evening.

"Egads," said Jude. "We've been waitin' here for hours. I guess we're getting stood up by the Tinkerbell fairy. Wonder what we should do now."

"I'm the Tinkerbell fairy!" squealed a high voice from the door.

"Anyone hear a pinging sound? Oh, sorry, that's my gaydar going off," said Ned'dog derisively.

The gay man was indeed Antoine. A tall and frail, wimpish boy-man with deep facial wrinkles and heavy eyelids - though being only middle aged - and with wispy dyed-blond-streaked gray hair. He wore a tight fuchsia silk shirt and too-tight cut off blue jean shorts as he thus sashayed with hands low in the air across the hotel's white marble floor into the bar.

"Last call!" Antoine mocked. "Hello, Dog-Fam-Bam! Was it a good night for you, dearie? Hmmm?"

"You owe me two hunnerd fitty. I need it. Give it up now, yanker," countered Ned'dog. "Or bust yo' ass outta here!"

"Tsk! Tsk! Such attitude you have today, dearie!"

"Yeah, yeah. Blow me a kiss."

Antoine reached into his button-downed fuchsia shirt pocket, pulled out three crisp benjamins, dropped them on the counter in front of the barman, and reached out a limp hand for Jude to shake. Ned'dog swiped up the money with a cold stare and put it in his pants pocket.

"Thanks," said the keeper. "Next time I'm not gonna wait that long for it. It'll be yo' ass."

"Wench," said Antoine, still holding his limp hand out to Jude.

"Am I supposed to kiss your hand?" Jude questioned. "Where's Paco?"

"Paco is, shall we say, indisposed for the moment. He asked me to come here and help you out for the evening. As if I didn't have other bigger plans myself. But Paco comes first."

"Indisposed? What the heck? We've been here for hours! I called him hours ago when we arrived in South Beach! Where is he?"

"Of course he is at his cheeky high-rise duplex penthouse in South Pointe. Who is this lovely Latino man next to you? He's looks yummy!"

"That's Hector. Lay off him. He doesn't swing that way."

"No, mon. Sorry, I doesn't swing dat way," Hector said with his arms folded, turning his head away, careful not to upset Antoine and make a bad situation worse.

"Fine. A pity. Sorry, but Paco can't meet with you until tomorrow morning. He has made a reservation, complementary for you for a large suite facing the ocean at the Embassy Suites up Collins Avenue. Dinner and drinks all included on his tab as you so desire."

"Yee-haw doggy!" said Hector. "AWESOME! This Paco be f'real!"

"Good. I'm hungry and tired," said Jude. "Best thing I've heard all the blessed day."

"Then let's leave, shall we," floated Antoine. "Before DogDamBam here blushes red."

"You color blind as well as stupid? I'm black!" yelled Ned'dog. "Call me 'your high-holiness'!"

"Knock-knock," lilted Antoine.

"Um, whose there?" replied Jude.

"Jamaican!"

"Jamaican, who?"

"Jamaican me crazy, wench!" laughed Antoine again as he threw his head back.

"I've had enough. Let's want blow this juice bar. I'll drop a final tip to his holy-highness or whatever and we can cruise," said Jude.

"Finally," coughed Hector as he wiped his hands on a cloth napkin. "We gets somewheres."

"My, my, my dearie! Never, ever give a tip!" Antoine said rudely. "Why would anyone want to tip someone that was dumb enough to take such a low-paying job in the first place? I don't know where their hands have been, can't be sure about the cleanliness of their plates and silverware. Or their methods of how the food was stored and prepared. I don't know if the cooks in the back are coming down with a nasty cold, sneezing in what direction, picked their nose, dropped the food on the floor and then tossed it back on a plate, who hocked a snot-load into the food, spit in it, used the bathroom and didn't wash their hands, scratched their butts or groins or whatever grossness they engaged in. I don't EVER eat out. I doubt you would leave a tip let alone come back here to this oh-so-fine establishment knowing what when on between the times you ordered and were served. This bar of DogFamBam's is a petri dish of bacteria and disease."

Ned'dog got angrier. "I get tipped for my good face-to-face customer relations! If there isn't a clean plate back in the kitchen to serve the bar-food because the dishwasher is out the service entrance smoking a joint, who gets yelled at for the delay? I do, that's who! Now, get your butts out of da bar so I can clean up and get me home to my woman! Now!"

"Wench," said Antoine a third time. "So much for customer relations."

Jude and Hector walked out of the bar, with Antoine gliding behind them slowly singing a Lady Gaga song.

"*...Caught in a bad romance! Caught in a bad romance...*," he continued on and on repeatedly.

"Blazes it's still hot!" lamented Jude. "I'm all outta perspiration. Soon I'll be sweatin' blood."

Once outside, Hector pulled from his underpants an already opened pack of Newports and matches that he had stolen from the bartender's stash behind the counter when DogFamBam wasn't looking.

"Oh, dear! I do sayyy!" yelped Antoine in front of the Bel Air. "Such a nice automobile machine! But, dearie, what's with all the bird poop on the seats? Hehehe! How utterly gross and unattractive!"

He was right; there was bird poop messed up all over the seats. A lot of it. There were seagulls nesting on top of the Delano, and the line of sight for their droppings was the parking space right below where the Bel Air was located.

Jude grimaced and walked deliberately back into the Delano to get some paper towels from the bathroom. Ned'dog was at the sink shaving himself. He put down the razor. "You do' wanna hear it, but I'ma gonna say it anyways. Read the bible! Learn somethin'!" castigated the bartender. Jude flipped him off.

Hector leaned against the car and fingered a cigarette and lit up. Antoine leaned against the car next to him and tore up a parking ticket that hung on the windshield. He was humming a Katy Perry song. "*Sun-kissed skin so hot we'll melt your popsicle!*" He sang the same line again and again, winking at Hector.

When Jude came back out from the hotel, he had his phone to his ear.

"I'm sorry, but I don't think I have any relatives or other close personal connections to the Ministry of Oil in Nigeria. Yes, I'm pretty sure. If you'd like, though, you can transfer me the money through Western Union first and then I will send back the referral fees for-... What? Seventeen million dollars can't be sent across the ocean, like, through Western Union? Well, then, mail the paperwork to me and I will call the U.S. Consulate there to get it worked out with my bank. Yes... Mail it to me. What? Any and all paperwork you can provide and-... Yes. I will send you the referral money in return. Yes, of course... I do promise! Trust me! My address? 1600 Pennsylvania Avenue, Washington, D.C. 20001. Yes, it's a house, no apartment number. I look forward to getting the letter and documentation from you soon, my brother. Okay... Right... Yes... No need to thank me... No. You are the one giving me the money. I should be thanking you. By the way, I like your accent. Do you have a boyfriend?" >click< "Okay, the Nigerian criminal hung up on me."

"I tried the same idea one time with a political fundraiser who kept calling Paco's condominium," said Antoine. "But it became tiresome attempting to maintain a conversation on a fifth grade level so that she could understand it. It must be difficult to function in today's world when the only multi-syllable word you know is abortion."

"You vote Republican?" Jude was confused. "That doesn't compute."

"Not really. I'm actually a true Libertarian. I don't like to pay taxes to house marijuana felons when I believe that marijuana laws should be relaxed. Kind of like Paco who doesn't want to pay his property taxes because he doesn't have his own kids in the public school sys—"

"So's your three hunnerd payment to DogFamBam be for some of da weed. I gots it now," said Hector. "And I'm da one who goes to jail for a dime bag minor drug possession."

"-tem. Just gut and shut the IRS, the DOC, both DOE's, the EPA. The rest of the alphabet burdens this country has to suffer. They're all unconstitutional. Of course this administration won't be the change needed. It was put in place by Divine Right of Kings. So to go against it is sin."

"Don't want to pay your taxes?" conjectured Jude. "Then we'll install a pay-per-crap toilet in your home. Only two dollars fifty per dump. Need to have the streetlight turn green? Please deposit a buck to get you to the next light."

"Oh, you're a boor," waved Antoine casually. "To sum up, as a gay man I just want the same rights as—"

"Cans you tells me what is a gay right?" asked Hector.

"I don't think gay men want to be married. You just want society to give you the a-okay to be gay. To have the government sign off on it. Then you would feel better about yourselves. But if I protested for heterosexual rights, I'd be accused of rape. Enough of this garbage. Can we please go to the hotel now?" Jude was testy. "I'm hungry and I'm beat!"

"Yeah. I be hungry, too. Anto here's prolly a eunuch anyways."

"Patience, dearies," Antoine alighted. "No need to be in such a hectic rush. Can't you relax a brief moment and enjoy the ocean air?"

"I was on the road for twenty-one straight hours!" Jude took a step towards Antoine in anger. "I haven't slept in almost two days! I'm beat and I'm hungry!"

"Careful. Care-fulll," Antoine held up his loose open hands and put his left foot forward, bending his knees slightly. "I trained Muay Thai at Pentagon MMA. Where we train, fight, win, repeat."

"I don't want to fight you, fag! But I will if I have to! I'm not effing messing around!"

Antoine stepped his left foot back and lowered his hands. "Mmm, 'kayyy. Back to my original point. Taxation is criminal. Like both of you think—"

"You know what your problem is, Antoine? Let me tell you. It's physical and biological. It's called recto-cranial inversion. You have your head so far up your ass you're blind!"

"You know what, dearie? I don't have to justify myself to you. I'm still going to keep talking about my dreadful taxes. If it doesn't interest you, then—"

"It doesn't!"

"Well then, anyway, I have to come up with over six grand in property taxes to Hialeah every year. Second half of the year's payment is due October 17th. And yes, my body is chafed already."

"Well, we KNEW that!" Hector and Jude both said laughing.

3 The Man, Paco, Lives

The next morning at the break of dawn Jude left Hector in the hotel room to sleep off a heavy rum hangover while he went out for a run barefoot on the sand. All Florida beach-runners know it, and Jude soon learned well, you gotta keep your feet step by step firm just along the line where the Atlantic Ocean laps the beach. His gate was swift, firm and steady. The run was so pleasant and the air was so fresh that he lost his sense of distance before deciding to run back. Twelve untimed forties for windsprints followed by some quick two-minute bouts of shadow-boxing. Jabs, crosses, and other air-strike combos along the side of the cabana by the pool completed the strong-hearted training. A curious flock of seagulls landed near him to watch a moment before he stepped to the side quickly with a jab-jab-hook combo, sending the unnerved birds flying away. Some young girls by the pool squealed at seeing Jude's now-topless sweaty muscular body glisten in the morning sun. A Haitian schoolboy wearing a crisp and new *Tap-Out!* t-shirt came up to him with a pen and pad asking for his autograph.

"Are you Nate Diaz?" asked the elated middle-schooler.

"Naw. But I could probably take him down hard and put him to sleep. In the first round. On a good day. Assuming he wasn't high on the ganja," laughed Jude as he took the pad and pen. "I don't know why his trainer allows it. His lungs have to be getting punished from that bad stuff."

"A friend with weed is a friend indeed," spoke the boy. "The best part of the school day is getting baked during 3rd period before lunch. Then you go out in the courtyard and watch the fights break out."

Jude looked him in the eye a second. "If you do MMA, don't do drugs, kid. If nothing else, it gets you gassed too fast in the fight."

"Beer pong okay?" the boy genuinely smiled. Jude turned again and stared at him blankly a moment.

"...Whatever."

"Can you show me some good Ju Jitsu moves?"

"Can't we just take a selfie together?" Jude was getting testy.

"Summer school science teacher caught me with my phone and took it away until the summer's over. She said 'Why else would you be looking down at your crotch and smiling?'."

"Hmm. I see."

"You finished working out? I wanna watch some more shadow boxing. Momma's not finished cleaning the hotel rooms."

"Gads, kid, you are pushy, aren't ya? I am gassed. Done. I am getting' outta shape fast on this Florida trip. The way I am now, I'd be gassed pretty quick against most of the UFC lineup. Why you wanna watch me train?"

"Momma doesn't want me to watch pro fighting on Youtube," said the boy sadly. "So she blocked it."

"Why's that?" Jude finished putting his signature on the boy's pad with an added drawing of a muscular arm.

"She says it's pointless and pathetic. She says it's not good role modeling. Or something," the boy shrugged.

"Hmm. Your dad here?" Jude's eyebrow furrowed.

"Don't know who he is. I've never seen him. Momma doesn't talk about him." The kid took a slow step back in shame.

"Yeah. Or something." Jude took a deep breath and thought a moment. "Hold up your hands, kid. Are you orthodox or southpaw?" The boys put up his dukes but didn't answer the question. "Ok, let's try orthodox like me. Stand this way. Left foot forward. No, hold your hands higher, you are gonna block your face. Everyone has a plan until they get punched in the face. That's what Mike Tyson says."

"Who is Mike Tyshen?"

"Manalive, I am old. Ok, make a tight fist and throw your hand straight forward. Like this. Like a snap. Turn your body as you step with your left foot. That's it. Step. Turn your shoulder. Let your hand fly forward. Snap! Better. Knuckles tilted down. Only the first two knuckles make contact." Jude rubbed the boy's index and middle finger knuckles.

"Like this?" the boy threw out another jab.

"Not bad. Now hit my hand, don't worry, you won't hurt me. Snap it. Knuckles tilted down. Again. Harder! Again. Again. I'm your corner! Jab! Harder! Harder! Jab, jab, jab! Keep going! Like you are taking down that schoolyard bully! Snap!... Snap! In his face! Again! Again!... Good! Again! Again! Nice! Again!"

The young teen missed Jude's hand and hit him square in the chin. Jude didn't see it coming. "Oh for eff's… Way to dust my chin, kid."

The boy stopped punching and smiled weakly.

"Don't sweat it. Are you gassed, son?"

"Yeah-h-h. I mean no! Let's do some more, sir! It's my dream to fight pro! Do you think I can beat up this guy, Ned'dog? He is a bully. He's huge! He comes at me all the time to scares me. One time, he pushed me down and busted my knee open. Look." There was a small scar on the boy's left knee.

"Um, I think I've heard of this guy. He work in this hotel?"

"Yeah! And he is mean to my momma and me! Momma won't bring me here no more when he is working."

"Be smart. The first rule of MMA is no street fighting. Why? There are no rules, and street fighting ends careers before they start. So be smart. I will kick his ass for you."

"I want to be there and help! When?" the young boy got excited again. "Show me how to punch again. Snap! Snap! My dream is to go pro MMA."

Jude laughed, "You're a trip, kid. I hope I have a son like you someday. That's my dream. I gotta go. Here kid, catch." Jude tossed up his sweaty UFC rashguard t-shirt. "It's from Diaz himself."

"Oh-h! Wow! Thank you, sir!... Heyyy mo-o-m!" the boy hustled off, clutching his prizes tightly to his chest.

Jude's brow dropped. He rubbed his sore chin and silently

watched the boy run away. He knew well what life was like for a fatherless teen boy. It's about that kid's age, when life becomes the proverbial be-yotch for males. At that precarious age, a boy without a father comes to realize that all the other boys are his competition, and you have no choices but to man up and compete nonstop or wuss out and have no self-respect. Worse, the other boys' fathers have the backs of their boys, and will fight for them against you, too. Still worst of all, the fatherless boy's mama being a woman was no help to him in his struggles, though she may try hard. A fatherless teen boy learns fast he has no one at his back. He is on his own. The fights only gets tougher as he gets older. And lonelier. With more to lose. Society is no help. Adult men today are too selfish and all wrapped up in themselves with pride. Boys without fathers never get initiated into authentic manhood. They fail to launch, and fearfully keep themselves safe stuck in the basement with the Xbox and Taco Bell delivery. The single mother tells her scared fatherless son that he can grow up to be anything. What happens? He listens to her. And he grows up to be a failure at being real. His mother can't understand it and gets angry at him. So he hates women. No good adult man tells him how to treat a woman. And he goes off and rapes the girl who laughed and rejected him. He becomes beyond frustrated by the bullies he doesn't know how to fight, and shoots up his school. The fatherless boys are lonely for life. Life in prison. That stinging thought ended Jude's workout.

He was now finished displaying his physical fitness in front of the curious onlookers and returning to the hotel room to rouse Hector. Jude toiled a moment next to the poolside tiki bar to enjoy the sun streaking across his face and skin. Not much was showing yet, however in time a deep golden tan would enhance the cuts and lines of Jude's well-developed physique. He wasn't a vain guy. Yet being a fit man meant everything to Jude.

It would be the only time in Florida Jude was of mind to train.

At the resort's back entrance, a photo shoot was in progress. An unshaven portly Middle-Eastern man in a blue speedo stepped closer to have a look at the model in the barely-there white bathing suit. She was smiling widely and standing next to a placard of an aerial view of the resort as the photographer clicked rapidly. The Middle-Eastern man rubbed the top of his scalp and let out a low whistle.

"Don't o'jectify me cuz I'm a woman!" the buxom model held out a pointed finger. "I'm studying to be an ak-triss."

The Arab man took a step closer for a better look.

The blonde waved her hands. "Get away! You're not my type. I don't like men with more hair on their back than the top of their head. Good things apparently don't come in small packages," she pointed at the man's speedo.

"Hehehe," gurgled the stout man as he shuffled his bare feet on the hot concrete. "Where you from, miss?"

The girl's eyes lit up. "New Yawk! Brook-lyn!"

"Can I has your nummah? I to take you to my yacht this evening."

"Shewah! Where are YOU from?"

"Dubai!"

"I wasn't talkin' to you, Mr. Piggy," she turned her pointed finger to Jude and batted her eyelashes.

"Baltimore," said Jude.

"Never heard of it. Where's dat?" asked the babe in earnestness.

"They say happiness can't be bought. I see it can be rented cheap," Jude commented. "If I am dissatisfied after twenty minutes, can I return you slightly used? Like at Sears?"

"Are you all deaf?! I said don't o'jectify me cuz I'm a woman! Where is that rent-a-cop prick, Schylr, to handle this?! Levin, help me, DO something about this man!"

The cameraman shrugged and turned his camera back on to film the scene. "Honey-Tots don't get eggz-ited. You are starting to perspire."

"Lotta good you are, Levin! Help! Schylr, where are you! Hel-l-lp!" She waved her arms frantically. The hot girl's voice started to scratch.

Jude flexed his pectoral muscles. "Allow me everyone to dissect this drama you never knew you needed. The Muslim man here has not had such experiences before. In America, the women willingly go half-naked to have their picture taken and be paid well for it. They call it a career. The straight men are blamed for this behavior. The gay men take the pictures and exchange clothes with the women."

"I no gay. So she no sleep with me on my yacht?" queried the Arabian. "I can love her for many hours." He scratched below his groin.

"No Paki, you no lucky."

The woman's spoke again louder and her chest bounced up and down. "Thaz right! You two mens' audacious ploy to get me into bed isn't gonna work! You hear me?! Isn't! Gonna! Work!... SCHYLR!"

"Audacious? My, that's a big word for someone who dropped out of school at third grade to be featured on the Disney Channel full-time. My kid loves Dora the Explorer. Or perhaps with that thigh-gap Hello Kitty is more your style?"

She put her hands on her hips. "I AM STUDYING TO BE AN AK-TRISS! WHY IS EVERYONE LOOKING AT ME?! LEVIN, TURN OFF THE CAM-ERA! I DON'T CONSENT!"

"You should relish the complements. I doubt anyone will remember your name in six years. Those fun-bags will begin to sag, too. That's what happens with silicon."

"WHY YOU BASTARD! THESE ARE REAL, I WILL HAVE YOU."

"Ha! You've had more front end body work than a Lamborghini after a Collins Avenue accident."

"DON'T YOU DARE O'JECTIFY ME! THIS IS A JOB!" She pointed at her chest. "THIS IS MY JOB!"

The women in the audience giggled. All the men cheered.

Red-faced she turned around. "WHAT'RE YOU ALL LAUGHING AT?! I HATE YOU!"

Jude grinned. "It's all good, girl. Be an influencer. You need to toughen up if you want to be famous. Ignore the haters. They are just jealous. They don't score hits like you do. That thigh-gap? Works for you. It's a poster-board advertisement. A veritable 'Bunny Ranch South Beach – Now Open for Business' billboard. They oughta put yer pic up on A1A."

"Honey, ignore him. He just wantsta get in yer panties," smirked Levin the Cameraman.

"That's what I was thinkin'. But," said the befuddled babe tilting her head slowly side to side at Levin. "I wasn't shewah. I like him. He looks great standing there in the sun. What a package! You think he likes to be filmed? We got a new series comin' up, don't we?" She turned to Jude. "Mistah, whatsyer name? Do you have a job to go to?"

"It's a little late in the morning, Miss. I am an early proctologist. Inspecting the crack of dawn."

A hefty, hairy, sweaty bespectacled man in a red polo with the resort name and emblem on it and loose khaki shorts ran into the crowd panting. He waved a black clipboard and pen and shouted across the din of the people standing around. "Get off the damn Facebook, people, and get back to work! My SNAP food stamps aren't gonna pay for themselves!" Though the man wasn't addressing them, the cabana boy and tiki-bartenders instinctively put their smartphones in their pockets and pretended to be productive for a few minutes. "Yo! Honey-Tots, adjust the white postage stamps you're wearing! I'm not paying you and the photographer half a G an hour to hit on the clientele! Time check on the camera spots, Levin? Levin, right? You have a camera and a man-bun but can't answer when I call you? Let's take some pics! Strike a pose there, Honey. Yes with the screen. Pretend to be human, will ya!"

"Awright awreddy. You don't have to be so mean about it, Schylr. I got standards, ya know," She pouted her lips.

The man smiled. "If you wanted to promote my resort with that pout and rant, then you succeeded. Not the way I planned it, but no one here is going to forget it. People look for drama queens like you at places they go because life is dull. Jesus is watching us; the least we can do is make Him laugh. Nothing funnier to watch than drama from a scantily-dressed New Yawk woman in heels in Miami. Now shaddap and pose. Cameraman? Levin, I got that right? Take the pics before she gets sunburned and sues. Sun-splashed South Beach sees another day with drama. The partners are gonna love the free exposure. *briefly kisses the girl on the mouth* Sweet! Like money."

Jude left the scene to go back to the hotel room, shaking his head as he walked, still dripping sweat from the hot sun. *I shoulda said something and blasted all of them narcissists. But unlike Michelle Obama, I've got outrage fatigue. So much for the public school system and the perennial lie that a government education will pay your bills. President Obama doesn't send his daughters to public school. Now you know why. She doesn't know where Baltimore is? 'I'm studying to be an ak-triss!' She probably gets her thespian skills from watching lawyer ads begging for mesothelioma cases. That cream-dream girl makes more bucks selling her body in photos for Instagram than a middle-class lawyer. It all works for her until the bloom is off her rose. Welcome to Obama's America, where any activity you get paid for is called a job. Those legs pay well. Dang, I wimped out big time on the training this morning. What a wuss, I am. Older and slower by the day. Woo-oo wee! Hot damn, that chiquita Honey-Tots is fine! Men and teen boys will mouse-click over and over just to see better pics of her half-naked. Zuckerberg racks up his clams on the ads. The men and boys won't even remember the name of the resort. But they will remember Honey-Tot's name and look for her again. More and more ad clams for the billionaire Zuck. What a scam. That's how Zuck can buy a politician. It's a felony to give a poor guy my earned pocket money to buy his vote. But a liberal candidate can promise tax-payer money – stolen by placing an IRS gun to the shmuck's head - to the poor masses to buy their votes. Ain't our republic great? Honey-Tots wouldn't know a voting booth from a math classroom. Ask her about the electoral college, and she'll say it's got a good football team. I guess Obama wants a better life for his daughters. For sure Honey-Tots has got nude pics out there in cyberspace. They all do. Google Images is your friend. Just gotta remember to delete the browser history before the missus gets home from slinging the hash. Porn is a problem for some men. I used to have a problem with porn. Now it's free. That Honey-Tots was once some man's little girl with an innocent ballet recital. Look at her today. That's what she wants. For you to look at her, but not objectify her. Not the life I want for my Chloe. Ugh, I need to call home. Look at Hector there, curled up in the fetal position with a pillow, all schweepy. What a pansy.*

Jude whapped him with a pillow. "Yo! Wuss! Get yerself up and outta bed! We gotta move!"

"Wha-? Boss, where ya been?" said a sleepy Hector.

"Checking out Honey-Tots."

"Hehehe. Now I knows you lyin'. Honey-Tots be a well-known porn star. She be an 'ak-triss'. Hehehehayyy!" Hector sat up in the bed.

"You know of her?" Jude dropped his shorts and grabbed a used towel off the hotel room chair. He took a sniff. "This towel the cleanest one we got?"

Hector pulled the pillow over his face. "Shewah, I knows her!... But that's a little suss. I'd rather see her nekid than youz."

Jude and Hector muddled in the hotel lobby for an hour or so next to the coffee urn and croissant table, waiting to hear what the next move should be. Schylr and Honey-Tots walked through. She spied Jude and turned up her nose, babbling incoherently about the nerve of 'gross sex addicts' wherever she goes hitting on her. Schylr put his hand around her waist. "NO YOU DON"T!" She swatted his sliding hand away like he was only putting one-dollar bills into her G-string. "I'm not that easy today!" Schylr rubbed her shoulder and put his hand around her again. She relented with a soft coo. Almost at the end of the hallway, she turned slightly to the side and looked over her shoulder. Jude was caught by her eye. She winked at him and bit the tip of her finger with a giggle.

"Da-a-mn, boss. I hope you gonna tap that?" Hector whistled low. He stretched his arms over the back of the wing chair.

"Not a chance. Not even tempted. Salma Hayek in a hot tub couldn't knock over this tower of celibacy. I got nothin' but Margarita in the steamy walk-in shower on my mind."

"What's up with dat? You never cheated?"

"Never. Been tempted many a time. No woman ever got over on me to drop trou' after my marriage, and she's not gonna be the first. My dad was a serial adulterer. One of the demons that brought him down. That aint' my style to give up the pillar and play adventurous nookie-nookie, and as a result lose the family and assets. Margarita and Chloe are gonna think better of me than that. I wish both of them weren't always recording our conversations for training and quality purposes. What's that nasty attitude's adolescent son gonna say when his best friend pulls him aside in the locker room and says 'Hey, dude! Check this! I found your mom's south-mouth on PornHub!' Honey-Tots is gonna be welcomed to the PTA by the middle-school principal and all the fathers for all the wrong reasons."

"She be hot to trot. Dang sure I'd tap it." Hector put his elbows on his knees.

"I was all for premarital sex until Chloe was born. I'm betting most fathers see it the same way."

Hecctor whispered. "I'm sooo desperate."

"That's why you will always be single. I gave up those swinging ways in my 20s. That was totally my choice. The right way they claim is it's one man and one woman, though that wasn't my reasoning. It was all the AIDS and stuff goin' 'round that stopped me from tapping randomly."

"So? You got eyes? You don't even look? He-e-ell, I'd consider marryin' her."

Jude crossed his leg over the other. "I look. Not long. Always without letting my mind wander. Mechanics appreciate a good body. That Honey-Tots is not wife and mother material, which is what attracts me. It's a shuck - I always look to see if there's a diamond ring on the knuckle. Ok, so, she's hot. For today. A plastic mannequin would be more agreeable and fun. No plastic surgery will save her from biological reality. She passes by and you can't look away now. Wait a decade for her train to wreck. You won't be able to look away then. She'll be clown-freakish."

"Who's that dude she wit'?"

"Schylr. The resort's owner. The flavor of the month. Rich coffee, rich chocolate, rich grass-hole."

"Wondah what his wife think'."

"Apparently, from the looks of today, two things. One, when they are apart, his lonely wife spends more time wondering what he's thinking than he spends thinking. Two, when they are together, she's thinking 'no respect' because he wears skinny jeans and a flannel short-sleeve. She admits to no one that she is waiting for the corporate bonds to mature. Because he sure won't."

"It's always the dudes wit' da big money. Money and power. Wimmen's aphrodisiacs."

"Without men, Honey-Tots would graze thrice daily at the Golden Corral and drive unknowingly with expired tags and the emergency brake on."

"Hehehe. The weaker sex."

"Women call themselves the weaker sex. It's a ruse to blindside men. Which isn't hard because most of the time men think with their little head. Breast feeding notwithstanding, a woman's chest evolved over eons primarily to attract men's stupidity."

"We can' help it?"

"No. It's biology. Just like the peacocks."

Hector put his hands behind his head. "Wish I had known dat when I was youngah. Coulda saved me a whole lotta hassle in court. Thanks, boss."

Later Antoine met Jude and Hector outside the gate of the half-circle entrance to the luxurious South Pointe building in South Beach where Paco held his penthouse home and office. He handed them a parking pass and key fob to get into the underground lot. Jude drove the Bel Air around the half-circle and back into the street to go through the electronic iron-gate and enter the underground parking area. Instantly Jude and Hector were stunned by all the exotic automobile machinery.

"Awe-some! Billionaires got it hot!" said Hector. "Check out all dis fine metal!"

"Yeah," added Jude meandering through the lot. "You don't see Lamborghini Gallardos anywhere in Baltimore. And look here are two of them. With offsetting colors. Parked side by side. Owner and his wife? Or mistress. I think that is a McLaren. Says *hybrid* on it. That's a mistake. The British are the last ones who should be making a car that's half-electric. Lucas Electronics downright blew in my Triumph TR7 when I was a teenager. That Aston Martin over there probably cost over two hunnerd fifty large. Blow a tire in that, and it will run ya almost twelve-K to replace. We are talking big invoices. Did they get this rich from good schooling? No one teaches you how to be poor. Like me. I have the desire to be like these accomplished men. Not the ability. This is America. Is it my fault?"

Jude and Hector rejoined Antoine upstairs at the large stately glass double-door entrance to the decorative building. A squat Caribbean-native doorman with a slight island accent stood wearing a full regal uniform in the stifling heat to help anyone with luggage or to assist the rich elderly New England snowbirds and wealthy South Americans – mostly Brazilians - who lived there to get out of their cars in the semi-circle. Hector whipped out a quick cigarette which dropped ashes in front of the building as he smoked. The Caribbean porter walked over with a small black broom and dustpan to clean up Hector's scattered mess.

"Mr. Trump doesn't pay me enough for this job, Anto," said the doorman. "You guys agoin' up to see Mr. Paco?"

"Yes, we are indeed, Hippo. He's expecting us. If that awful Trump doesn't pay enough, ridicule the tyrant on Facebook until he does. Even Satan can't deal with scorn. I am perspiring here, people. Let's enter and be refreshed."

"Scorn. If I remember correctly, I believe Trump was the almost the Reform Party candidate for President in '99," Jude proffered. "He even proposed a 14.25% national wealth tax. The peacock megalomaniac has got some balls. If he ran for President today, he'd have more than his fifteen minutes of hate on Twitter from both parties."

"Oh, Trump won't run for president," said Antoine. "It is far beneath him to do so. He would rather sell overpriced timeshares in the Berkshires. Hahahahaha!"

Once inside the building, Jude felt the overpowering presence of money. Opulent fresh red and white roses were on the front desk that was as ornate as any first-class hotel's. Qirmen Persian oriental rugs, immaculately woven and now being vacuumed by a young Haitian maid, lay on the floors below the building's tenants' Ferragamo and Gucci sandals. In the corner were soft, luxuriant gilded-covered silken chairs and a low green marble-top table where a few dark-skinned men in cashmere-mink navy blue suits sat discussing West-African oil reserves and holding small mugs of gourmet Cuban coffee poured fresh from the wet bar near them. On the walls were assorted contemporary art works by artists whom Jude had never heard of. This made Antoine turn up his nose to explain that artworks were well known in Miami circles and in the upscale locales of Rio de Janeiro and Buenos Aires.

The gentle elevator up to Paco's penthouse duplex on the eighth floor was all mirrors with a chromed and leather bench seat. Both the elevator and the hallways were brightly lit with LEED-certified soft industrial lighting. The elevator porter was dressed to match the doorman who picked up Hector's cigarette mess outside.

Answering the door to Paco's condominium penthouse duplex was a young, vibrant and very tan Brazilian hottie wearing an almost-see-through silk sarapé and Jimmy Choo stilettos. She softly introduced herself as Vanité with her palms turned up . She was all smiles to see Antoine come in and kissed him gently on the cheek. Without saying a word, she led Antoine and the two Northerners through the over-four thousand square foot home. The sweetness in her giggled nervously when Hector told her she was "Dang! So fine. Like white wine. But you ain't mine!".

Paco was found within his office sitting in a high-back calfskin leather wing-chair behind a large mid-century mahogany desk, facing the windows overlooking the Atlantic with his back to the guests entering the room. He had a mixed drink full of ice in one hand and a gold chromed cordless phone receiver in the other. Two plasma TV's were hung on the wall to the far side of the desk. On one, a Fox News morning commentator was berating a seasoned Democrat politician about the Syrian conflict. On the other, CNBC showed the morning stock calls, with Jim Cramer saying he was bullish for the day. Still with his back turned, Paco spoke in broken English and Spanish into the phone.

"The doctor says you only have six months to live, grammy? *Creo que no.* He's been saying that to you for five years now. What? *No se.* What? Six months? That's not long enough for you? Then move to Detroit. I've been there. It will feel like ten years. What? No, I'm not being difficult. I just don't know what to tell you. I'm sorry, Nanoo… You're welcome, Nanoo… I'll send the car to pick you up and take you to the hairdressers tomorrow at 10am. Yes, I am sure you will still be here with us tomorrow. You will wake up fine and alive. You're welcome… Okay. I'll call you tomorrow evening after I speak with Valenton. Yes, I will speak to him and set him straight. Okay, Nanoo. Goodbye, grammy."

Antoine lowered his eyebrows and cleared his throat, "Ahem!"

"Sorry, gentlemen, but when my Nanoo calls everyone else gets put on hold. Now, what can I do for you? Buy you some real clothes?"

Jude and Hector quickly inspected their clothes with confusion.

"I'm very well aware of your Nanoo, Paco dearie. She will live until tomorrow, you say, but what if she doesn't? You didn't see her today, then. That would be a mistake."

Paco waved a hand and threw his head to the side. "No biggie."

"This is the chappy with the Bel Air. A very nice automobile. You'll agree when you see it. Hopefully the bird poop has been cleaned out of it—"

"It has!" said Jude.

Antoine cleared his throat again. "I assume you wanted me to have him park it in the underground lot, right? In your guest spot? See that on the screen? I heard about this earlier today. The Pope castigated Obama for jumping to a rash decision to have a military conflict with Russia in Syria. You know, Paco," Antoine's eyebrow arched. "I am sick of paying property taxes to Hialeah. So I'm getting serious about selling my pad and buying the houseboat to live on. If you'll help me out financially, that is."

"So you have told me before. Too many times. Come on in, good sirs," Paco offered. "No matter about the conflict with Russia in Syria. I wouldn't worry about it. Obama is higher than Pope Francis. Everyone knows that. Maybe not if John Paul the Second were still with us."

"Refer to Greek tragedy for illuminating parallels. Let's make this quick," said Jude. "How much you offering me for the Bel Air? Come see the car. It's pristine. Even virginal. Test drive it if you wish. I don't like to have my time wasted. As I am sure you don't either."

Hector pulled a cigarette from his pack of Newports.

"Please smoke out on the balcony, my good man," said Paco as he turned a half-circle in his chair. "Smoking's a gawd-awful expensive habit. Marijuana is more expensive, and makes you a financial loser. That lowly cuck Ensminger at the building's front desk is always complaining about being down to his last dollar before his paycheck comes. Beggin' me for a tenner in the tip jar every Friday. Yet he hangs out in back of the service entrance smoking a spliff at any free moment he has. Just getting' high and listening to Bob Marley. Maybe that's no so bad on second thought. Beats making sandwiches for a living.... As we were discussing money, Antooo, before Nanoo called, I was going through our house account bank statement," he held up a white bank sheet. "What's with the sixty-four or so ATM withdrawals all in one place in three months?"

"Well, Paco, dearie, I will not bore you with the details about my proclivities at the drag strip clubs. But let's just say it wasn't frivolous spending. Hehehehe!"

"Look!" interjected Jude. "You want to come see the car or you want to b.s. all morning? What's your interest in my baby anyway?"

"I want you to show it at the South Beach classics on Wednesday. After that, I'll take it. All cash for you in low-denomination bills."

"What price are we talking about here?"

"Dat car not gonna win no prizes, Jude," whispered Hector.

"Shut up!" bellowed Jude. "We'll stick around until the show is over if you cover our hotel—"

"Done!" reacted Paco.

"-But if you pass on the car, then, I'm gonna be ripped."

"So I see," said Paco turning his chair to the other side. "By the way, you are both sweating on my genuine teak floors."

"It's ten thousand degrees out there in the heat," said Jude.

"And if I want you to show the vehicle at the Fort Myers Classics as well? Can you stick around for that? I'll treat you to my guest house on Sanibel for your stay there. For as long as you so wish."

"Depends," Jude took a step forward. "Are you sure we're talking an all-cash buy? I can see you can afford it. But why go for my car? From so far away?"

"You are friends with Filiberto. I owe him a favor. Actually, several favors. He claims your garage in Baltimore is having money problems, and I'd like to help, if I can. I don't hand out money, but I do buy nice things as you can see. Look around my space. I like nice things. You met my Vanité. One of my finest objects, she is."

"Isn't she a bit young for you?"

"A man is as young as the woman he feels. Can I get you a drink? Let's sit out on a balcony. There's three of them to choose from. Wrap around. Choose one to relax on. I'll be with you all in a short moment. I still have a few calls to make first." Paco turned his back to the men.

"The jet-tub Jacuzzi on the balcony is fun!" Antoine remarked. "Maybe we can all jump in and get to know each other better. Woohoo!"

"We don't have swimsuits," Jude was testy. "And I'm not getting in a Jacuzzi with you to check out my package. That's for dang sure."

Paco turned back around with his phone in hand. "Ah, ha. Hmmm. Would you please excuse me? Antoine, make yourself useful and fire up these fine gentlemen some cocktails. Anyone like Pusser's rum? I'm a Bushmills 1608 Scotch whisky drinker normally. But today I felt like a mango daiquiri."

"It's eight-forty-five in the morning!" Jude was flabbergasted.

"And you're in South Beach," retorted Paco. "Not Baltimore. Take a chill-pill. Lighten up and enjoy yourself. Even alcoholics like me and your friend here can enjoy SoBe."

"Yeah, bruthah, lighten up!" smiled Hector. "Gots any tequila, *hombre*?"

"Better brands than what you are used to tippling, *hombre*."

Jude shrugged, and he and Hector were led by Antoine through the glass and steel sliding doors onto the balcony facing the Atlantic. A large eight-person Jacuzzi sat on the side-deck. Large white metal glass-topped tables with matching enamel etched seats awaited their presence.

"Man," said Hector. "This condo is da ballz. Wha' you think he drop for it?"

"Money to burn means money to earn," Jude shook his head. "No idea. But based on his accent and his rich casual attire, I'm thinking he didn't make his money the old-fashioned way by earning it. Something doesn't add up about this dude. He keeps saying he wants to buy the car, but won't bother to come see it or tell me a price. I don't get it. And only after it enters a second rate classics show? What's up with that?"

"I don' know for sure, man. Thinks the guy is illegit?"

"I don't know. But I am curious which of the exotics in the parking garage are his. If he has thoroughbred stallions in the stable, what's he need with my mare?"

"Dunno bro. He gots a big statue of the Virgin Mary. Didja see it?"

"Yeah. Usually guys like him with money spend a lot on art. But not religious art. Must be his Spanish heritage. Or Catholic guilt. I fail to see how an ivory statue of the Virgin Mary distills your soul after you've raped the masses. But to each his own folly. Money, money, money."

Hector grabbed a folded beach towel lying on the back of a metal chair and wiped the sweat off his brow. Antoine came outside shortly after and set down two cocktails in Collins glasses and a pitcher with more of the same mixed drink on the white steel table where Jude and Hector were seated.

"I thought we was gonna be drinkin' tequila?" whined Hector.

"You will drink what I bring you, dearie," Antoine responded flatly.

Vanité followed closely behind with a tray she brought forth holding a plate of sliced and diced citrus fruits and grapes and two open cups of vanilla Greek yogurt. She lilted a giggle when Hector smiled widely at her, and then quietly excused herself.

"Dang. She be fiiiiine," Hector marveled.

"There, gentlemen," said Antoine. "All nice and settled in for the good morning. That should serve you well until lunchtime. At which time I will fire up the grill for some Kobe ground beef burgers for you all to enjoy. That's Paco's favorite lunch. A gourmet burger with homemade avocado dressing. For *moi,* I don't eat any meat. A burger would be the last thing on my menu even if I were starving. My system would kick it back as if it were roadkill."

"Then you can eat dis here yogurt," said Hector derisively. "Real men don' eat no yogurt."

"Very well. I don't wish to insult you any more than I already have. Paco wouldn't have it. I will just throw… them… away," he fluffed. "You will wait for the gross red meat for lunch, I do assume, yes? How dis-*gusting*!"

"So? You don't eat meat," Jude said. "Do you think you are morally superior? Meat allowed our brains the fat and protein needed to evolve. Or did they not teach you that at Berkeley? Vegetarians are literally making mankind stupider. Good job on that."

"Ken youse order us a pizza or sumpin'?" Hector asked sheepishly.

"Better ingredients. Better pizza. Papa John's?" Antoine added.

"Papa John's Pizza. That motto's a vile sin!" said Jude.

"If it's a sin, what is *I'm with her 2016?"*

"That depends on what your meaning of 'is' is," redirected Jude.

"Well bully for you, sir! Now, gentlemen, if you would give me leave, I am going to partake in some grocery shopping. I will be back just before noon to prepare lunch. Paco will be off the phone in a moment. He's talking to his personal banker at Goldman. The money-man is jetting in to Miami tomorrow on a private G4. And you know what they say about bankers. When they take Viagra, they grow taller. Bwahahahaha! I mean really. Did Jesus hate anyone? Certainly not the gays of his time like Herod and Pilate. He just condemned the bankers in the Temple," Antoine quipped. "Don't you just hate Jewish bankers?"

"Not really. I might really be an anti-anti-semite."

"If I had Paco's money in the bank, I'd be helping the poor and the homeless vets right here in Southern Florida as Jesus did in His time. But Paco is such a brute. A tight-fisted manimal."

"No, you wouldn't," said Jude. "You're doing nothing about the homeless here in Miami or anywhere else right now. Why would you completely change with sudden riches? You know you wouldn't. Money won't change who you are. It only amplifies your character."

"You hate me because I am gay, don't you!" Antoine put his hands on his hips.

"I don't hate gays," said Jude. "But I don't think you should have the right to demand a church wedding and a civil marriage license with the threat of a high-profile lawsuit. I don't think you all really want to be married anyways. What with all your vamping and cavorting. And rampant promiscuity. You just want society by the government's proxy to say that what you do in your bedrooms is right and acceptable, that's all. I agree with Pat Robertson, though, that Facebook needs a *vomit* button for when I see a picture of a gay couple kissing. Keep it at home and in the dark."

"Cretin! I am a Born-Again Christian! I am a man of God! And at the same instance I have every right to act on ALL of my biological sexual feelings whether you bigots agree to it or not!"

"Or not, then. You gays need to stop living through your genitals," Jude waved a hand up. "There is so much more to life than that."

Antoine stammered a moment, turned his back, and marched away fuming.

"You done did it now, homie. You done chased the homo away," laughed Hector.

"Yeah. Whatever. I'll leave him alone now. He is confused enough about himself. Let alone about real life. Too much soy in the latte will do that. If he lies to himself - what should I worry - won't he lie to me as well? I didn't add anything to that diatribe of his that wasn't true. The homosexually transmitted AIDS kills more gay men than guns. Time to ban penises."

"What is dis we is drinkin' anyways?"

"I'm guessing *mojitos* from the look of the mint sprigs."

Hector dove into the fresh fruit slices, but Jude was being more mindful. He wasn't so sure that this was going to be a good deal, selling the Bel Air to Paco. *Why didn't Paco immediately go down to see it? And why is he so keen on keeping us here through lunchtime? All in all, I'd rather be inside in the air conditioning eyeing that Brazilian arm-candy Paco owns,* he told himself in his mind. *She is one hot chick. Foreign dudes with money always score the finest toast. That's just the way it is. Poor American saps like me who bust to survive in the middle class have to settle for what's in front of us: the average baby-bearing woman.*

"I am not sure I like dis *mojitos* drinks."

"Actually, it is *cachaça.* The finest you can find outside of Brazil. Sorry, gentlemen, to make you wait," Paco strolled out the patio to the balcony holding his Pusser's mango daiquiri. He pulled up a hefty metal seat and slowly plopped himself down into it. "I had to call my nephew, Valenton. Nanoo is worried about him. Strange kid I got for a nephew. He's part of the Occupy Wall Street crowd. My parents left Buenos Aires for a time and came of age in the early 1960s at Haight-Ashbury, so I am familiar with the protest mindset. Young people are still idealistic, and that's good, but what the Occupy protesters of today lack is a sense of purpose."

"They've got the campaigning down to an art," said Jude.

"Yes, but they can't seem to come up with any reasonable solutions to the problems. Like other protestors in the past used to. Instead, we hear their now-demands that most twelve-year olds of my time would have recognized as being ridiculous. Valenton doesn't understand the First Amendment. He doesn't understand economics. He apparently doesn't understand the nature of business. And he definitely knows nothing about human nature. All that core missing and still he holds a Columbia degree in journalism that I paid for."

"Where's his dad?" asked Jude.

"His dad. Valenton's dad. His dad was my brother. Dad's deceased. Made millions at and for Goldman Sachs. Which is not a big deal like everyone thinks it is. Getting filthy rich at Goldman Sachs is like being covered in sawdust at a sawmill. He was shot in Quito, Ecuador when he was down there to negotiate a treaty on oil rights exploration. *Bang!* Shot dead right in front of his horrified son and daughter and niece in the town square. Assassin never caught. Rumor has it is was an activist for the local indigenous tribe there. That's probably why Valenton is so screwed up today. I financially support him and even help out his friends some with cash as he wishes, but—"

"But what troubles me most—" Jude cut him off. "-is their collective delusion that they represent the other ninety-nine percent of America. They don't. Not even close. They represent a very small fraction of people who firstly grew up privileged and still believe that they should receive all the desires of their hearts just because they exist. They want sunny days in Miami and bowls of mixed fruit and nuts and ponies to ride. When the sky is cloudy and no ponies can be seen, they want the government to fix it. Just because it's the white guys' fault for the internet being down at Starbucks."

"Right! There were a few protesters in the 60s whom we look back on and laugh at now. I presume that future generations will look back at the Occupy movement, scratch their heads, and ask themselves how indeed the world continued on despite them," said Paco sarcastically.

"Yeah. They're that insipid," Jude put in. "Historians in other countries are gonna say America started downhill when Twitter and the words *influencer* and *triggered b*ecame a household name."

"Valenton is so outraged that he now tells me he is not going to white man's graduate school as I offered. He instead is going to search out an internship with a third-generation welfare family and write a blog of it as his life's experience. Because in the welfare state we are becoming due to bipartisan political policies there will eventually be no work, no jobs, just a universal income. He wants to learn the in's and out's of living off the government welfare check and being a demanding liberal. I told him to try to move to Chicago or Detroit in winter to really get a feel for what it's like. Hahaha!... I still have to cover his Verizon cellphone bill. That I am sorely aware of. I have no idea why a cell phone bill can be such a huge expense for these kids. Small for me to pay. But still."

"Who needs a job when you have an unlimited data plan?" Jude laughed.

"He lose his daddy, man. Lighten' up on him," said Hector dryly.

"He didn't have to suffer the oppressive threats of a father telling him what to do and beating his ass in a drunken rage. It's counter-intuitive, but not having that hell, that's how he ended up screwed up like he is. He's forever soft and weak. Uncompetitive.

The kid may choose to never bust his ass and work a day in his life. Why should he? With Paco spreading the family his wealth, he may not have to. Will he ever be educated enough and disciplined enough to solve the so-called problems in America? A country he disdains? The problem actually is: he is maladjusted and he isn't well informed. *'Wherever the people are well informed they can be trusted with their own government; that whenever things get so far wrong as to attract their notice, they may be relied on to set them to right'*. Thomas Jefferson said that. Great American he was. We need men like Jefferson to run our country again. Real men like my father and grandfather. Reagan and Nixon. Not this pansy Obama we have in the White House exposing the world to his faux outage on Twitter."

"You hate because Obama is black. That's unsettling to you. The most dangerous man in America is a man of color with an education and with a purpose. You are telling me you want the country to be run by old white men," interjected Paco. "That's racist."

"I have no problem with you or Hector or anyone foreign or domestic of any color who want to work in our government. Elected, appointed, it doesn't matter. But look at the demographics. Know what I'm sayin'? Asia for Asians. Africa for Africans. But white countries are for everybody. Think about it. All white countries and only white countries are being flooded with third world non-whites without an education. Whites are being forced by progressive law and false guilt to integrate with the immigrants so as to 'assimilate' to their being rather than the other way around. Blended out of existence. Forced assimilation is genocide when it's done to Tibetans in Tibet and Uyghurs in China. It may not be a violent genocide when it's done to whites in white countries. But I have read the U.N. Convention and it says genocide is defined as quote *'deliberately inflicting on the group conditions of life calculated to bring about its physical destruction in whole or in part'* unquote. The persons carrying out this genocide against whites say they are anti-racist and white men like me are the racists. What they are actually is anti-white. Especially anti-white male. The biggest demographic. Of which I am."

A white pigeon flew onto the railing near Paco, strutted a bit, then fluttered away.

"No, I think you are the racist and won't admit so. Isn't your wife's family from the Dominican Republic?" asked Paco rhetorically. "That makes your daughter half-Hispanic. Brown-skinned."

"Touché. How do you know so much about my family?"

"Filiberto, of course."

"Filiberto has told you way too much about me, and I don't like it. But you are right, my daughter is half-Latina. I didn't know what box to check off on the last national Census form that came out in 2010. There was nothing to check off for Mestiza, which is what she is. Mestiza is half-white, half-Indian. That's my best guess, anyway."

"So what you did?" asked Hector with a bunch of grapes in his mouth.

"I drew a big asterisk and wrote 'Mestiza' next to it for those questions concerning Chloe."

"Hahaha!" belly-laughed Paco. "Of course the bean-counter at the Census has no idea what Mestizo means. The computer kicked it out and the poor shmuck didn't know what to do with the form so he probably tossed it. You just royally screwed up America's demographic counting."

"Quite right," said Jude while drinking from the Collins glass. "As long as it doesn't infringe my right to bear arms, I'm okay with it being screwed up. Now, about the Bel Air. Do you want to go see it now?"

"Not just yet. Let's talk some. Pundits on CNBC expect the stock market to go higher today, but fall over two hundred points by the end of the week. Obama in his infinite wisdom wants to go full-blown into Syria against the Russians. I'm not sure how I will approach my trading this week. Decisions. Decisions."

"Only because Obama wants Israel to be attacked in retaliation. What dominoes fall in the far future from Obama's planned blitzkrieg into Syria will be like a winter blizzard following into a Christmas Eve fire. Let's go see the Bel Air."

"Are you a Democrat?" Paco alighted.

"I would be if JFK and Dr. Martin Luther King were still around. They may have been socialists. But Obama promoting and supporting homosexuality? Meh. I'll pass."

"Dr. Martin Luther King was a socialist because he didn't have any money," Paco took a drink. "Of course today, any socialist who actually has money is called a globalist. Can you say you are conservative? Or liberal."

"A conservative. Non-believer. Meaning I don't go to church. As opposed to a liberal non-believer who wants God and priests silenced."

Paco raised his glass casually, took a drink, and raised an eyebrow. "I apologize to you, gentlemen, but I am busy at the moment with some loose ends. I do have good news for you, Jude. I just got off the phone and entered the Bel Air in the classics show here in South Beach. And I paid for a complete interior and exterior detailing at Catty's shop. Here is a card with the address. When you go there tomorrow, tell Catty I sent you. He will know to treat your baby well since I bring all my cars there. And I have even better news for you, Hector."

"Really? Whassup?" asked Hector still eating grapes and spitting out the seeds over the balcony.

"You met Vanité, my model hostess? She told me about your lively comments to her that made her blush."

"Really? She do? Whas da good news then?" Hector was excited and curious and sat up straight in his metal seat.

Paco smiled widely. "The good news is—"

"Yes?! Yes?! I'm hearin' ya!"

"When you leave—"

"YES!?"

Paco leaned over the table to get within inches of Hector's face and whispered gently, "I'm sleeping with her."

4 Life in The Fast Lane

Jude and Hector spent the rest of that day walking around South Beach and eyeing the hotties in their skimpy outfits bobbing in and out of the exquisite boutiques and delightful cafés of Collins Avenue. The two men snacked on some Cuban sandwiches a street vendor sold to them cheap after Hector chatted him up in Spanish about the World Cup qualifiers. After a long day in the blazing sun, the miscreants crashed at their hotel with a pitcher of Captain Morgan rum punch poured over ice melting in the Waterford highball glasses the hotel concierge brought up to their room. Jude felt uneasy still about the whole situation. He was nevertheless content with the hospitality Paco was showing them. At least for the moment.

The next morning Jude and Hector gathered themselves early and headed to a certain florissant café just north of South Beach's hotel district, where Jude drank a French smoothie.

"I like South Beach," Jude remarked. "Cars, bars, and movie stars. Plenty of sunshine. Paco sure has it nice. Doesn't get any better than this. I wonder if I can get a job here. I wonder if Margarita and Berto would be up for moving down here and opening a garage. Berto would be up for it. I'll have to check in with Margarita on that. She probably wouldn't agree to it. Too many beautiful women around."

Hector wasn't listening. He was at the counter hitting on a young British maiden who was in Miami on an extended vacation.

"I like what youse wearing. Hehehe. Can I try it on?" He grinned widely.

"Gay men make good friends because we can exchange clothing tips. Is that what you meant?" the girl asked sarcastically.

"Hahaha! Youse talks so sweetly, yez. Such a fiiine accent. Can I ax you yo name, girl?"

"Catherine Mary Henrietta Potter," she smiled back at him. "You definitely talk differently from the other American men I have had the mis-pleasure to meet in Miami. Can I ask where you are from?"

"Yez you can. I is from Puerto Rico. The Island of Song, girl!" he leaned on the counter towards her at the cash register. "And you is one fiiine chick. Yez. Hehehehe!"

"Chick? Oh, you must mean 'bird'. In England, men refer to girls as birds."

"Birds? Wha for? Why's they be callin' you birds?"

"Probably because we are always being chatted up by worms. Have a lovely, lovely day," she grabbed the box of exquisite pastries from the cashier and walked briskly out the door.

Jude spit out a mouthful of his smoothie and broke out laughing. Hector stood there a moment completely at a loss for words. "Dang. Fogget me going to England, homie. Them girls gots a bad attitude across the pond!"

"Never mind. You always strike out anyway, Money. This or that side of the pond. Must be your mustache that's the problem. No matter. You know, I can't seem to get a hold of Margarita. I've tried calling her cell, our home number, her mother's house, so many times this morning. Look, even Filiberto isn't answering my calls. I think that's a bad sign. Maybe we should cut out and drive back to Baltimore with the cash we have left. This Paco guy doesn't add up right to me. The more he talks, the more the creek seeps into the buyer's hole he is digging. I'm gonna keep raising the sales price in my mind until I get some kind of sign out of him he's serious to make the deal. My granddad told me often, expectations will rise over time. For now, it doesn't add up."

"Leave? F'real? I'm enjoying m'self in Miami. Hang in until the show on tomorrow, boss. We can gets the Bel Air detailed this morning and all real nice for the show. Paco is still covering the hotel costs fo' us, ain't he? Can't beat that with a baseball bat. Filiberto done gave you da cash to spend on what yous wants. I hear some hot Brazilian model named Gisele wearing a thong and crop top and nuthin' else is gonna lead the parade at the show. I gots ta see that. Hehehe!"

"You're thinking with your little head again, but okay, why should today be any different. I just have a bad feeling. Margarita isn't answering my calls, and Chloe's birthday passed. I don't know if she's so ticked at me for coming down here in the first place or the phone's been cut off. The bill is probably sitting on my desk at the garage and I forgot to pay it. No way to pay it now from here."

"Fogget about it. It'll all be cool. Let's get shaking. We's in South Beach!"

Jude gave in to Hector's badgering, and the two of them drove the Bel Air to Catty's Garage and Detailing over near *Calle Ocho* in Little Havana just as Paco told them to. Catty was sitting in his office when the Bel Air pulled up in front of the large office window. The red faced man left his office quickly to go behind the building adjacent to it, came back, and met Jude and Hector in the parking area, where many classic vehicles sat waiting to be worked on.

"Greets, gents," said Catty. "This must be the car Paco wants me to handle. She sure is a beaut'. You guys wanna come in for a moment and see our warehouse?"

"Natch," said Jude. "I'm always willing to have a look at another man's garage. What kind of metal and fiberglass monsters do you have in there?"

"Come on in and see!"

The three men walked into the expansive garage. Hefty air conditioners were blowing so hard there was frost on the expansion chambers leaking condensed water. Hector immediately started griping on how cold it was and stepped back outside. Jude continued further on inside with Catty to have a look at the cars the mechanics were working on. Several mechanics in oil and fuild stained work clothes milled about and paid no attention to the two men entering the garage. Straight up in front of them was a '64 Corvette getting a total frame-off restoration. Jude picked up a bolt of Turkish leather and commented that he had never seen such quality goods for a seat.

"It's also for the dash. Same leather Rolls Royce uses in their carriages," said Catty proudly. "It ain't cheap stuff, so we charge accordingly. Most of the cars here are owned by Dolphins players. Like that Lambo Veneno in the corner. It's owned by Lamar Miller, the running back."

"And this L-88 'Vette?" asked Jude.

"You got a good eye for cars. It's owned by the wide receiver, Brian Hartline."

"I know my cars," he smiled.

"Cars are better to know than women," laughed Catty.

"F'real?" said Hector grimly holding his cold self as he rejoined the two men. "I don' think so."

"Sure. A car doesn't care if you get in another car," Catty rattled off. "A car will give you the same cool ride any day of the month. A hot car and a cool car are equally thrilling. A car doesn't even have a birthday. A car has no mother or mother's birthday. If a car is late it probably won't cost you twenty years of your life. If you are in one car and admiring other cars, no problem. Cars never leave you. You can sell a car you tire of. Rent it out. Even simply ignore it. If a car starts deteriorating, you can restore it. I mean REALLY restore it. If you can't get in a car and drive it, just about any lubricant will work fine. If a car starts getting loose, you can tighten it with a wrench in seconds, while drinking a beer. You can rub your car's exterior ten percent a day for ten days, or all at once, starting and stopping whenever you want, and rub it any way you want. If your car has a sagging rear end, sixty-five dollars for air shocks and you are done for another fifteen years."

"Never thought of it like that," remarked Jude.

"I got it memorized for any occasion," Catty winked.

"Huh. Fo'get da cars. I'll takes the hot honey-bun at the counter there, thanks," said Hector.

"You mean Grace?" asked Catty. "She's taken, brother. She's the lead on the Dolphins cheerleading squad. Hangs with the Patriot's Tom Brady and Gisele when they're in town. I keep her around because the men with money all drool over her and give me their business. Besides, she's my niece."

"I like that Detomaso Pantera over there. A '74?" Jude asked.

"I think it is a '73 actually. Good call though," said Catty as he walked over to the Italian supercar. "The owner of this one wishes to remain anonymous for now. He's paying me over eighty large to restore it to standards. He has all the papers and its repair receipts. His father was the original owner since it came off the boat. I think his dad must have dragged it some for the quarter mile back in the 70s. Still no spider cracks at all in the fiberglass. Really a solid supercar. It could sell for a third of a million easy once restored."

"Something I'd like to own myself one day," said Jude. "I love Italians. Got three of them in my garage that I'm working on now. I'll never be able to own one, unfortunately. That kind of money to own one is way beyond me and my abilities."

"As Einstein once said: it's all relative. If you've got tons of money like Paco, it could just be a drop in the bucket. What about you, guy, you got the clams to buy such a vehicle?"

"Me?" said Hector. "I wear my shoe soles until they are so thin, I can steps on a gums wrapper and tell you what flavor it be!"

Catty laughed. "You know what we call an Italian homosexual?"

"No," said Jude, as he checked under the Detomaso's engine cover.

"A guy who likes exotic women more than exotic cars!"

"Funny. Or not. Whatever."

"The owner of the Pantera is a car nut and he loves to show off his metal and glass. If you'd like, I can invite you over to his club this evening. Invitation only normally, but I know the bouncers. Or, actually, they know me. Plenty of young ladies to meet there."

"I'm in f'real!" Hector locked in.

"Owners of clubs always have the green and the ladies," said Jude from under the engine cover. "They get the Alpha male athletes to drop their wads of green easy at the bar. Losers like

Hector follow along and go broke trying to keep up. I don't get it."

"It's quite simple," said Catty. "You rent the VIP area to a top local male celeb, and invite every good looking girl in the place to enjoy an open-bar. Bottles of your choice of alcohol run six hundred dollars a pop or more with so many lovely lady waitresses doing all the pouring. Lebron and Dwayne and the other guys on the Heat probably only drink about five percent of the thirty-thousand dollar tab. The rest is spent on lowering standards and creating open minds for bad decisions."

"Great stories come from bad decisions," added Jude. "I've always wanted to get with Alpha males like Lebron and jump around in their worlds. If you can get us into the club, that would so very much rock my world."

"Hey whas with that dark room behind dat large silver-streaked door?" asked Hector. "Why's they be takin' the Bel Air in there?"

"Uhhh... That's where we will, umm, detail the Bel Air. Don't worry. Come. Let's let the workers do their thing. I'll get you guys an Uber to wherever you need to go for the day. Or if you prefer to drive yourself, I can lend ya my airport car, if you're careful with it. The Ferrari 512 Berlinetta Boxer you saw parked out front. It's all mine," said Catty proudly. "Better than a wife as we discussed earlier. One of the few things my ex didn't get from me in the bitter end."

"Airport car?" the two men asked in unison as all walked outside into the heavy heat.

"Yeah. If I have to pick up or drop off a client at Miami-Dade airport, this's the car I use. Here's the keys. You're welcome to use it for today. If you need to put gas in it, just bring it back here and one of my men will fill it up for you, no charge. It's a gas guzzler at high speeds. You think you can handle this beast's twelve cylinders? It'll haul ass on A1A down to the Keys."

"It's yours?" Jude stepped to the side. "How'd you get it?"

"Got it at a police auction for a good price. I ran the numbers and found it had been abandoned in Fort Lauderdale by some

Middle-Eastern prince who was in a real hurry to get out of the country. I heard he was wanted for murder. The police confiscated it and then auctioned it off for just pennies of what it's real worth is."

"Don't tell me; let me guess. The interior smelled like curry, old sandals, and body odor. That's why it sold so cheap," Jude quipped.

"The dude who 'bandoned this ride officially loses his 'man card'," said Hector. "Check dat. Revoked!"

"Must've had a deep, dark secret to be such in a hurry to get out of the country. Call girls murdered, maybe? Or maybe he insulted The Prophet in some way and a fatwa was called on him."

"Peace, gentlemen," said Catty with a wave. "Make peace with the Muslims. They are our friends, even if they have different beliefs than we do. I say peace because we have so little of it left in the good ole U.S.A. What is our present government going to do to bring the peace back to this divided nation? Nobody is happy."

"I know, I know," threw in Jude. "Our forefathers would be shooting by now."

"*My peace I leave you. My peace I give to you*. Jesus said that," quoted Catty. "Good Man, that Jesus. If only President Obama would be gracious to say the word 'peace' in English once in a while, instead of in Arabic."

"Like my daddy always said: *Peace for the world, my ass. Every man just wants a piece of the world's ass,*" offered Jude. "I ain't religious. Except about cars."

"That's your choice. So, if you like the Boxer at the end of the day, I'll sell it to you for two hundred even," said Catty.

"I see. It's a sweet ride. But maybe not two hunnerd grand sweet," Jude frowned. "I wouldn't kick it out of my garage back in Baltimore for leaking oil. Hope my own Italian jobbies will bring such a price when they finally sell. After the loans on them are paid off, I should do well."

"As Einstein once said: it's all relative. If you've got tons of money, it could just be a drop in the bucket," Catty grinned widely.

"You said that before. I think that's your canned answer for everything that costs a major body part."

"You want to talk or drive?"

"Can I drive it to heaven? Without repenting of my sins?" asked Jude rhetorically, rubbing his hands together. "We are off, Hector… Off like a prom dress." Jude opened the bright red door.

"I would do terrible things to own dis car," said Hector as he ran his hand across the shiny roof before opening the passenger door. "Maybe not kill a man fo' it. But certainly there be terrible things I'd do to own her."

Someone from the office came on the loudspeaker and called Catty to hurry to an issue in the garage mechanics' bays. He scurried off without a final word and just a wave of the hand.

Jude didn't know what to say next. He just stood there a few moments next to the open driver's door of the low-slung Ferrari 512 BB. Never had anyone lent him such a fine supercar - and without questions asked about his driving skills! The car's candy-apple 'Hello, Officer' red enamel paint glistened beneath the noon sun. Jude flicked a large bug off the BB's slick roof and shook his head in disbelief. Both men hopped into the cream-colored interior and settled in the immaculately clean Recaro seats. She smelled so sweet and clean on the inside. Jude fired up the twelve cylinders, and the car roared to life. He grabbed the Brabant steering wheel with both hands.

A smoky tire burnout and a minute later the two of them were cruising the speedy Italian vehicle down *Calle Ocho* towards the center of Miami passing slower-moving cars with horns blaring.

"If I had heavy-loads of laundry coins like Paco," said Jude. "I would spend my life dealing in fine vehicles such as this one. Faster than a 16-year-old's sex habits."

"No spider cracks in the fiberglass now. I sure bet it gonna have lots o' spider cracks by the end of the day. Haha! Lessee what this baby can really do," said Hector. "Less hit the highway."

"Forget it. I'm not risking to redline the engine in this machine that ain't mine."

"F'real, man?" said Hector in disgust. "Can I drives, then?

"When hell freezes over from global warming."

"Dang, man. Uncool."

"Anyway, I'd rather be riding in that Vette we saw. Better straight-line speed times in the 'merican built muscle machines, I always say."

"Does that mattah?"

"Not really. If you're upset with the zero to sixty time of this Ferrari steed—" said Jude as he pounded his foot on the gas; the car peeled away from the stoplight. "-then set your alarm clock for three seconds earlier."

Hector paused a second looking right at the wide-smiling Jude, then laughed and clapped his hands in the air.

"Hahaha! F'real, homeboy! Lemme drive her!"

"Hello, Hector. This is your pharmacist. You need to check your messages. There's been a mix up in your meds. Don't drive or comment till you speak to us first."

"Dang, man. You be sucking."

"Yeah, I be sucking alright. Like most of my career and my marriage. I be sucking bad. Ain't nothing but a shuck. Buffalo Wild Wings for lunch?"

The Ferrari turned the next corner like it was on rails, and the two men smacked hands in the air. They were free for a day of fun in a car they once only dreamed about riding in. For now, like a classic 1970s road show, cruisin' was heaven in their hands.

5 The Bel Air Stands Alone

The South Beach Concourse show proved to be an event definitely not for the faint of heart. Lots of young lovely ladies in designer outfits and draped in lots of jewelry hanging on the arms of well-tanned, wealthy men from all over the world. Everyone was checking out the classic and uber-luxurious steel, fiberglass, and chrome that set apart the car owners and dealers from mere mortal men. Some of the cars had price tags on them. Some would be up for auction later in the week. Jude's Bel Air went down the street parade with Paco waving a hand from the driver's seat. Antoine and Vanité sat up in the back sipping from champagne flutes. Jude was proud of his car, as the detailing by Catty really brought out the beauty in her. But he was still not convinced that Paco was serious about buying her straight up. A price hadn't been set yet, and Paco hadn't been answering Jude's many calls to him. When the Bel Air passed Jude and Hector standing by on Collins Avenue, Paco saluted them both with a wave and made a rubbing sign with his thumb and forefinger – money, it meant. Jude took a deep breath and sighed. Shaking his head, he had his doubts again whether it was a good idea to leave Margarita and Chloe all alone as he did for so long. Margarita still wasn't answering his many attempted calls, either. Jude didn't know if she and Chloe were staying at her mother's, or even where else his wife and daughter could be. Drips of sweat fell down the sides of Jude's eyebrows and streaked his cheeks in the hot sun.

At the end of the parade, Paco climbed out of the Bel Air without opening the door and stroked a hand slowly across her hood. He had seen a car just like this one wrecked in Buenos Aires as a boy when it had crashed head-on into his father's Mercedes 450SL convertible, sending his father straight to the emergency room. The accident left him to come out a paraplegic who could no longer speak without slurring his words. The driver of the Bel Air was drunk, but he was also the son of an Argentinian General of the Army, and a case was never brought against him. From all the pain surrounding the crash and the ensuing years of Paco's father being in a wheelchair until he had a stroke and passed away at the young age of fifty-four, all Paco recalled of the incident was showing up with his distraught mother after it happened only to see the once beautiful Bel Air being towed away completely totaled from the wreckage sight. That image stuck in his mind years on in. Paco knew then that somehow, someday, he would own one of those same cars, and by owning it he would take his mortal revenge. Now that he was leaning against Jude's Bel Air, he mentally noted to himself that any price Jude asked he would meet. He would certainly pay a king's ransom to have this baby as his own personal ride - for whatever rides, even money making ones, he desired.

Jude and Hector met up with Paco and company at the end of the parade route where all the classics and modern moveable art were being shown. They strolled along the grassy concourse together to marvel at the fancy steel and fiberglass, forged and molded by men of skill to impress men of means. Paco recalled to Jude and Hector the ex-wife of his youth being somewhat of a marvel herself, especially after her breast enhancement the top plastic surgeon in Miami performed on her. He wished he had kept the receipts from the surgery bills, he joked to Jude, because he asked for custody of the hooters at the divorce proceedings. At the very least, he continued on, he should have gotten visitation rights granted by the judge. Jude let out a bellowing laugh. Paco verbally pointed out Antoine's breasts which sagged down to the top of his belly. But his ex's were surely still in place, he figured.

"I don't get it," said Antoine, dizzy from the blazing sun.

"I'm sure you don't," said Jude. "I bet you have to have the jokes on Bazooka gum wrappers explained to you."

Jude moved on ahead of the group and started to chat up a chap who was rubbing a chamois on an orange 1970 Ford

Mustang Boss 429. A small sign in the rear window read, "For sale. Principals only." But no price was listed on the sign.

"She's done undergone a complete frame-off restoration," stated the car's owner proudly with a smile. "I found her in a junkyard in Georgia in '87 and fell in love with all the rust at first sight. She's been restored to pristine condition. With the 429 engine I had to find separately since hers had been ripped out and done gone when I found her. I wish they'd bring back lacquer paint. This orange enamel stuff's just doesn't work for her. I've had to repaint her twice, and the lacquer paint they used to use would really bring her to her original life. Dontcha think? You interested in a quick buy?"

"Mmmhmm," said Jude, as he looked under the hood. "That is one smooth powerful engine. American motor companies don't make 'em like that anymore. A new Corvette or Ferrari couldn't beat this 'Stang in a quarter-mile. No chance. Such a rarity. I doubt I could find a perfect 429 like this in all of Baltimore County."

"The words 'frame-off restoration' would seem to be a lie," interjected Paco. "If there wasn't much left of her when you found her in the junkyard. Especially given the missing engine, it's more of a 'recreation rebuild'. It's always interesting to me to see how a car owner spins the tale of his machine's provenance after the car has been gutted and left to die in a barn or junkyard. As in 'Oh, by the way, I have the actual original revolver Samuel Colt made. Sure, it has had its cylinder, grip, hammer, and trigger replaced multiple times, but I'm telling you it's the real deal just 'restored' to original condition.' You say you can't afford to keep her anymore?"

"Lost my Disney job to an H-1B visa holder," lamented the Boss 429's owner. "Thanks to Obama."

"Why's that Obama's fault? It's your choices you're making," said Antoine. "You could be making better choices with your life."

"I did. I am. Stop leaning on the car! I spent the first five years of my young adult life drifting from minimum wage job to minimum wage job. Barely able to keep a roof over my head, and food on my table. I decided I was not getting anywhere, so I joined the military. After my tour in Desert Storm, I went to school, graduated with degrees in software design and mathematics, and finally began a career as a software engineer with Disney in Orlando. I made good choices, and all of it served me well for a long time. Then, all of a sudden, it happened. The execs at Disney Corporate with the help and blessing of the Obama Admin took my job away by bringing Jalafreezy and Jasmine and all the rest from India with an H-1B visa program to replace the engineers in my department."

"You still live in America. Big chances here you can't find anywhere else in the world," Antoine continued.

"Yeah, bud, yeah. I get ya. But get this story. Years ago, I believe in the late 70's or early 80's, a family in my neighborhood emigrated from Uzbekistan to America. They had lived and moved around Georgia for a number of years before settling near me. The father bounced from poor job to poor job to poor job, barely making ends meet. The father finally decided he had had enough of his horrible way of raising his family and moved his wife and younger children back to Uzbekistan because, he said, the problem with America is that though you can succeed greatly, you can also clearly fail miserably. At no fault of your own you can fail and still get no adequate help to lift you out of absolute poverty. He said he would rather return to Uzbekistan because, although you might not ever have much, you were always able to eke out an easy and manageable living on bread and cheap Vodka and whatever vegetables you could grow in a garden. Which is more than he ever had here working his tail off. Sure, you say, a lot of immigrants come to the USA. But few of them or their children ever make it to the big leagues in society. Most of them stumble around for generations upon generations, getting nowhere. Which is how I feel right now after Disney dumped me. Nowhere."

"Well, good sir, we have support programs both public and private in this country to help those like you who need it. There is a group of people that I am aware of who seldom hold jobs. While

I would not want to live at their level of existence, they seem to manage just fine."

"Your gay friends who don't work a job even part-time?" Paco entered. "Heck! They live life barely a day at a time. And live like crap as well!"

"I've never taken a dime from government or any charity," the Ford owner said a frown coming to his face. "Well, the government did pay for my education after the military with the GI Bill, I agree to that. I don't look down on a person in need. I do think people need to be responsible for themselves. Charity breeds dependence. I bought and restored this Mustang myself. Top to bottom. Front to rear. Blood, sweat, and tears. Too bad I'm broke and hafta sell her."

"And what if you were a thirteen year old girl from poverty who got pregnant and received no help from the baby's daddy?" Antoine brought up. "I know, I know, she's thirteen, she should have had more sense, right? What if you had been busted for that joint you smoked in high school and the military wouldn't take you? Or gotten a tattoo around your neck and face? What then? What if the government had not offered you college scholarships and the GI Bill and all that helped you all along through your career after the military tour? What if you had been saddled with caring for a family at seventeen because your daddy was in jail or was shot in a drive by? Seriously. What if your education had ground to a halt in eleventh grade because you had to go to work at minimum wage to pay the rent and buy groceries for your fatherless family?"

"Anto!" halted Paco.

"No! Let me finish! What if one job wasn't enough and you had to work two and by the end of the day all you could do was crash into a bed, let alone finish high school? And taking classes to become a software engineer? What if your momma had gotten sick and had no medical insurance? And you had to work minimum wage and had to steal the difference from the register you worked to get money for her medical bills? Not everyone is you, buddy. There is more to this world than your philosophy encompasses, Horatio. Decent people realize this and want to help others. Some do not look for every excuse under the sun not to help."

"What-ever", the Ford owner flipped himself around and returned to buffing the car with the chamois in his hand. "You assume too much about me. I have compassion for, and I am willing to help, those who cannot help themselves. Including your example of a thirteen year old single mother. I'd rather help her than see another abortion happen. But I am not going to engage in 'what ifs'. It's too tiresome and gets me nowhere fast."

A wrinkly and overly-tanned elderly man in a red and yellow Hawaiian shirt and grey camping shorts and Timberland sandals with black socks hobbled around from the back of the Mustang. He took a look at Vanité and smiled.

"Poverty. There but for the grace of God, go there I," the old man began. "I like what you said. I am now retired and lucky to be living the best times of my life. You can see many people my age on the street and under the bridges who should be able to say the same. I have here my successful adult son who probably learned a lot about drive, determination and living within your means from the days when we were about fifty dollars away from homelessness. He was in middle school. Look for the lesson or blessing in every situation, people. I am an educated person and worked hard to achieve my education goals to land the job I dreamed of. All that before having a family. I had a home and savings. Then catastrophic illness struck. I was just nearing the end of a three-year probationary period at work and was deemed 'unsuitable' for tenure due to an 'unreliable attendance pattern'. I'll spare you the medical details, but four years later I reapplied for the same job and was rehired. Between those times we almost didn't make it. If not for a few loyal friends and a few affordable California campgrounds and an old VW minibus, I know for sure we would have been on the street. I am an intelligent and educated person who never had any problems with addictions. I had an advantage in dealing with my near desperate situation. Can we only guess at the feelings of total desperation that so many of the homeless are experiencing today? Especially our returning veterans who absolutely deserve whatever it takes to get them back on their feet. My experience has taught me that a fiver or ten-dollar grocery card, a new pair of thick warm socks, along with some eye to eye contact while saying 'I pray things will get better for you' is sometimes all it takes to make a homeless person's day a little better. If you are ready to tell me that an EBT food card may not be used as intended, all I can say is: that's between God and the recipient. Having compassion for others is between God and me. Before passing judgment on a fellow human being, please pause for a moment and consider: there but for the grace of God—"

"Thanks, as always, dad," said the Ford owner stopping his father's soliloquy, grinning faintly and standing up straight. "Just for being my dad."

"Wealth is not always a viable choice, I readily admit," said Jude with arms folded. "Unfortunately, the same goes for poverty. However, most every person I meet is self-made. Only the rich admit it. C'mon. Let's go. I'm not interested in this car or this conversation. I want to talk about the Bel Air, Paco. Now. You with me or not?"

"And if I'm not?" Paco raised an eyebrow, lying through his bright white teeth.

"Then forget it! Hector and I are leaving this hellacious heat right now. Gimme the keys! And the gas tank better not be on empty!"

"I don't have the keys."

"What the heck? Where are they? Did you lose them somewhere in the last ten minutes?"

"Relax. Catty is taking the car back after the show to do some more detailing. It's sitting there getting judged right now in the show. Yes, relax, because I am still interested in buying. Don't get so ripping upset. There's more to life than cars and money, you know," Paco walked on, waving a hand.

"Says the eccentric millionaire with a full stable of Ferraris." Jude got frustrated and headed towards a hotdog stand to get a can of cold Canada Dry ginger-ale as antidote to the scorching sun bearing down on him. He was startled by the price. "A buck-seventy-five for a cold can of soda? I mean, W.T.F., dude?!"

"Welcome to South Beach," said the vendor without batting an eye. "Don't like it, leave. Hialeah isn't but a bus ride away. Getcher drinks there, bub. Next!"

Not a moment later a mocha-colored ultra-thin tall woman with blonde streaks wearing a gold-colored bikini and expensive designer sunglasses walked by Jude and stroked his arm lightly breathing, "I'll give you anything you pleasure for two hundred dollars. Take me wherever you want to go, my man. I'm yours for the taking."

"Thanks," countered Jude as he gruffly handed over the two dollars to the vendor and popped open his can of Canada Dry. "But my wife will give me anything I pleasure for dinner at Applebee's and some new mascara. Try your luck with that guy over there, sugar-sweets." Jude pointed a stiff finger at Hector a few steps down the street.

"Ugh!" screeched the girl bitterly. "He's so heinous!"

"Maybe you could take him home. For foreplay, he could hose off all that make-up you've got caked on. Invite a few Kardashians and make a party of it."

"HEI-NOUS!" she repeated as she turned her slim legs left and headed slowly down a side-alley.

"Yo, bay-bee!" Hector yelled after the sultry woman. "Yo Happy Meal ain't even amusin'! Youz a rip off, girl!"

"Moron and idiot!" she screamed back at him.

"Yo, lady! You need to get that stutter fixed. Or understand what the word redundant means!" Jude added.

Hector started to walk towards the woman to carry on, and then thought better of it.

"Heinous, she called him. That means he looks broke to her," said Jude to the vendor. The vendor shrugged and smiled.

A sunburned beggar in ripped sneakers and cut-off shorts and no shirt shuffled up to Jude asking for spare change. "Here's a quarter," Jude flipped. "Go call someone who cares. If you can find a payphone."

The panhandler flashed Jude his fancy iPhone, and pestered him to 'lend' a twenty-spot.

"Mama always said, lending money to strangers and sex with strangers is best left to the professionals. Actually, she didn't say that. But she would have."

The beggar came up close and pushed Jude back a step.

"Get away from me, man, and don't touch me again before I hurt you!" Jude shouted. "I work for a living! You should try the same!"

Paco could sense the consternation Jude was effusing about the delay in the discussion about the Bel Air, and decided to play it against him. He sauntered across the street at a steady gate, away from Jude, lifting his sunglasses onto his forehead to see if he knew anyone on the grassy concourse. Antoine, Vanité and Hector were lumbering behind him blindly. Hector was beat, and looked like he could use a good cold shower as he was dripping with sweat.

"Anto, you don' sweat, man?" said Hector as he pulled off his Baltimore Orioles baseball cap and wiped his brow with his hand. "You is as dry as crabs on a prostitute."

"I don't sweat, dearie. I perspire. And by the way, I don't perspire in public. If you know what I mean," Antoine chuckled to Hector.

"Dang, man. Youz disgusting, fo' sho'."

"Paco, dearie, I hate to bring it up while we're having such a fun time, but you know it is payday. You know me and my money problems."

"No, I don't know your money problems," laughed Paco. "Never had to experience them myself. Tell me again what your money problems are? C'mon, Anto. Entertain me. I'm so bored."

"My car is broken-down. My boy Friday ran away. My son is gay, and my seventeen year old daughter eloped with a broke old man. I have no money for my alimony, let alone food and liquor. I can't work with my dreadful illness. Oh, geez, dearie. Where do I start?"

"I would ride a camel across the hot Sahara desert with Roseanne singing the National Anthem to me before I'd let myself end up with a life like you have, Anto. God forbid—"

Antoine put his hands on his hips. "Okay, then, Pacooo. Shall we discuss YOUR real desires for the Bel Air? With our friends with us here to witness?"

Paco turned to face Antoine head on. "Shut your mouth now or you'll get not a nickel from me! Hear me? Not a nickel! I know YOUR secrets as well! Junkie—"

"I have no secrets. As for calling me a drug user, I think your tin foil hat is on a bit too tight today, Paco. Seek professional help."

Paco picked open his wallet and pulled out fifteen benjamins and foisted them to Antoine's open palm.

"Is that all I'm worth to you, Paco? Fifteen hundred dollars for two week's work? Glory me. I thought I meant more to you than that. After all I have done since you got back from motor-boating in the Keys. You think you won't have enough money still to buy the glorious Bel Air automobile and—"

Paco raised his fist to Antoine. He huffed and nervously handed over to six more benjamins.

"Settle down, Pacooo. It's all good. Okay. Well, I shan't complain anymore. Thank you. This will tide me over for a while. At least a little while. A few days at most. Oh, my Lord, Paco, you remind me of my Uncle Stingy. When he farted, his ears popped. Maybe I can get a second job parking cars at Cristina's on my off nights."

All around the slowly sauntering group, led by Paco, were the most beautiful, stylish, wealthy, and envied people in all of Miami-Dade. The moneyed men and their arm-candy strolled gaily around the vintage and exotic metal, commenting and striking up conversations with the vehicles' owners. Some men were making deals. Others merely showing their admiration for the loveliest cars that could be shown in all of Southern Florida.

Jude's phone rang just as he was going to suffer Paco another complaint.

"Layden here."

"Jude? It's Berto. Mr. Wright from the bank came by the shop today to find you. I told him you were out scavenging for some particular spare parts. I didn't tell him you were in Florida. He was ticked. He took a good long look around the shop before he stamped out and left in his BMW. Before he left, he said he 'would be back imminently'. And that if he couldn't find you, then 'bad things could happen'. I don't have a good feeling about this."

"Thanks for letting me know. I'll give him a call in a day or two after he settles down and b.s. him up a bit. The shop mortgage is overdue. He just wants the payment now. I can make him wait on the payment on the Italians. Your friend, Paco, hasn't paid me yet, but he will. So he says. I'm gonna shake that mother down in a minute and give his butt a whooping if he doesn't square up with me."

"Please don't do anything rash. Paco will pay up. He just likes to go on his own schedule. Like you do with the mortgage payments. And your marriage."

"Oh, shut the eff up."

"Hang loose a day or two. I'll call Paco in a moment and tell him you're rushed."

"You don't have to call him. He's here with me now. Wanna speak to him?"

"NO! I mean, er, no. I'll call him later. I have to clean up the shop. Good news though for you. The Jeep owner came in to pick up his ride. He paid me in caaaaash. That should cover the parts and supplies bills for the time being, eh? I will write the checks now."

"And the utilities, please. They're in the desk drawer with the checkbook. I forgot to pay them in my rush to leave Baltimore. Yes, good news there that money came in. Good to know. Yes, go put the cash in the account immediately once you're off the phone. Write checks today to the parts vendors and utilities. But don't let Mr. Wright at the bank see you put the money in the account. Use an ATM. Unless he checks our account at the bank, he won't know the money's in there until it's already spent. Hopefully Paco will pay me now and I can get some more money in the account to cover the mortgage and loans."

"Fine. Just do me a favor I'm asking. Don't tick off, Paco. We need him. More than you know. My hottie sugar-momma is the one who introduced me to him in the first place. I think it's actually his credit card you are running up a bill on, by the way. I'm not sure how my lady and Paco are connected, but—"

"We haven't run up a bill on anything. Bare necessities. What's your deal with Paco anyway? Why would he give your old lady the credit card and then she gives it to you to give to me? This guy doesn't add up, I tell ya'."

"Please for the love of God just don't tick him off, okay. We need him. I'm gonna hang up now and do what you told me with the Jeep cash. I can come in tomorrow and clean up the shop. I wish Hector were here to do it. Hector is still with you, no? Or did he get himself locked up again?"

"Hector's here, too, in this blast-furnace heat. Get off the phone and go do what you're supposed to do. We'll talk later. Ciao, Berto."

>Click<

Jude fell behind the group as he was talking with Filiberto and lost them for a moment. His phone rang again.

"Hello? Oh, hi! It's you again! How are you, my Nigerian friend, Ntube? I'm sorry about the boyfriend comment I made. Totally inappropriate. I already have a boyfriend anyway. Now about the ten million you are going to wire to me…What? I sent the retainer money you asked for. Yes, I sent it Western Union. They would only take one thousand five hundred dollars at one time. I'll have to send the ten thousand over in several days. You say you haven't gotten it yet? I sent it to you. Ntube Ogasawara. Yesterday morning my time. It should be there by now, I would think. Let me check my Western Union slip. Hold on a second…Mmmhmmm…Oh, dear me, I'm sorry, Ntube. I blew it and sent the money to Niger, not Nigeria…What?...How far is

Niger from Nigeria then? That far? Okay. I'm sorry, brother. Maybe you can catch a bus or camel caravan there to ge—"

>Click<

Jude smiled freely as he ambled along in search of the others. He found them a little while later looking over a 1984 Ferrari 512BBi, which he didn't recognize at first was the one he had just driven a day earlier, owned by Catty. Jude leaned against the car.

"Paco, can we talk now?" Jude started in. "We need to consummate this deal. I'm tired of waiting on you."

"Espera, fortunato!"

"Sorry, Paco. I don't speak *taco*."

"What do you speak?"

"English, profanity, and sarcasm. Nothing else is necessary in America."

"You obviously haven't been in Miami long enough," said Paco as he walked away from the conversation. "Spanish is going to take over America. You will be left out."

"America is a melting pot. Not a stew. Assimilate or get the eff out."

"Spanish is going to be the main language in the USA. Then English will be foreign to most. It's coming. There is nothing a bigot like you can do about it."

"For now, Hollyweird and The Oscars call Spanish a foreign language for their movie award categories. No different than Russian, French, or any language NOT English. Make something of that, you freaking liberals," Jude finalized.

"I like French," said Antoine. "Very good mustard. Better than Heinz."

Catty came out of the Ferrari. "I picked up some Japanese last year… Those two girls were the best group sex I ever had. Hahaha! Hey Jude! I'm taking the Bel Air to, uh, detail her some more. I've seen some spider cracks in the paint on the hood and both fenders could stand to be, uh, re-chromed. Cool with you?"

"As long as I get paid by Paco here first what I'm asking. And I'm asking one hundred and ten thousand, cash. I don't give a rat's behind what you do with her. Set her afire under this blazing Florida sun for all I care. I need the clams."

Paco reached into his off-white blazer and pulled out a thick envelope he handed to Jude. Inside were two hundred crisp new century-notes. "I don't want to buy her just yet, Jude. But let me rent her for two more weeks. Just to check her out some. See if I like her. Here's twenty thou. That should cover me renting her for the rest of the South Beach show. You can then drive her for me to Fort Myers car week. If I still want her after that show, I'll get you another hundred thousand. Cash again. If I don't want her, you can drive her back to Baltimore with this slimeball Hector who's drooling all over my Vanité. No charge for all the detailing I'm covering for ya' either. Trust me or take a walk."

"This is a Zapruder moment," said Antoine sarcastically.

A hundred and twenty thousand! thought Jude. *That will cover the mortgage and the Italians' loan for a year and a half at least! We can surely get the Italians rebuilt by then! And then. And then…what?* His face fell when he thought about losing the car his grandfather and father had owned and passed along down to him.

"I need to call my wife," Jude demurred.

"Is your wife mail-order?" quipped Antoine.

"No. Is your boyfriend inflatable?" countered Jude as he dialed. No answer on the other end. "Can I see the car once more before Catty takes her in for the detail?"

"Too late, sir," said Catty. "I just had her driven off by one of my mechanics. He'll go over her engine as well. Her oil is black as pitch."

"There's nothing wrong with her engine," Jude stepped towards Catty. "I rebuilt that engine myself last winter. So if you mess with her engine or the transmission any, and I don't get paid, there will be blood!"

"No biggie, Jude. We just want to run some, er, diagnostics on the engine."

"Diagnostics? What the heck are you talking about? She hasn't needed diagnostics on her since you were standing on your toes adjusting the tin foil on the rabbit ears to eliminate the white noise of your black and white television!"

Paco laughed behind his teeth and reached out a hand to Jude. "I think someone needs an herbal enema."

"I'm not playing here!"

"Then it's a deal. You'll drive her in two days to car week in Fort Myers. While she's showing there, you can stay in my house on Sanibel Island. I'll even let this gross Hector of yours stay with you if he will keep away from my Vanité. I'll probably have to throw the bedsheets out after he leaves."

Hector flipped him off.

"Fine," said Jude, shaking Paco's hand firmly. "Two weeks. That's all I'm giving you. Hector goes with me. You cover the housing. And that loser Antoine there stays here in Miami."

"Me?" Antoine asked with his hand on his heart. "What on God's green earth did I do?"

"Nothing," Jude replied. "I just want you to keep your gay hands off the car."

"I was kinda hopin' that, um, wouldn't you like me to drive the Bel Air to Fort Myers for you? You can ride along with Paco in one of his finer sports-cars. You'll get there quicker."

"With you going twenty-four miles per hour and the emergency flashers on the whole way? Forget it. Not even if Jesus commanded me to allow you to."

"Don't be so crass. If Christianity were criminalized as a punishable offense, would you be convicted? I sincerely doubt it. Paco, dearie, I thank you heartily for the money. I'll be heading back to the penthouse to clean up and take your shirts to the laundry, if I may take my leave now." Antoine raised his nose in the air.

"Be gone with you, Anto" said Paco. "Stay out of my liquor cabinet."

"As for me, I'm heading back to the hotel now for a long cold shower," said Jude. "Dang this city is a scorcher. I'll be at Catty's in two days. The Bel Air better be ready to drive to Fort Myers. I'm calling all in, gentlemen. No funny stuff."

"It's a done deal," Paco miffed. "Nothing to worry about. Continue to stay at the hotel as my guest. Or, if you'd prefer, come to my condo and stay with me and Vanité. I would enjoy the company."

"I vote fer stayin' with Vanité," giggled Hector as he munched on a corn-dog. "She be like Baskin-Robbins. Thirty-one-derful flavors."

"Not a chance," said Jude. "The hotel will be better for us. I'll be at Catty's in two mornings. Like I said, no funny business. Paco, point me to your bank's closest branch so I can wire some of this cash back to Baltimore. My old lady needs to eat and my kid needs new shoes."

"Go back to your hotel get your shower first. There's a Wells Fargo bank across the street and a block or two North. Go in and tell the manager Graciela that you are a guest of mine. She will take care of wiring that money for you. Tell her to charge the wire fee to my account. She'll do it."

"Thanks," said Jude calmly. "I guess I should first call my honey to tell her I scored some clams. That should make her happy. 'Scuse me a sec."

Jude turned away and tried calling Margarita's cell phone again. No answer. Then he tried calling Margarita's mother's home. No answer. So he tried to call Filiberto back to see if he had been by the house to check up on Margarita. No answer from Filiberto.

"Farkle," said Jude. "I'm stuck down here in a hot paradise with twenty large on my person, and I can't even call home to celebrate my casino winnings."

"Don't worry about back home right now. It will all be okay in due time," smiled Paco widely. "Trust me."

"I'm working on trusting you. You're not making it easy on me."

Paco grinned. "By the way…Do you know how to say 'trust me' at Goldman Sachs?"

"No. I don't suppose I do. Humor me," said Jude flatly.

"It's very easy. Pay attention. *Trust me*?"

"Trust me?"
"Screw me."

6 Doc Ford's Cures All

Jude and Hector woke up bright and early in plans to hit up Catty's and pick up the Bel Air for the road trip to Sanibel. After munching breakfast at the Florissant café, the two blokes took an Uber to Catty's garage. The gaunt and derelict Uber driver went on and on joyfully commenting about their plans to take Alligator Alley from Miami-Dade across the belly of Florida and have them end up on the West Coast. After every sentence he spoke, he used his arm to wipe his nose and snorted.

"I nevah get over dere," said the transplanted Jamaican-New Yorker driver. "It's where the beautiful sunsets and 'the green flash' are more highly esteemed by the *touristas* than the grand yachts to their owners here in Miami harbor. I love it dere. Da money be here, though."

Jude had enough of this kid yapping on and on about Florida, just as he just about had enough of Florida. When he and Hector jumped out of the Uber car, the interior door handle came off. Jude just shook his head and went to find Catty. Hector had mercy on the young guy and tried to put the door handle back on. To no success.

"It ain't gonna," projected Hector, look for the loose screws and fiddling with the door.

"S'okay," said the Uber kid. "The biggah problem is the broken brake pedal. I have to use this stick to push it into the floor boards." The driver held up a grandfather's cane. "So far no accidents. Well, no major ones."

Catty was nowhere to be found. The hot-number Grace at the garage office gave Jude the Bel Air keys on a shiny gold key fob that was engraved with Paco's initials. "Pretty bold of Paco," commented Jude as he turned away from the nubile woman.

"The car is fully gassed up," said Grace with a gleam in her eye. "Have a nice ride."

"Mmm," mumbled Jude as he walked out of the office.

Grace giggled sweetly and gave a flip of her ponytail.

Before Jude and Hector left, Jude lifted the heavy hood and checked the engine compartment of the Bel Air, just to make sure no tampering of her OEM components was done or anything was ripped off by Catty. He grabbed a dirty rag by the side of the garage.

"Yep. They changed the oil, like Catty said he would. Nice of him to do that for us. I guess that means we can make like a holy priest and get the flock out of here."

"We bettah fills the tank, too, boss," said Hector. "Anto done told me dat Gator Alley is long as long can be. And there ain't but one gas stations along the strip. I don' wanna be stuck with no gas broke down in some gator 'fested area, mon."

"Tank's full, thanks to Catty again," said Jude as he fired the engine. The Bel Air's engine rumbled loudly. "Finely tuned like a Stradivarius violin. Gotta love that sound. The Bel Air can go four hundred and fifty miles on a tank of gas, unlike most cars of today. Of course that full tank will run you over eighty-five dollars at today's gas prices."

"Then less go, *hombre*!"

"Top down or up, Money?"

"Down, baby, down!"

Off towards Alligator Alley the pair went, following Miami's toll road, and hitting the Everglades just before noon struck.

"You know, sumpin', Jude?" asked Hector.

"What now? You don't want to go to Puerto Rico after all? You like Miami?"

"Naw. That's ain't it. It's I gots a bad feeling about this Paco dude. He just ups and gives you dat big cash and promises you a lot more than the car is worth if you just show it at Fo't Myers car week. Dat don' make no sense to me."

"I getcha. But big cash is hard to resist. A very bad thing about money, my momma always said: It makes you do things you didn't really expect you'd ever let yourself do."

"I guess dats why Ima always be broke, then!"

Just over three hours later across Alligator Alley and along the I-75 highway which runs up along the Gulf Coast, passed Naples and Bonita Springs, Jude agreed to make a stop in Fort Myer's at the insistence of Hector who was complaining about his empty stomach.

"We need gas, too. Paco said he would meet us later this evening on Sanibel, and according to my Tom-Tom GPS, we are about a half an hour away from the Sanibel Bridge. We've got plenty of time to enjoy a sandwich and a beer or two somewheres. You know how we can find the right place where to eat and drink?"

"No clue, boss."

"We ask a local! See that independent no-brand gas station and garage at the corner there? Best place to inquire on local eats."

Jude pulled the Bel Air to a stop at the gas station at the corner, right next to the gas pump where on the other side was a well-tanned young woman with a blond ponytail and bright red tank top with no bra standing next to a dark green Mazda Miata. The license plate had the initials MJ on it. Jude smiled and waved to her. The young girl feigned a look of boredom and didn't acknowledge Jude as she pumped gas into the Miata. She went inside to pay for her gas, returned, and finally gave the time to Jude.

"Maryland plates?" the sun-kissed babe asked rhetorically.

"As Sarah Palin sez 'You betcha!' Baltimore to be exact. You ever been there?"

"I went to Towson. Graduated last year."

"Towson's a good school. Know a good dive to eat and sit a spell around here?"

"I don't. But go inside and ask for Donald. He's the mechanic. He's from England, but knows everywhere and everyone in this town better than anyone," the girl said as she started up the

Mazda. "I'm from Estero down the road. Donald services all my family's cars here."

"We passed Estero on I-75. Nice looking area. Thank for the tip, hon'."

"Anytime, Baltimore," she flashed a smile as she drove off. The Miata's small rotary engine hummed as she entered the main roadway.

Nice girl, thought Jude. *Man, if I were younger and not married, I'da pursued that tail.*

"Hey, Jude! You gonna find us some food and beer, o' what?" yelled Hector impatiently.

"Yeah. Hold on."

Jude went inside and asked for Donald. A well-groomed and clean-cut man folded his arms and leaned his belly on the store counter.

"Donald Volvo here," said Donald with a devilish grin.

"Donald what?"

"Volvo. Like the car. Let's not make an issue of it."

"I'm not making an issue of it." Jude looked around the shop. "I'm just a man pregnant with liquor and my water broke. Where's the gynecologist-urologist?"

"Bathroom's back there," Donald pointed.

A gaunt African-American man in a seer-sucker suit and a pekoe hat on his head sat in the corner not far from the door to the bathroom. A half a bottle of Maker's Mark Bourbon and a full shot glass were perched on the running shelf along the window. The man and Jude traded nods. Then the man said squarely, "Whassa mattah? You never seen a black man so finely dressed? Adam and Eve were black, dontcha know. They were made of dust. What color is the dust?" The man let out a hearty belch. Jude paused a moment in contemplation, and turned himself towards the bathroom. He returned quickly without having relieved himself. The man in the corner was swigging a double-shot of Bourbon.

"Not enough O's in smooth!" laughed the man holding the shot glass.

"Who sprayed all over the wall and toilet in the bathroom?" inquired Jude with a twinge of disdain in his voice. "I haven't the slightest clue why trannies want genderless bathrooms seeing that nastiness in there!"

"Excuse me, sir!" said the man with the alcohol. "Did you say on the floor or the wall?"

"On the wall."

"Oh, well then, not me."

Jude inspected his shoes.

"Can I help you, Fletch?" asked the clean-cut man behind the counter.

"Uh, yeah... But... um... Sorry, the girl I just talked to out at the pumps said Donald was the mechanic. You're not wearing any fluid stains on you."

"Don't mean I ain't the mechanic. Just means I gots no work today. Whatcha need, Fletch? Gas? Oil? A Pepsi? To get laid?"

"Yes, gas," Jude pulled out the credit card from Filiberto.

"Sorry, Fletch, cash only here."

"Oh. Sorry. Here's eighty in twenties. She can't hold more than that. If you tell me a good place to respite for a few hours not far from the bridge to Sanibel, you can keep the change after I pump."

Donald grinned and stepped back to put the eighty dollars in an old mechanical cash register on the shelf behind the counter. "I have a bar I love. It's not flashy or filled with hot chicks in bikinis sucking down daiquiris. It doesn't have a thousand TVs with sports on 'em or some staff with matching uniforms. But they do sell cut bait if you need some for your fishing on Sanibel. They make their own home-made hot sauce and serve up fresh grouper sandwiches. The waitresses greet you with a smile when you enter, and they always remember me when I come back anytime. The female bartenders even ask me to go home with them, but I'm betrothed." He winked and showed Jude his gold wedding band. "The old men drink green label and hand me juke-box money because we listen to the same country music. That old, crazy hillbilly-looking guy at the end of the bar every Friday and

Saturday night, his eyes light up when I walk up because we are about to have the greatest conversation ever had. I love this bar because it's my kind of place and it's the people and food and not the name or alcohol that makes it awesome."

"Cool. Sounds like the right place to hang this afternoon. What's the name?"

"Not sure it has a name."

"Then where can I find it?"

"Not sure I can get you there from here."

"Wha—?" Jude started, then caught on. "Oh, I get it. You're a comedian. You sure you want to be a stand-up comic? Thanks for nothing. I'll be pumping my gas and be off your station then. Criminy—"

"I asked ya before if ya wanted to get laid."

Jude stood there and looked at the man incredulously. "You British are so superior, ain't ya? Do you know where you'd be without us Yanks? Eating knockwurst with sauerkraut and doing the duck-walk!"

"Britain was doing fine in the war until America decided finally to show up."

The black man sitting by the door let out a hearty laugh from his belly, slapping his thighs, "If the Church does nothing beyond perpetuate the faith that Jesus loves us unconditionally, then it will have done enough. Everything else flows easily from that ironclad belief. Think about that on the road to wherever you're agoin'."

"I have thought about it often enough. I ain't religious," countered Jude.

"In the happy moments, praise Jesus. In the difficult moments, seek Jesus. In the quiet moments, trust Jesus. In every moment, thank Jesus. Praise be to Jesus in Heaven! Yassir!" the black man slapped his knees again, laughing and hollering loudly.

"Okay, Britain. Can I at least get the key to the woman's john to drain the lizard before I fill up? Men's room is nasty. Or is there comedy in that, too?" asked Jude.

"No problem, Fletch. Do you need some help in there? Or can you handle it yourself?" said Donald flippantly as he went and sat next to the black man, holding a Snickers Bar and an open can of Dr. Pepper.

Jude used the woman's bathroom, commenting to himself that it was remarkably clean for being in a gas station owned by a jackhole. As Jude was walking out, the black man grabbed Jude's arm sternly. Jude smelled the heavy alcohol on the man's breath. The man looked at him sternly, as if the two were going to fight. He took off his hat and leveled a heavy brow. "Son, Jesus has only got three answers to a prayer. Now pay attention. They are: *Yes. Not yet.* Or, *I have something better in mind*. Let that work its way into your soul as you leave the station to wherever you're agoin'."

Jude smirked at the quirky black man, "Like I said before, I ain't religious", and went out to fill up the Bel Air with unleaded gasoline. *Dang,* he thought. *I should have asked that wanker Donald if he had any lead additive to coat the valves. I doubt Catty took care of that.*

"What took ya so long, boss? Where's we headed to munch?" asked Hector enthusiastically.

"Dunno. Everyone here 'cept that gal in the Miata has their head up their collective arses."

"We can't be delaying the trip no mo'. We be hittin' Sanibel, then, I take it? All straight up?"

"Yeah. I guess. Pull my cell phone and call Antoine. Maybe he knows a non-gay locale we can enjoy on Sanibel before we meet Paco later this evening at his beach house."

Hector rang Antoine, who sounded perturbed by the call. *"What, Hector? Why on earth are you botherin' me? Are you calling me for bail money?"*

"Naw. That ain't fonny, Anto. Judes wanna knows if you gots any place you cans recommend on Sanibel Island for us to enjoy afore we meets Paco later."

"Just you two going in? Or did you pick up a meth addict nymphomaniac or two on your way?'

"Yes and no. Just us, fonny mon. And Judes says no gay places, please."

"Unfortunately there's nothing gay on Sanibel. Don't worry about that. For you men, Doc Ford's all the way."

"Cool. We'll blow it up later. Bye, Anto."

"You know, Hector, I really should keep your number in my phone so I know not to answer it. Ciao, ciao."

"It be Jude's pho—"

>Click<

"You knows, for being a poof, Anto ain't that bad a guy," Hector called out to Jude. "Tho he cans be rude some."

"Yeah, yeah. Maybe his hormones haven't arrived from Canada this week. Just a minute more here and I'm done. Doc Ford's he said? Filiberto told me the same thing before we left Baltimore. Lotsa eye-candy for you there, Money."

The black man with the pekoe hat stumbled to the door and shouted out to Jude. "Jesus never allows evil to occur without allowing for a greater good to come from it. Think about that as you go wherever you're agoin'."

"Dream on," retorted Jude loudly. "That's like saying what doesn't kill you can make you stronger. Well, it may not kill you, but it can cripple you for life, anyhow."

"Love thy neighbor, son!"

"Only if thy neighbor is the key to instant wealth!" Jude shot back without turning his head.

"Be careful, son! I think the devil is wanting to sift you like wheat! This I know in my heart of hearts!"

Jude turned his head. "Ha! The devil. Like I believe that nonsense. Evil is as man does."

The black man put his pekoe hat back, his head hung low, returning slowly to his seat with the Bourbon, mumbling, *"Trust in the Lord forever. For the Lord, the Lord Himself, is the Rock Eternal.* Isaiah 26:4."

"You know, something, Hector?" Jude redirected as he kept pumping the gas into the Bel Air. "Ever notice the number of young males not marrying? Why is that?"

"Dunno. No clue," Hector shrugged.

"I'll tell you. Because so many good, religious people did zip while women's groups removed fathers from families. Guys aren't stupid. They know marriage is a bad investment. A man is only one woman's phone call to a divorce lawyer away from losing his kids, his money, everything in his life."

"I takes it you still can't get a hold of Margarita in Baltimore?"

"I wired her some big money when we were back in Miami. So why isn't she answering my calls? She should be happy to have a couple large in our bank account now. It's hers to spend as she wishes. I left a message saying just that before we left South Beach. Still no call back from her. Nothing. I can't win in my marriage. It's the whole universe against me."

"I hears ya. Dat's why I ain't married."

Jude finished pumping gas. The pump read eighty-two seventy-three. Over the eighty dollars Jude had given Donald. Jude climbed over the Bel Air door to the bench seat and fired the engine. He let off the emergency brake, and quickly pulled out of the station. Donald came running out of the garage after him. Jude flipped him off as the two men sped away fast.

"I tink," said Hector. "Dat marriage is dying because women are easy to bed nowadays. Why limit yourself to one woman when the liberated women are there for the easy plucking?"

"Again, what have the Jesus people done in the past fifty years while the National Organization for Women held congressional hearings on laws to make men irrelevant in marriage. Except to be money-mules. What have the Jesus people done while feminists demonized men and made public school hellacious for boys? A young boy is criminalized for playing tag at recess. There is just something fundamentally wrong with our society for making a thirteen year old middle school boy sit in a chair for seven hours. I blame it on the liberalized women."

"I dunno, Jude. My gran'father done left my gran'mother in Old San Juan with seven children and one on the way, which was my father at the time. My gran'father never came back none. She ended up bein' a very strong and determined woman. Never had no education. Couldn't read or write. But she wuz the most lovin' person I ever knew. Cooked up some fine meals, fo' my family and my cousins. All of us. All of us together in one small house. She wuz a good woman. As wuz my muthah."

"How did you say you lost your father?"

"I thinks it was murdah. My muthah never came clean on me on dat. He wuz fifty-fo' years ol' when I was born. Din't know him well anyways. He wuz always drinking cheap rum and smokin' a spliff on the back porch. He come back late at night drunk and high. My muthah gets up every time and makes him a big plate o' eggs and pinto and black beans with lotsa hot sauce. Then he be fightin' bad with my muthah till the morning hours. He done gone and gave her black eyes so many times, I done lost count of dat happenin'. Such a dang shame cuz my mother loved him so. It wuz painful to see. I don' miss any of dats from my childhood. I wish my muthah done had it bettah. She deserved so much bettah than what my daddy done gave her. Which wuz nuttin' but trouble inside and out."

"Sorry to hear that. Your mother sounds like a fine person."

"She sure wuz. A saint. Saint Isabel. How 'bout you? You never talk 'bout yo father, yet here you is in yo' pappy's car."

"He left me and my siblings alone with my mother. I don't really know what happened. It was all hush-hush in our house. We can talk about it some other time. I want to focus on the road. Just let it be said: Not everyone has a '*Leave It To Beaver*' scenario for their childhood."

"That really sucks. Sorry, bro."

According to Jude's Tom-Tom GPS, the bridge to Sanibel was not far away, just down McGregor Avenue. Instead of trying their luck again and asking at another filling station, the two decided to take up Antoine's advice and make it all the way to Doc Ford's on the island. The bridge toll was their first shock of Sanibel Island.

"Eight bucks to cross this bridge?!" asked Jude incredulously to the toll-keeper.

"Yessir. Or you can get a SunPass and it is only two-seventy-five each time you come across," answered the gritty toll-man.

"How much is the SunPass?"

"Seventy-six dollars. Annually."

"Forget it. We ain't comin' across this bridge any more times anyway. Here's a twenty. Break it."

The toll-man handed Jude back a crisp tenner and two crumpled ones. "Have a nice day on Sanibel. You boys going fishing?"

"Not fo' fish," cracked Hector with a wide grin as Jude pulled the Bel Air away from the toll-booth.

Not long after crossing the long bridge from Ft. Myers to Sanibel, the men got their second shock of the island. Less than a mile into Sanibel on Periwinkle Way, a motorcycle police officer in reflective Rayban sunglasses pulled him over. The officer took off his helmet and got off his bike slowly. Jude put his hands on the dashboard. Hector followed his lead.

"You know why I pulled you over?" asked the motorcycle cop as he leaned with both hands on the Bel Air's door, a bead of sweat dropped from his cheek.

Both Jude and Hector still had their hands on the dashboard. "No. Can't say that I do, officer."

"The speed limit's twenty-five. You were doing twenty-eight. Driver's license and registration please."

Jude pulled his license from his wallet and asked Hector to look through the glove compartment for the car's registration.

"Sorry, officer. I didn't see the speed limit signs."

"Where you miscreants headed?"

"Burning Man. I guess we have to scratch making the pyrotechnic opening celebrations."

"Funny guy," The cop looked down at the license. "Funny doesn't work with me. Lessee... Layden... Jude... I knew an old Tom Layden in Illinois. Ornery farmer not worth a hill of beans. You men got any guns on you? Or you been drinking? Out of the car, driver."

"No, sir. No guns," said Jude complicitly. "No alcohol."

"You. Slim," the cop flicked Jude's license between his fingers. "What's your name?"

Hector looked down, "Joe."

"Joe what?"

"Joe... Mamah. I be Spanish, suh."

"You got any ID on you? With or without that name, wiseguy?"

"No, suh," Hector lied. "No ID."

"And may I ask why not, fella?"

"No law in the land sez I gots to carry ID, is there, officer?" he held his palms up and shrugged.

Jude tried for a little more levity. "I recall years ago that the boxing champ Mike Tyson left his Rolls Royce on a New York highway and walked away because he was DUI and didn't want to get caught. He called the State Troopers and told them to keep the car. Hehehe. Funny, no?"

"Amusing," said the officer with no facial expression. "Make me laugh harder and I'll lock you both up for days."

Jude took a step back from the car and the policeman.

"Don't make a move, son. Stay right where youse at. I'm serious."

Hector kept picking through the glove compartment. "Jude, mon, there ain't no registration papers for the car in here."

"You sure?" Jude asked nervously.

"Dang, mon, yes I'm sure. Ain't none."

"Officer, we can't seem to locate the registration. Sorry?" Jude sheepishly grinned.

"Wait here," said the cop. "Don't get back in the car. Got it? Or I'll tighten you up."

The police officer went back to his motorcycle with Jude's license.

"Farkle," said Jude. "I know the registration was in there when we left Baltimore. I made sure of it. Let me ring up Catty. Maybe he knows where it is.—Hello? Catty?"

"Yes, Catty here. Is this Jude? I thought you'd be calling me. How's the Bel Air running? Purring like a kitten, eh?"

"Not bad. Not bad. She's running fine. But we got stopped by a motorcycle officer here on Sanibel, and we can't find the registration. You don't happen to know what happened to it, do ya?"

"Lemme check with Grace. Hold on."

"Catty is checking with Grace."

"Sweet young Grace," said Hector.

"Jude? Grace said one of the office girls took it out to make a photocopy of it for the South Beach show and forgot to put the original back in the car. We have it here in the office."

"Oh heck, great, that's terrific. I'm screwed now. Thanks, Catty, thanks for nothing. We are totally blown now. This cop here is mean as a wildcat in heat. I'll call you again." Jude put his phone back in his pocket when the officer looked at him.

Jude stood there next to the car. Hector sat still in the front seat leaning against the passenger door with his arms folded. Both men did not make a sound. Time went on for a few moments before anything else happened.

The motorcycle officer hobbled in his thigh-high jackboots back to the car. "Well, your license is clean, but since you don't have the registr—"

"I just called a good friend in Miami. It's in his service garage."

"Registration," repeated the officer gruffly. "You will have to leave the car here and I will have to have it towed to the island's impound yard."

"Impound?!"

"Hand me the keys to the car. A tow-truck is on its way and should be here soon. If you say the registration is in Miami, then get it here quickly and show it at the police station and you'll have your nice car back unscathed and at no cost to you. Assuming there are no issues with the registration when we do a search of it on the database. You didn't steal the car, did you, men?"

"JUDE!" yelled Catty on the phone. Jude pulled the phone from his pocket. *"Jude? JUDE!"*

"Dang, Catty. You still on the line? You hear that? The very nice officer here thinks the Bel Air's stolen."

"Yes, I heard. I'll do a FedEx personally right now. I'll send the registration to Paco's house there directly." Catty sounded unusually nervous on the phone and hung up quickly.

"Officer, I do apologize. The registration will be coming by FedEx. Hopefully tomorrow we can present it at the police station."

The officer handed Jude a folded paper map with penned directions to the police station and impound yard on Sanibel. "The yard is only open 9am to 4pm for pick up, but you can show up at any hour to let us see the registration. I warn you, though. If you are lying to me, we send impounded cars every month to Fort Myers to be auctioned off for whatever they sell for. And if it's stolen, you both could get locked up good and well. I'm letting you off with a warning on the speeding," he wagged a thick finger in Jude's face.

"You have my word. I'll show the registration at the station as soon as I get it. It's coming to a friend of mine's house here on Sanibel."

"Then enjoy your stay on the island. Here's your license back. Good luck," said the officer sarcastically as he went back to his Harley Davidson bike.

"Thank you, officer." *Why the heck did I just say thank you?* Jude smacked himself on the forehead.

"Suck," said Hector. "What a ways to start our island vacay."

"Yes. This does suck royally. But I am waiting here until the tow-truck comes. No way I am letting them drag my baby away tail-up. They better use a Low-Boy to haul her."

The hefty motorcycle cop sped away on his bike with heavy exhaust, leaving Hector and Jude standing by the Bel Air with no car keys under the hot Florida sun. Leaving them wondering if a tow-truck was indeed going to show up.

"At least he didn't give ya a ticket, boss," said Hector "That be lady-luck lookin' out for ya this time."

"Why would the cop leave us here alone? Shouldn't he wait until the tow-truck comes? That's what they'd do in Baltimore. Or any other place for that matter. Is it because he trusts us, or is he in a hurry to get out of this blasted sun? It's burning hot out here and we gotta wait until the tow-truck comes? This sucks awful. Big time."

Hector lit up a menthol and took a long drag, releasing the smoke through his nostrils.

"How can you smoke them ragweeds?" Jude asked with consternation in his voice.

"Easy. You just inhale. Unlike Bill Clinton."

Minutes passed. Then a half-hour. Then an hour. The hot Florida sun blazed on the exposed men like fire.

"Heck," said Jude. "I got a bad sunburn coming up on my arms and the back of my neck. You are lucky to be a darkie, Hector."

Hector fingered menthol after menthol. He had weary eyes. "Mon, I totally take back all those times when I was a young'un and din't want to take a nap."

"Yeah, I can't remember the last time I wasn't at least kinda tired in life. You never know when it's gonna strike, but there comes a point when you realize you are not going to do anything else productive for the rest of the day."

A few minutes past the two hour wait, a Low-Boy pulled alongside the Bel Air. Both Jude and Hector were hot and sweaty, with their shirts soaked from the long wait sitting by the side of the Bel Air.

The driver snorted out the window. "You gentlemen have the altercation with the Sanibel police officer? This the Maryland car I am supposed to take to the impound yard? One of y'all's name is Jude Layden?"

"Yeah, it is," said Jude flatly. "Take good care of her will ya? Here's a twenty to be extra careful."

"She's a beut'. Glad I got the Low-Boy today. Usually I get the wrecker."

"Sees? Lady-luck be smilin' on ya still, boss," said Hector with a nudge.

The driver climbed down out of the truck and grabbed the twenty from Jude to put into his sweaty pants pocket. He had a large solid silver cross hanging on a leather necklace on the outside of a crisp and clean white t-shirt that read in big black letters *Who Would Jesus Bomb*?

"Thanks!" the driver said. "First time on Sanibel?"

"Yeah, it is. Thus far this island sucks. Toll-booth rip-off. Car getting towed. Stranded on the side of the road in this oppressive heat. Opposite of gilding the lily. We had a barely passable experience already in South Beach and this makes it materially worse. You ever been to Doc Ford's?" asked Jude. "Can you tell us how to get there from here?"

"Nope. I've never been there," said the driver as he struggled to unload his trucks' straps. "House of the devil. But you'll need a ride to get you there from here. Too far to walk. Sun or no sun. It's on Captiva, not Sanibel. Unless you want to go back to Fort Myers Beach. There's a Doc Ford's there, too."

"Captiva? What's a Captiva?" questioned Jude.

The truck driver looked at Jude like he was a child. "You're on Sanibel and you've never heard of the better island Captiva?"

"No, I haven't. I ain't from around here as you already figured out."

"Captiva Island is at the north end of Sanibel. Doc Ford's is part of the South Seas resort on Captiva. You'll definitely need a ride to get you there unless you have a couple days to walk No, I'm not giving you a ride."

"What cab company is on the island?"

The Low-Boy driver started the winch to bring the Bel-Air onboard. The winch groaned under the weight. "Sanibel cab'd be too expensive. It's a rip-off. You'll need Uber for a better deal. It'll plum get you there faster cheaper."

"Oh, wait, forgot. Wait a sec till we grab our bags and stuff out of the car. Then you can take my baby away." Jude climbed up into the halfway loaded car to get the gym bags.

Jude and Hector watched as the Bel Air was well-strapped and securely loaded onto the Low-Boy, with Jude checking the straps himself before he would let the driver take her away. When the

Low-Boy did leave, it spewed a large plume of diesel smoke that choked the two abandoned misfortunates.

Jude let out a heavy sigh and slumped his shoulders.

"Ways, Jude, ways. What we gonna do now?" Hector lit up another menthol. "I'm outta smokes, too."

"Hector, use your brain. It's that lump three feet above your butt. I suggest we find Doc Ford's on Captiva, wherever that is. Paco better be at his house tomorrow if we don't get there for the FedEx. Or we are really fried like an oyster. I don't know about that Low-Boy driver with my car. I know I gave him a twenty-spot, but even so, if a blue-collar man is talking nice to you, something is definitely wrong. He should be cursing your arse out for nothing. I know I would if it were my job to tow cars on a hot day like this."

"It's cool. The dude's a Christian. Din't ya see his shiny cross around his neck? You gonna check with Uber for a ride?"

"What choice we got? I don't know where the heck I am. Do you?"

Hector shook his head.

"Do you know any-thing, Money?"

Hector shrugged. "Newsflash: Kim Kardashian's surrogate is pregnant. Updates at eleven."

Jude rolled his eyes and checked out the Uber App on his Samsung cell phone to set up a quick pick up from the closest corner of Periwinkle Way and Casa Ybel Road.

"My phone battery's dying. Almost dead. We gotta find an electric outlet. Man, is it hot out here. I'm dying myself. What a crap-assed day."

The Uber driver showed up within minutes in a late-model mint green convertible Mustang with cream interior.

"Y'all are waiting for me, right? Y'all wanna go to Doc Ford's, right?" the driver asked. "That's what is says on my app."

"Yeah. Uber. Take us there," commanded Jude. "Now."

"Sanibel or Captiva location?"

"What? A dude we just talked to told us it was on Captiva. He must want us off his island."

"Which one you wanna go to? Rabbit Road or South Seas? Sanibel or Captiva?"

"Take us ta Captiva," interjected Hector. "I done had it with Sanibel. This place done ticked me off so much already."

"Doc Ford's Captiva South Seas resort, check. Hop in."

"You don't even look old enough to have a driver's license, and you drive for Uber?" questioned Jude to the youthful Mustang driver.

"I'm actually not supposed to be driving this car. It's my dad's."

"Oh, great. Just don't get stopped by the cops, cool, kid? We've already been introduced to Sanibel's finest."

"No worries. My dad's a Sanibel motorcycle cop. Let's ride."

"Da-ang," said Hector as he put out his last cigarette on the pavement. "Prob'ly the same cop who stopped us and took aways the Bel Air. What a coincidence."

With both men in the back of the Mustang, the young kid shifted into gear and began the drive down Periwinkle Way, turning onto Palm Ridge Road, and, blowing through the stop-sign intersection, made his way onto Sanibel-Captiva Road.

"Kid, you just blew a stop sign!" Jude warned.

"There's been a lot of changes on the island. I'm not sure that stop sign still works. That's J.N. 'Ding' Darling's Wildlife Refuge and conservation area on the right."

"We don' need no tour," commented Hector dryly. "Just get me to ma meal and cocktails."

"Excuse him. He has a fine line between boredom and hunger. I've heard of that man, Ding Darling," alluded Jude. "He graduated from my alma mater, Beloit College, in 1898."

"You went to Beloit College?" the kid asked happily over the sound of the wind rushing by the Mustang.

"Yep. Graduated in 2002."

"I'm applying there now. I hear it has a cool liberal arts scene."

"Careful. A liberal arts education is to some people just a participation trophy. I disagree. The benefit of Beloit and other lib colleges is the relationships you develop with the professors and the great alumni network."

"I want to major in English," the boy thumped.

"English major? Like that'll get you a good job. Try Economics. It's the same with all mid-west liberal arts colleges. It's a cool place to be if you're a lib and like protesting daily. The fraternities are awesome to be a part of. I was in Sigma Alpha Epsilon. You can make some good friends in one pretty easily. There's forever and a day of good beer in Wisconsin. For less than four bucks you can get a case of good Wisconsin beer. You can even get a case of bad Wisconsin beer for two bucks. Nowhere else in the world can that happen. The winters are rough. If you need the sun, then I wouldn't consider going there for college. It snows five months out of the year. I'm talking snow measured by feet. With cold grey skies eight months out of the year. Stay down south if ya need sunny days."

"I'm thinking of becoming a cop. Like my dad. He—"

"A cop? Your generation can't even argue over the Xbox controller unless violence is thrown in gratuitously."

"Y'all need to stop and smell the bougainvillea when you are on Captiva," said the boy.

"Is that like stop and smell the roses? Roses are too expensive. I will stop and smell the dandelions," deadpanned Jude

Multiple bicycles and runners, all well-tanned and sweating profusely, were going both directions alongside the road in the designated lane. The kid kept to the speed limit. He spoke about all the places on Sanibel and Captiva where Jude and Hector could enjoy a fine meal and boat-drinks. "Hey. What can I say? It's heaven here. I never go off the islands," the boy chimed.

"You are gonna be shocked dead by Beloit, Wisconsin."

A little while down San-Cap road, the kid spied a turtle in the middle of the road. He stopped the Mustang in the breakdown lane and got out to carry the turtle across the street. "Turtles get hit all the time. You gotta watch for them. They're protected. The manatees are protected, too."

"A manatee? What the heck is dat?" asked Hector.

"Oh, you should see one while on Captiva. They hang just underneath the surface of the waters by the docks at South Seas. They're a funny sight. Slow moving. Called a sea cow because it's the only mammal in the ocean that's vegetarian," the kid chuckled. "We're now at Santiva. Here's Bowman's Beach. Good fishing here. Cross the bridge and we're onto Captiva. Almost there for you gentlemen. So close. Lee Majors lives over in that house. You know him? From '*The Six Million Dollar Man*' TV show and being married to Farrah Fawcett? Sad news at her passing away. I personally like reruns of '*The Fall Guy*'."

The Mustang drove through the Gold Coast of Captiva where all the mega-mansions of the island's ultra-wealthy spend their winters. Jude wasn't paying much attention to where they were going. He was more concerned about the Bel Air. He pulled from his pocket the map of Sanibel that the policeman gave him and had a look at it before stuffing it into a pocket of his gym bag. He and Hector hadn't had the chance to do any laundry yet on their trip. Their reused clothing was getting mighty ripe.

"Shirts get dirty. Underwear gets dirty. But good khaki shorts never get dirty, and you can wear them forever," noted Jude to the bewilderment of the other two in the car.

"We're now just going through the center town of Captiva," pointed out the kid.

"Hey, dere's a store. Can we stop? I need some smokes," asked Hector with a hint of pain in his voice. "Spot me the money for a few packs of menthols?" Jude quickly flipped him a twenty dollar bill.

"That's the Island Store. Don't be shocked at the prices," said the kid.

Hector went in while Jude hopped out to mull around and try to call both Paco and Margarita. The cell phone signal was weak and so was his battery. "Hey kid, you got a mini-USB charger in your dad's 'Stang?"

"Yeah. You can charge your phone while we wait for your friend. Does he know he smells bad?"

"Oh, he knows."

About two minutes later Hector came out from the Island store with his head down and mumbling under his breath. He handed Jude a few ones and some small change.

"That's it? From a twenty? How many packs did you buy?"

"Jus' two." He ripped open a pack and pulled a cigarette out to light up.

"We're gonna sit here a while as my phone charges. You don't mind, kid, do ya?"

"No problem. By the way, I turned off my Uber app before we left Sanibel. You mind paying me cash for the ride?" The kid flashed a smile.

"Can do. How much?"

"Fifty bucks sound about right?"

"FIFTY BUCKS!? Are you out of your mind, spanky?"

"What did you expect? The islands aren't cheap. I'm not supposed to be in this car. I better get home before my dad's off his beat."

"Here's two twenties. You better take it, or I'll report you to Uber."

"That'll do. I can only stick around to let you charge your phone for another coupla minutes. You guys can walk to Doc Ford's from here. It's a straight shot down the road to South Seas resort. Doc Ford's is right there near the entrance."

"What are you gonna do then, kid?'

"Go home and sit and do Facebook," replied the boy.

"You're gonna waste the rest of your day on that crap?"

"If I didn't have Facebook, I'd be bored."

"Boredom is a luxury."

"Doing Facebook and other social media well is my ticket to higher education. *Sitting here in my room, safe here inside my womb. I touch no one, and no one touches me.* Simon and Garfunkel."

"Sure thing. That'll get you into Beloit College. Being a loner in your momma's basement pimping time on Facebook. What're you scared of? People?"

"Nope. Not scared of people. I can be better off as a loner. What'll get me into Beloit College is a quote from Steve Jobs, the ultimate loner. He was a big time stoner. He died worth ten billion dollars. *'Everything around you that you call life was made up by people that were no smarter than you and you can change it, you can influence it, you can build your own things that other people can use.'* I'm gonna create new technologies no one knows about yet. Great and wondrous new technologies."

"You're saying that's gonna be your budding career outlook today on Facebook? Followed up with a degree in English from Beloit. I got it."

"I hafta start somewhere. May as well be updating my Facebook wall."

"I can't imagine the irony here. Here's a piece of advice: you - not Facebook or Google or Apple - you have to be the inspiration, the motivation, and the ideas you want to make the world a better place. I used to want to change the world. Right now I'd be ecstatic to change my underwear."

"I'll probably be downloading porn. To be honest with you" said the boy glumly.

"You better find a best friend to erase your computer history when you die," pointed out Jude.

"Have you heard about all the great advancements in cloning? I want to be a part of it!"

"Just don't clone yourself. One of you is difficult enough for the world to deal with. Go on. Get out of here."

"I forgot to tell you. There's a water shortage on the island."

"So?"

"If it's yellow, let it mellow. If it's brown, flush it down."

"Get out of here, kid. Gimme my phone first."

The young driver handed Jude his phone and charger and started the engine. "Time for Facebook and porn."

Hector leaned on the driver's side. "Don' you gots any hobbies to be doin'?"

"I have my pet hermit crabs."

"Pet… crabs?" Jude was nonplussed.

"Yes. They make great pets because they don't run away. You can even neuter them yourself. Byyyeee!" He shifted into gear and peeled away in a cloud of dust down Captiva Drive back towards Sanibel.

"I guess if your father is the island's cop, then you can pretty much drive any way you want," Jude said.

Hector lit up another cigarette. "We gonna make it to Doc Ford's now? I been hungry for hours."

"These feet were made for walking."

Walking down Captiva Drive towards South Seas, Jude and Hector were passed by many cars going to and from the resort. One car, a Mercedes convertible with a manatee on its Florida license plate, stopped just in front of the two stragglers. The driver, a tall slinky girl with red highlights and designer sunglasses offered them a ride.

"Sure!" said Jude, as the two of them stepped forward to meet the car.

"Byeeeee!" laughed the girl as she pulled away, leaving the two men in her wake.

Jude stood there for a moment. Never in his life had something like that happened to him.

"Wench... Now I sound like Antoine. These islands have been such a hit with me. I need a drink badly."

The two men were close to passing out from exhaustion. Fortunately Jude and Hector were not far from Doc Ford's. They passed a mini-mall with a Starbucks on the left, and wandered onto the South Seas resort.

"There you be," said Jude. "Unless that's a mirage. The way today has gone, it very well could be."

Hector dropped his menthol cigarette and stamped on it. "Fo' sho'. Let's go on in."

Doc Ford's was hopping with people of every variety milling around. Hedonism and diversity at its best. Everyone had boat-drinks in hand, listening to Jimmy Buffet's *A Pirate Looks At Forty* playing over the speakers in all corners of the bar-restaurant. Jude and Hector blew passed the bouncer and went straight to the zinc bar counter. Two women talking there took a whiff of Hector and walked away holding their noses.

"Anto can't like this dive. The bar-stools aren't upside down," Jude nudged Hector a step away from him.

"You men need something? Or are you lost puppies?" asked the wispy brown-haired bartender with an Australian accent. "Welcome to Captiva Island. Where every day is Saturday night… and Saturday night is New Year's Eve."

"Straight vodka on ice for me," replied Jude matter-of-factly.

"You want straight vodka? Are you an alcoholic?" asked the barkeep as she wiped the counter in front of Jude.

Jude winced. "Okay. Then a slight vermouth droplet in with the vodka. Just a drop."

The woman perked up. "Oh, that's so pretentious! If you just want to drink vodka straight, then say so!"

Jude gazed at her dumbfounded a moment. "Rum punch. No ice!" he flashed back.

"I'll be havin' a rum punch, too," said Hector nodding. "Wit plenty o' ice."

"Which rum would you like? We have Gosling's, Captain Morgan, Pusser's, and rail."

"Rail. For both of us," said Jude before Hector could speak.

Hector scowled at him, "Ways to be cheap, boss".

The bartender began to mix up the drinks in front of the two men who were now seated on wooden barstools.

"Where yo' from?" asked Hector. "I likes yo' accent. Let's blow it up some."

"Australia. No, I don't qualify for Obamacare. It's one of the first questions people ask me about my working in America. So let it go, mmm, okay?"

"That is okay," said Jude while grasping his rum punch. "Obamacare only means I can get my penis cut off and a boob job for free."

"I been wonderin'. What does they do with all de cut off penises?" asked Hector curiously.

"They go into the National Organization for Women's lock-box."

"Oh," said Hector. "Din't know dat."

"You men missed the book signing," said the barkeep. "You shoulda been here an hour ago. What's with the gym bags? You guys look like sandy-murky water. Healths-a-poppin' you didn't come here from a work-out."

"Book signing? By whom?"

"By whom? Seriously? You must be new to Captiva. Randy Wayne White. The most famous book author on the islands. He's promoting his latest book *Deep Blue*. I haven't read it yet. But I plan to at some point soon. Enjoy your drinks. Sixteen-fifty. Cash or shall I start you a tab?"

"Gads. This ain't a cheap dive," said Jude as he pulled a folded twenty-spot from his wallet. "Go ahead and start mixing up another round as we will be done with these in seconds. We are gonna tie one on today."

"Aiiight. Done. How much rum can you drink, mate?"

"Um, I—"

"If you have to think about it, you're in the wrong place. No amateurs here. Professional drinkers only."

"I guess," Jude threw up his hands.

"Just to let you know. There's a water problem on the island and—"

"If it's brown flush it down. If it's yellow, something or other?"

"Exactly. You know the islands well!" she shouted above the din in her Australian accent while turning her back.

Four rounds and almost seventy dollars later, Jude and Hector were lit up and loud like Fourth of July fireworks. They could barely sit on the bar stools and had to lean on the zinc counter to keep themselves up straight. The Aussie bartender pounded on the zinc to quiet them down. Jude's phone rang.

"Layden heah."

"Jude? Paco. Anto told me you called. Did you make it to Doc Ford's?"

"Yesh Paco Mr. Taco. We're heah now on Captiva at South Seas. The rum is exsheptionally de-lish!"

"Just don't drive the Bel Air while you're tanked. We don't need you

to get stopped for a DUI."

"Couldn't get stopped if I wanted to. Copsh already confiscated the ca—"

"The Bel Air has been confiscated? Is that what you are telling me?! Please tell me that isn't what you mean! What the heck happened?"

"Copsh already confiscated the car," Jude repeated louder with weariness in his voice. "It's somewhere like the po-po station on Sanibel. We can't get it till Catty Fedex's the car's regishtration to your houuuse."

"Gads! We can't lose that car! Losers! I knew you'd blow it! Man, oh, man, OH MAN! We can't lose that car!"

"Whash so special about the Bel Air to you, anyway, Paco?" Jude stiffened. "Of all the carsh out there in 'Merica, you want my baby. Whassup wit dat anywaysh? I want some transhparency."

"Transparency is another word for Obama meets Orwellian. It's more of an urban myth. Oh, man! Did Catty say he sent the Fedex yet? If not, I can bring the registration with me when I drive over tomorrow. Man, oh, man, OH, MAN!"

"You mean to say you're not gonna be heah tonight?" Jude was confused. "What're we shupposed to do for to-night? Hector and me are—"

"Sorry, fellas. I've been held up here in Miami. I'll be there tomorrow night. Just sleep on the beach by South Seas. You sound drunk enough to sleep in a cattle car. Sleep it off on the beach till morning. I'm gonna call Catty. We need that car, I'm telling you. You couldn't even drive it across Florida without screwing it up, could ya? What the heck is wrong with you? You and Hector are like herpes. Just when you think they're finally taken care of, they come up and ruin your life again!"

"What-ev's,"

"Man, oh man!"

"Yeah, yeah, Paco. Blow me a kish, pushycat," said Jude as he clicked off his phone. He was so ripped at Paco for reneging on the stay-over at his place for the night it started to sober him up fast. Still he wasn't sure how he was going to break the bad news to Hector. Hector, meanwhile, was hitting on the bartender.

"Eh, tar-bender," Hector laughed incoherently. "Where'd you say you gots dat awesome accent?"

"Australia!" she yelled back at him.

"I remember the Crocodile Dundee commercial where he goes and says he's gonna throws some shrimps on the bar-b. You and me. We be making a good couple with our accents. Whass yer name?"

"Wish," she batted her eyelashes.

"Really? Wish. How I wish—"

"You just keep on wishing because I'm a taken woman."

"Dude," Jude stepped up to Hector.

Hector turned back to his friend and sat on a stool with his arms folded and eyes closed. "Blow it up."

"Bad news. We're sleeping on the beach tonight. Paco dissed us big time."

"No mattah. We can stays here all night long in da bar! Woohoo!"

"Not in my bar, you're not," said the barkeep. "I'm done serving you lushes."

"Well then, can we eats? I done fo'got to eat," said Hector grimly.

"Make it quick," said the bartender as she wiped down the bar one more time. "I'm off shift in twenty minutes. The guy taking my place doesn't mess around. If you're a drunken mess in his bar, he'll kick your butts right out. You know you guys look like poor tippers. Don't let your tight sphincter kill you. Loosen up, or you'll back up and die."

Hector pointed to something on the menu that he was hoping with his bloodshot eyes looked like chicken wings. Jude passed on the idea of eating. Yes, his stomach was empty as he hadn't eaten all day, but he was still flipping angry at Paco for dissing them. He wanted a cold shower and a clean towel to wrap himself in and a cool pillow to lay his head on. What choices did he and Hector have? Only sleep on the beach as Paco instructed him? He didn't even know where to find the beach when they would leave Doc Ford's! He was dead exhausted from the heat, the hassles, and the rum. Jude took a seat in the corner by the now-silent jukebox with a pitcher of ice water for a few minutes to clear his head and get fully sober again. He nodded off and leaned against the wall. *How the heck did I end up like this? Where did I go wrong in life? I should be back in Baltimore sleeping off this buzz next to Margarita. Does Filiberto know what's going on? I could choke that bastard Paco.*

Hector came up to him. "Jude, wake up. You see that bald-headed guy with the lumberjack beard? Coming back from the bathroom I asked him why his head was upside down!" laughed Hector.

"Sicko. You're a mess."

"Yer a mess, too, boss. Looks at the mess we're in now."

"Maybe so. But as a good man I own my own messiness. Hurry yerself up and finish eating. Ima 'bout to pass out here," Jude spoke quietly, not looking Hector in the eye.

"Can't you hang for a while? I wuz hopin' to scam for a steamer. Ima thinkin' to get lucky!"

"No dice. A two at ten p.m. is a ten at two a.m. Let me save you the trouble. My buddies at Sigma Alpha Epsilon always said it: friends don't let friends beer-goggle."

"You really missed yer callin'. I wish ah knew what it is."

When the hot wings arrived, Hector took a bite out of one and bit off part of the bone. It crunched in his mouth. "Mmm… Not bad."

A few minutes later the wings were gone. Jude continued to sober up gulping down more glasses of water with a lemon squeeze. He finally had enough and settled up the tab with the Aussie bartender, taking back the cash he had been giving her and using the credit card Filiberto gave him. He wrote on the credit card receipt a fifty-dollar tip and gave the barmaid a castigating smirk. She returned a chilling Chesher-cat smile. Jude hustled himself and the reluctant Hector towards the door.

"Where's da beach?" shouted Hector in a stumble.

"Can't you see? The beach is straight ahead of you!" yelled the bartender. "You can't miss it. March your way down the beach a bit away from the resort so the South Seas security doesn't bust your loser butts for being drunk on their turf!"

"I will never recommends this place, Doc's whatever-the-heck it is, to any of mah friends," said Hector defiantly, flipping off the bartender.

"Wow, I do mean, wow. You have so penetrated my thin skin. That doesn't make any sense, Sheila," replied the bargirl. "First, you probably don't have any friends. And even if you did, they'd probably not like you enough to follow you to Captiva from whatever hell-hole you are from. Yes, I think our bar will survive just fine without your fictional friends' business or Yelp reviews!" She washed up a Martini glass and hung it up in the wood sleeves above the zinc bar.

Jude turned and frowned weakly as the two men stumbled out the wooden door of Doc Ford's. The bartender yelled after them again, "Don't ask me to apologize! I won't ask you to forgive me!" Jude slammed the door shut.

The two drunks fumbled across the parking lot, through the thick flora and grassy path, straight onto the Captiva sandy beach.

"I'm done beat. I feel awful," Hector groaned.

"I'm sure. She said we can't stay here. We'd be busted by security. We gotta move down the beach some away from the resort, or we're sure to get our arses busted. Better to sleep on the beach than in a jail cell. Less go."

Not even forty paces down the beach, Hector stopped his stumbling. "I don' feel so good," he held his stomach.

"We gotta keep goin'. We need to go to be out of sight. C'mon. Just a little bit farther."

"Mmmfghhh", muffled Hector.

"What are you trying to say?"

"Mmmghtth."

"Hector, for pete's-sake. Buy a vowel."

Hector let out a heavy wretch, throwing up all the chicken wings and hot sauce and rum he had forced down his gullet back at Doc Ford's.

"Fogget it, Judes. Ima cashed," he said as he held his gut tightly. "Can ah get any help here? Any pepto-bismol or sumpin'?"

"Way to go and toss your groceries on the beach. That smells worse than you do. I guess the rum and wings were too much for you. We gotta keep moving. There's a spotlight down the beach a bit more. I can see it from here. Let's go near it. There may be an outdoor shower at a beach house we can quietly sneak into. Both of us could use a good showering."

"I'm done cashed," said Hector again as he dragged his body along, drifting in and out of semi-consciousness.

Down by the spotlight, just off the beach line, there was a clothesline with some towels drying off in the dead of the night. Jude ripped down a bunch of the towels, laying two larger ones side by side for him and Hector to sleep on, and making lumpy pillows out of two smaller towels. The two men took off their shoes and let their feet become cool and sandy.

"Feels so dang good to set yerself down, don't it?" relaxed Hector.

"Yes. Yes it does," exhaled Jude. "Thankfully it ain't a million degrees right now."

"I gots to get to Puerto Rico soon."

"I get it. You will, Money. I promise you that. I will get you there."

"Boss?" asked Hector as he stretched himself out, scrunching up the small towel again for a tighter pillow.

"Yeah, Money."

"Ain't it true the unexamined life ain't worth livin'?"

"Yeah. That be true, my friend. My life for sure works that way."

"Mmhmm. I sees… uh… boss?"

"Yes, again."

"Explain the world ta me? I be here looking up at the shiny stars and moon and all. None of it makes no sense to me. The world and all, I means."

"I wish we had been here for the sunset. To see the mysterious green flash."

"Mysterious what?"

"Never mind. God is playing a game using men as tokens. That's how I see the world. You won't get any more religion outta me than that."

"Ok on dat. Any advice?"

"Not much I can offer you. My daddy did tell me something when I was young that I won't forget. He said, '*A working man does not have time for relationships*'. It's a pity, no? All my relationships are with customers at the garage. It's all business, nothing more. My daddy also said, '*Always, always, always be here now*'."

"Was yo daddy old when he done died?"

"Old enough, he once told me, that when he saw a pretty girl, he got a lump in his throat, instead of his pants. I was too young to understand that."

"Oh."

"Funny, right?"

"Yeah. Fonny. Did he ever compliment you?"

"Once that I can remember. I was about nine years old. Not long before he died. I had just scored the winning goal in the final seconds of a semi-final game in the local soccer tournament. He said, '*You're gonna be a big man, someday, son. I'm proud of ya.*'. We won that game, but lost the championship. I cruised myself on that compliment for two weeks."

The two men fell silent a moment, listening to the rustle of the palm trees above them in the wind. The sound of the sea waves was melancholic to Jude.

"Boss?"

"Yes, yet again."

"Berto done told me once dat yo daddy off'd hisself. Dat true?"

Jude sighed. "It's true."

"How'd he done it? Can I ask? I don' wanna push ya none."

"He swallowed a bottle of sleeping pills and followed with some cheap whiskey. All alone in his big farm house in the hills since he and my mother were separated. My mother told me at the time he was stressed with bills and it was an accidental overdose. Drop by drop over time the words came out of her and I finally understood that he took his own life."

"Pain. Man, that be harsh to deal with. How'd you gets yousself through it being so young and all?"

"I meandered through all the emotions for years. Mostly falling to pieces at the mention of his name. I never have gotten over it. It especially hurts when I hear some religious jerk say that people who commit suicide are bound for hell."

"Damn. That be harsh. I'm sorry. I gets to understand you nows. You's a good man, boss."

"I wish my Margarita saw me as a good man. Right now I'm sure she doesn't."

"Margarita's gonna unnerstand jes fine. You waits and sees. She gonna be lovin' ya good when all is done and settled and you gots that money from Paco."

"I'm not a praying man, but I do hope so."

"I'm sorry you had such a bad childhood. I can relates. As I done told ya today."

"It's okay. I appreciate that... and you. Get some sleep. Tomorrow is going to be an eventful day. I can tell you that. We will have to see how we can get you back to Miami soon so you can head to Puerto Rico. You're running out of time before the warrant is out for you."

"I miss my own Island of Song. It's the place of my chile'hood."

"We'll getcha there. Don't worry about it now. Sleep."

Jude lay there with his arms folded and his legs crossed staring at the stars above. Hector turned his back to him and softly sang a few lines of a song he learned when he was a child.

"So I'ma sad to say I be on my ways. Won't be back for many a days. My heart is down; my head is turning around. I had to leave a pretty girl in ole San Juan town. Mmmhmm."

Jude soon heard wheezing which let him know that Hector was now asleep, putting his heart at ease. Jude breathed deeply as he sank into a contemplative moment, wondering just how he got to where he was and what would happen next. He was unsure about Paco. He was unsure about getting the Bel Air back. He was unsure of everything and anything that tomorrow could bring. That was all he knew and could admit to himself.

The spotlight still shone in the dark night. No one was around to notice the two interlopers crashed right there on someone's property next to the beach underneath the palm trees. It was probably illegal for them so stay there, or so Jude thought. Jude didn't care. He was comfortable on the warm sand with the cool breeze which brought the smell of the sea and its sounds and the bright shiny moon above looking like it was cut out of the dark night sky.

The mental anguish from the recent days' episodes that Jude was suffering would have harmed a weaker man. Yet Jude had hearty resolve. He had learned that from his strict grandfather at a tender young age. More than that; Jude did not choose to carry himself as a weak man. Not a bold man, but not weak man, either. As the day had passed, he felt himself suddenly feeling harder, stiffer. Like having a core of steel. He thought a bit about his father and his youth. Would his father be proud of him now? What about selling the Bel Air? This bothered Jude much as he tossed and turned himself gently on the towel he lay on.

At long last, he finally fell asleep on the warm sandy towel next to Hector in the chilly sea breeze. What Jude didn't know was that both Margarita and Filiberto were trying to call him at that very moment, and Jude's phone was out of reach of a cellphone tower signal. Margarita didn't bother to leave a message, but Filiberto did. Jude wouldn't get the urgent message from Filiberto until over a day later. That missed call would unfortunately be very costly in so many ways for Jude.

7 It Has Been Said: The Devil Wears Prada

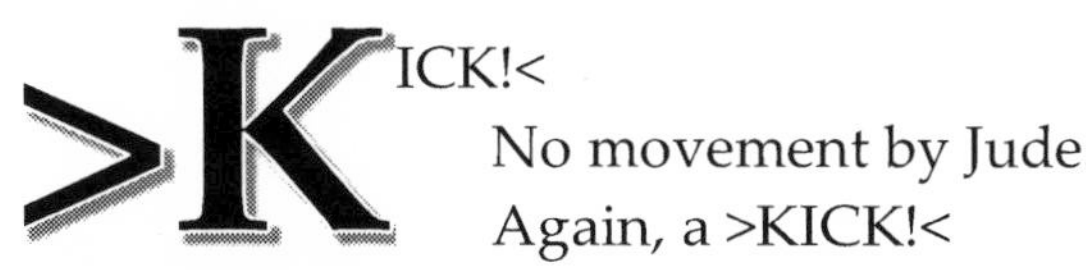

ICK!<

No movement by Jude.

Again, a >KICK!<

Jude rolled over and held his hand to cover the morning sun from his eyes. Standing before him was a deliciously charming, slender blue-eyed brunette with perfectly coiffed hair. She was adorned in a red and yellow Prada outfit, something similar to what Hillary Clinton would wear to a campaign pep-rally. The woman smiled and kicked Jude again, this time not as hard, more like nudging him to address her.

"Hey! I got it the first time," said Jude.

"Don't have a hissy fit. It's too early in the morning. You'll wake the sand scorpions" chuckled the quick-witted woman. "You're on my formerly clean beach towels!"

"Scorpions?! Uh… Sorry. Was I being quiet too loudly for you?"

"Poisonous snakes usually is the bigger problem. Coral snakes. You don't look so derelict like that guy over there.—"

It was true. Hector had rolled several feet away from Jude in his sleep.

"So why are you sleeping in front of my house on my formerly clean towels?"

Hector was still fast asleep though the sun shined brightly and the beach was hot. "Sorry," said Jude grinning. "We needed a place to crash for the evening. The sandy beach here was inviting. No one was around. Your clothesline had these large towels, and, well, um, I just took advantage. I'd be happy to pay to have them laundered for you."

A sand-piper flew down and landed next to Jude and cocked its head sideways. Jude was nonplussed at both the bird and the woman.

"No need. I'll have Beatrice do it. In the meantime, can you tell me why you made it all the way to Captiva and then decided to sleep on the beach? Did you pass out drunk and leave your car somewhere? I don't see any liquor bottles around you. Did you throw them in my trash bins? Don't you have a car to get off the island? Or are you fugitives fleeing the cops and looking for a safe space with coloring books and cute puppies?"

"Egads. So many questions," Jude held his head with his hand. "And me with a bad headache. Bad buzz."

"So, then tell me. Why are you here laying on my towels?"

"Wellll… It's a long story actually. Let's assume you'll be bored or pissed after thirty seconds of me speaking, and we'll just skip the question. Okay?"

"I've got time to chat. All the time I want. Come to my deck, and you can shower outside underneath it. That ragged dark-skinned derelict under the cabbage palm tree is with you, I suppose?"

"Yes. That's my personal emotional-support human, Hector—"

"Phew! What is that smell he is emitting? I'm nauseous."

"And I'm Jude. Forgive him. He has no control over it."

"And I am Lilith. Pleased to make your acquaintance," she held out a slim hand with a diamond on it that went knuckle to knuckle. "Come have a shower if you want. You look like you need one badly. You both smell like sweaty socks and rum. Your man-friend boyfriend emotional-support animal whatever-he-is can sleep off his drunk a little while longer. Snakes will avoid the smell. Black scorpions? Might not."

"A shower. Best thing I've heard in two days, actually," smiled Jude widely. "Much appreciated."

"Welcome to the Stafford," said Lilith as she waved a hand. "The nicest beach house north of the Gold Coast on Captiva. That is only my own opinion, of course."

"It looks lovely from the outside. Simply grand."

"When you are, uh, first cleaned up, then I will take you inside. Oh, I get so few visitors this time of year. Would you like to have some breakfast?"

"Second best thing I've heard in two days," laughed Jude.

"Eggs? Or are you allergic to real food?"

"My herbalist tells me that the term 'egg' imposes low self-esteem on unhatched poultry. I believe the correct PC term is 'spring oval'. Please get with the program."

"I see what you did there. You like your comedy. Great. Whatever peels your banana. Well, then, take my sandy towel and go under the deck. You can undress in the shower. Hang your clothes over the side while the water's on. Soap and shampoo should be in there on a shelf. That is if Beatrice did her job correctly," sighed Lilith. "Let me look in the house. I may have some clean clothes for you and your boyfriend."

"Not necessary, but thanks." Jude strutted under the deck and on into the shower. He looked into the full-length mirror on one side of the shower and saw the unkempt and unclean person he had become. *Gads.* He thought to himself. *I am so looking a tad bit rough around the edges. And here this nice Lilith is offering me her home and breakfast. What's up with that?* He undressed himself and turned the water on. Cold refreshing water spurted from the shower-head at a pulsating, massaging flux. Jude lathered himself up head to toe with Irish Spring soap not once but twice, and then squeezed some Renee Furturer French shampoo into his hand and washed the sand and oil from his hair until it squeaked between his fingers. He was so refreshed in the shower after being out in the hot sun all day yesterday and sleeping in the sand overnight that he spent nearly twenty minutes underneath the comforting, cold pulsating water. Jude dried himself off with another towel and quickly dressed in his ragged, overused clothing, throwing his boxer shorts underwear he deemed no longer wearable into a trash can that was underneath the deck by the carport. When he came out from under the deck, Lilith tossed him a faded pale-green Hermés polo shirt and some orange and yellow Nike running shorts from the level above.

"You can wear these," she shouted down. "They were left here some time ago by someone or other. I'm not sure who actually. They're sure cleaner than what you have on. I think they'll fit you fine."

Jude went back into the shower to change clothes and tossed his dirty ones into his gym bag. He couldn't believe his luck. Some new, clean duds to put on, and soon some breakfast. He hadn't eaten in over a day. Why was this sweet and gorgeous woman so nice to him? Any other woman anywhere owning a beach-front property in Florida would have told him to get the heck off her land. Yet this toasty woman, Lilith, was welcoming him freely. His mind wandered a minute to think of Paco and the Bel Air as he looked out over the vast Gulf of Mexico beyond the white-sand beach. Then he glanced at Hector, covered in gritty sand and sweaty, still sleeping under the cabbage palm tree out of the direct sunlight. Jude went over and grabbed Hector's gym bag and came up stairs to the top level of the deck. Lilith sat flinty-eyed with legs crossed at the knee. Bagels and cream cheese spread with smoked salmon and capers were laid on a shiny silver platter placed upon a black wicker table.

"I don't mean to be forward," said Jude reluctantly. "If your Beatrice is going to do the towels for laundry, can she add our clothes here? We, um, haven't had them washed in days upon days. It's a long story."

"Ugh. How gross. Fine. Beatrice won't mind. Just don't open those bags with whatever is in them in front of me," said Lilith. "I get nauseous easily. Smells bother me so." She took a bite of a toasted sesame bagel with salmon spread and cream cheese. "Care to join me?" She pushed a wicker chair with her foot casually towards Jude. "Would you like a rum-runner? I make the island's finest."

"It can't be eight in the morning," Jude was confused by her asking this question.

"Then a mimosa perhaps? I have a fine bottle of La Veuve Clicquot champagne in the fridge. Let me go get it and a couple nice champagne flutes. The orange juice is fresh squeezed by

Beatrice. I picked out the nicest oranges yesterday at Publix. You must try the juice."

Jude looked down the deck and over at Hector, who was still passed out. *I guess he did drink a lot more than I did,* thought Jude to himself. *Poor guy. I'll let him sleep it off.* He picked up a piece of salmon with his recently cleaned fingers and placed it in his mouth. The salmon was fresh and melted on his tongue. He just couldn't believe his luck. *Today could turn out to be a fine day,* he thought, having forgotten about his cell phone and the need to check for any messages. A delicious breakfast was in front of him as he sat in the wicker seat next to the railing of the wooden deck that overlooked the white-sand beach and onto the Gulf Sea beyond. He was oh-so-satisfied with just that.

When Lilith returned with the open bottle of expensive champagne, she started on Jude. "I'm so awfully lonely these days. Captiva Island can be such a bore. Other than the Sandpipers skitting across the sand by the surf, I don't see many live beings. I'd love a good discussion about identity politics. What are your thoughts?"

Jude sipped some champagne from the tall crystal flute. "I'll be happy when America finally moves to a post-identity society. Right now an American's identity, be it their race or sexuality or color of their skin, defines them. Rather than their personal experiences or what they know and believe. There is somehow no room for an unbiased discussion among those who are defined differently from one another. It's just not allowed in our country at this time. I don't know how we got to this point, but I'm not happy about it." He picked up another piece of salmon and dropped it into his mouth.

"Spoken like a privileged white man." Lilith waved a hand to swat a fly. "I am a white woman. Both a majority and a minority. I don't know what it feels like to be a man. I don't think most cucks know, either."

"Unlike in Japan, the majority race in America allows the minorities to vote. That's enough progress for me. How can you be lonely when you are married?"

"I'm not married!" Lilith threw her head back. "Oh, you mean the diamond. A gift from an old friend. Long since passed away. Robert Rauschenberg. Have you ever heard of him? He was a world famous artist who lived just down the beach here a ways. He dilly-dallied in New York City's art scene with Andy Warhol and Jackson Pollock before moving to Captiva. The man left behind a huge estate that went nowhere. I think it's still in probate."

"Never heard of him. But that is a fine stone you have there. I don't think I've ever seen a diamond that large before."

"I've seen bigger. And not just engagement rings. The things that have always held people back: marriage, religion, and capitalism. All poison for women."

"You sound like you need a job… and need to get laid," Jude said somewhat unabashedly as he shifted in his seat and grabbed a poppy-seed bagel half to spread some cream cheese on.

"Mmmhmm. That could be. In due time," her eyes glimmered in the sun. "This woman doesn't need marriage, religion, or capitalism to have a good life. I tend to agree with the notion that women get more dissatisfied with marriage over time than men do. I suppose you were a George W. Bush supporter back when. Even with Mr. Obama, liberal America is in its death-throws, I fear."

"I think I've got the picture now. Let me get this straight: cops are criminals, criminals are victims, people that don't work should be entitled to a free ride, desecrating our national flag is the new national past-time, the trans-gendered are now called heroes, a Navy Seal sniper is a coward, Obama whom you support negotiates with terrorists, we supply guns to drug cartels but disarm law-abiding Americans, people who flip burgers should be paid more than the military personnel who put their very own lives on the line every day for you to live in a lovely house like this, and somehow, some way, it's still all Bush's fault many years later?"

"Yes. In fact, I can and do agree with all that. Mostly. May I add that marriage is also a dying fad."

"Marriage is dying because most men now aren't stupid enough to sign away their house, savings, retirement and future to a witch who will cheat on him after two years only to have some scumbag judge force him into eternal poverty. Guys are wising up."

"Women have the goods."

"Women have the goods and use them to their advantage. When the goods go stale in twenty or so years, they have a tale to spin to take advantage again. Why does it take twenty-five years to remember a sexual predator was—"

Lilith beamed and cut him off. "The philosopher Schopenhauer argued with his friends who claimed there was no greater ecstasy than lying with a woman."

"Lying is what I am talking about. Relationships with women are all dishonesty from the get-go."

"Not a success with women, I take it?" she grinned. "I had a brief same sex dalliance in college, but I have always been more attracted to men because of their foreignness. Problem was my ex worked 18-hour days. I never saw him. That your toy down there?" She pointed at Hector.

"No, definitely not. We are not gay. Thanks for asking."

"But no women, either? I'm surprised. Being asexual is a novel idea. What's it like to spore?"

"Oh, I've had plenty of women," Jude beamed. "I'm just commenting that there is no same sex attraction here with this man or any man. And then there's always one subtle woman in a man's life who—"

"Always one," she nodded with an arched eyebrow. "How do you treat her? Do you know what Maya Angelou said? *People will forget what you said. People will forget what you did. But people will always remember how you made them feel*. I see you eat with both hands. Cretin. And, by the way, everyone is a little gay. Each in his or her own way. I'm sure of that."

"Am I making you feel uncomfortable with my hands or my speech? I am a mechanic. I have to be ambidextrous," fronted Jude with a mouthful of bagel, lifting his palms up to show his calloused hands to Lilith.

"Not in the slightest. You couldn't knock me off my guard with a cannon. So, do tell, is there someone special in your life? You're not wearing a ring," Lilith lilted.

Jude thought for a moment as he chewed his poppy-seed bagel. If he said *yes*, then that would probably mean the end of this great hospitality he was receiving, and he still was hoping to get the laundry done by this woman's maid, Beatrice. But if he said *no*, then he would be dishonoring his betrothed wife, Margarita, his marriage, and even his daughter Chloe.

"No," it was painful inside, but Jude lied. "I'm still searching for that right someone."

"Oh, I am always so not content. Real men are so hard to find. All the best ones are taken," said Lilith out of the corner of her mouth.

"I said no," Jude furthered without thinking it through. "There's no special someone in my life. You?"

"I envision my ex now as a skinny jean-wearing hipster vegan with androgynous thick-framed glasses, driving around in a pink Prius with a *2016: Ready for Hillary* bumper sticker telling people how progressive he is. And yet… and yet… I was once married to him because of all that. At least he hated guns. I hate guns. You're not carrying one with you, are you? Or sandy-pants over there still asleep. He doesn't have a gun on him, does he?"

"No, we don't carry. But I like my guns the way Obama likes his voters: undocumented."

"The Second Amendment isn't going to help you any when their tanks roll over your house. You're a little man yodeling in a big canyon, and nobody's listening."

"Your ex reminds me of a joke I recently heard. How can you find a vegan in a crowded room full of people?" cracked Jude.

"Um, I don't know," Lilith was complacent.

"Don't worry. They'll tell you and everyone around you. Hahahaha!"

Lilith waved a well-manicured hand. "I guess. I like how you punctuate your ignorance with certainty. It's starting to get hot out here. Can I show you the inside of the Stafford house now? We can finish breakfast later in the dining room. Beatrice will come by to pick everything up and bring it in. Just leave your gym bags by the front door leading to the lower level. Beatrice will know what to do with them as she takes the towels from the bathrooms to be washed."

"Superb. Whatever peels your banana, as you said. It is a lovely house from the outside," said Jude.

"Then come on in and see the better part of it. Your banana and all."

Lilith led Jude inside and showed him the high vaulted ceiling lined with teak wooden beams. The kitchen had Sub-Zero stainless-steel appliances and a wine cooler that stretched half a wall. Walking through the kitchen was like walking into a Williams-Sonoma store. Past the kitchen was the living area where everything was covered in mauve colored Corinthian leather, including the tops of the carved wooden end tables. Jude was about to take a seat on the inviting couch when Lilith grabbed his hand to lead him onward. They passed through the dining room, where fine Lennox china and Gerber silverware and Baccarat goblets were perfectly laid out, with a beautiful rose and baby's breath floral arrangement in the center of the lengthy dining table. All as if the doyenne was expecting to have a grand dinner that evening. With a few more steps, Lilith led Jude into the master bedroom. She took a seat on the edge of the bed and crossed her legs at the knees, leaning back on her elbows. "Come sit with me, Jude? Just for a moment?"

Jude walked past Lilith on the bed and further on towards the master bathroom.

"What's your fascination with the bathroom? Need to use it?"

"Naw. Just curious about bathrooms. A fixation for me. Because you can sleep or screw in a bathroom. Using a bedroom as a john is unsanitary," said Jude retreating back into the master bedroom near where Lilith was seated.

With a glimmer in her bright eyes, and a casual stroke of her soft hand on Jude's elbow, she softly spoke, "Jude. I am not content."

Jude thought a moment about what that meant, and then realized he was indeed in the house's master bedroom. Lilith's bedroom, it was. A woman's bedroom. He looked at the silk bedspread with a marble headboard on the king-sized bed. Fluffy red velvet-covered pillows lay all around.

Jude absentmindedly sat next to Lilith while looking around the bedroom slowly and silently. There were no visible signs that another male had been there previously that day or any time before. He suddenly thought about something his mother once told him as he was leaving for his first year of college in Wisconsin: *Most people think happiness comes from the right job, the right salary, making the most of the opportunities in life, when in reality, happiness comes from relationships. A true happiness is that one which is cultivated in the heart and grows.*

Lilith reached up and stroked Jude's face. "You look tired and lonely, too." A tear ran down the side of her cheek. Then another. And another. "I am so not content," she repeated softly. Jude leaned over and gracefully kissed the tear on her chin, and then her nose. Then her lips. In a few moments, both were undressed and inside the luxurious spun-silk sheets. Not for a moment did Jude think of his wife Margarita back in Baltimore. He had already disowned her earlier verbally, and now she would not return to his mind as he consummated his relationship with Lilith. Adultery ensued, surprisingly with no guilt feelings summarily popping up inside him. All Jude could focus on during this sensual time with Lilith was her moaning over and over, "Oh, Jude. I am so not content."

And then it was over. Like after all great love-making sessions for men, Jude fell soundly asleep. Lilith got up immediately and left the room, shutting the door quietly behind her.

It wasn't a restful sleep for Jude. He tossed and turned about on the bed like a sluggard in his fitful unrelaxing sleep. Just over three hours later, Jude woke up clear-headed and scared.

"Oh, my God! What have I done!" Jude exclaimed out loud. "I can't believe what I just did! And I forgot about Hector! He's probably wondering where the heck I am right now!" Jude put on his new clothes without showering and went out into the living room, calling out for Lilith. No response. Lilith wasn't in the house; she was gone. On a low, wide wood and black marble chest by the front door were Jude's and Hector's old clothes all washed and neatly folded. The gym bags were even washed as well. Jude put the clothes into the bags and ran down from the back-deck stairs to the ground level. The late-model black Vanden Plas Jaguar he had seen earlier in the carport was gone. He ran out from under the deck to the cabbage palm tree where he left Hector sleeping earlier in the day. The Latino was leaning his back against the cabbage palm, with a half-empty six-pack of Corona beers and a small silver plate of sliced Key Limes next to him. In his hand, he held a lit-up marijuana joint.

"Hector! What the heck? Where did you get all that?"

"A nice Haitian woman brought da beers to me from out da house. I think she said you wuz sleepin'. That's what I was thinkin', anyways. I couldn't unnerstand her very well. How many times can I nod my head and smile before I have to say 'what?' when I don't unnerstand a foreigner? Wanna a beer? Look at dis view. This ocean be trippin' me out."

"Not right now. Did the Haitian woman give you that spliff in your hand as well?"

"Heck, no. This was in the pack of Newports I swiped from that jerk bartender, DogFamBam, at the Delano Hotel our first night in South Beach. Hehehe! Shoved the pack down my underpants afore we left. I done kept it hidden. I just been waitin' for the right time to enjoy it. And now is the right time. Care to have a toke? Look at dis view." He reached up his hand with the joint in it.

"I couldn't hide anything in my underpants," Jude said, trying to lighten up his mind and soul with some humor. "They're filled with natural ingredients."

"Have a toke, will ya?"

"Forget it. Not now. Dude, I am in such big trouble," Jude stammered with a crack in his voice. "I did this woman who lives here. Now she's boogied. I don't know where she is. I done cheated on my wife, brah!"

"So? You did her. All she needs to do is get a big shot o' penicillin. Dat's all. Bad decisions make for good stories. Don't remember where I done heard dat, though. Nice shirt you got on there."

"I'm so gonna burn for this. I've never cheated on Margarita before. Never. But here, our clothes are washed clean and in the gym bags. We need to get the heck out of here, Money. Where's my phone so I can call Paco to come get us?"

"I ain't got yo' phone, homie. And why does ya and Berto always calls me 'Money'?"

"You ask me that now because you are high as a kite? Cuz you ain't got any money," said Jude kicking through the sand around Hector. "Where the heck is my phone?"

"I said I ain't got it. And if I ain't got it, I ain't got it. If you ain't got it, then I don' know where it done went, dude." He took another drag on the marijuana joint.

"Oooohoooohoooo…," Jude held his head with both hands, still searching the sand for his phone. It was nowhere to be found. "I'm dying here. Where is my phone? It's lost in the sand somewhere. Let me go back inside to see if there's a phone in Lilith's house. We have to call Paco now. I mean right now! The Bel Air—"

"We ken go back to Sanibel and hook up with him at his house. I think I gots Paco's address done written down on a matches pack in my pocket. Anto done gave it to me afore we left South Beach in case we gots lost."

"Sometimes you do amaze me when you use your brain. Tell me Paco's address. Maybe the phone operator will give me his home phone number if I give her his home address on Sanibel. I will go back inside and look for a phone. I'm in some serious deep doo-doo. What was I thinking? I'm going back in. Is that a good idea? At least she didn't steal my money. The envelope is in the gym bag."

"Suits me well if you go back in. I'ma gonna sits here and enjoys my stuffs. Look out over the ocean. You evah seen anything so beautiful in yo' life? The ocean is a real amazin' thing."

"You're stoned. It's not an ocean. It's the Gulf of Mexico. But no matter. I'll be out in a sec. Hold on here and don't go nowhere."

The glass door at the deck was locked. Jude ran down the stairs and around to the front of the house. That main door was locked as well. He ran downstairs to the guest house to see if Beatrice was there. He couldn't see into the tinted windows. Jude didn't know that Beatrice was in the guest house kitchen out of his line of sight and that she wasn't about to answer the door for him. He ran back to Hector to look again for his phone. After scrambling around in the sand for several minutes, Jude gave up. The phone was gone, and he had no idea where it went. Could Lilith have it? Or did Beatrice pull it from his pockets when she did the laundry? Did he leave it in the house when he went inside? Jude was beside himself with terror. If he couldn't find that phone, he had no way to call Paco. Or Catty. Or the police station regarding the Bel Air. Panic struck him hard and he started to tremble.

"Jude, mon, takes it easy, will ya?"

"Hector, shut the heck up for a minute. We gotta get out of here before Lilith gets back. We need to get to Sanibel. It's going to be a long walk. Maybe someone will pick us up from the side of the road if we set out for it now."

"A long walk? I ain't up for no long walk. Dat be a buzzkill fo' me. Why you wanna go and leave this bootiful place? White clouds, blue skies, nice shade under dis palm trees. Look at this little lizard here lappin' at my feet. Ain't he cute?"

"Will you please shut up?! C'mon, let's go. Long walks are good for the soul. We can walk the beach until we hit the main road and keep walking it back to Sanibel's center. Someone will surely pick us up."

"Shuck. Aight. So we heads this way, right?" Hector took a swig of beer.

"I was wrong about your brain. You have two. One is lost, and the other is out looking for it. The Gulf is in front of you. We need to go left. Let's move."

"Okay. Can I bring my Coronas?"

"No, definitely not. Leave them right there. We don't need no more police action coming at us. Got it?"

"Suck, man. Dis was the best moment of my time on the islands." Hector wobbled to stand up, shaking off the sand from his butt and wiping his legs.

"Sna-a-ke!" pointed Hector. Jude jumped back fast and looked down. "Oh, boss. Sorry 'bout dat. Your zipper is undone. Hehehe!"

"Gimme a heart-attack, why dontcha, Money?"

Hector and Jude set out to walk down the beach to head towards Sanibel. There were lots of people on the beach by now. Hector smiled each time they passed a pretty woman. Jude wasn't much interested in enjoying the walk as he knew that the two men had a long way to go ahead of them back to the center of Sanibel to try and find someone who would know how to get a hold of Paco. After all, weren't people on the islands close in touch with one another? The closed-in island community would make it easier to find Paco, right? That was Jude's hope.

A beautiful flock of lofty White Ibis flew out of the seagrasses across the beach.

"You know. I don' like dese islands," said Hector.

"Oh really? Why's that? As if I give a rip."

"Too dang… white. The clouds is white. The birds is white. Every person is white. Ain't no diversity. That Haitian woman back at that woman you slept with's house was the only minority

I done seen since we gots here. No blacks. No Latinos. Not even a Puerto Rican like me."

"Yeah, well, wait till Obama and the liberals flood the U.S. with more immigrants. Then things will be different even here in whitey-land. The Democrats are clueless on it. Don't you wonder what the LGBT and La Raza and Black Lives Matters groups are gonna think of Islam and its Sharia rules? The Muslim men keep their women and children in line. Muslim men know they are men. From Indonesia to Tajikistan to Morocco, not a wimp or pansy or girly man among them. Even though I have no religious preference, I guess the Muslims are not so bad after all."

"My mutha always said we needs to keep da peace with da Muslims. She said they be good peoples likes us. We gots to love everybody, ya knows. But what-ever. I'm done beat up bad with dis walkin'. How much longer you think we needs to go? I never did see what the draw is to be a Muslim or any religion."

"For Islam, the draw for me would be the seventy-two virgins in eternity thing. And keeping the women in line."

"Yeah, dat's it. Seventy-two virgins. S'prised Bill Clinton hasn't converted yet."

"I think he already did. Killary must not be happy about that. Prolly will come out sometime during her campaign that Bill hits the Mosques on Fridays to scope chicks. Problem is the men and women are sep'rated at the Mosques. How will Bill hit up the babes on the other side of the screen?"

"Killary, hehe, that's a riot! You know, while I was sittin' there tokin' today under the palm tree, I was saying to m'self how great it would be to win the lottery. Then I thought what a bad idea it would be. I would prob'ly just sit on the beach in Puerto Rico and get high all day and drink lots o' rum."

"Other than me not toking the Mary-Jane, I fail to see the downside to your argument. The lottery can—"

"Oh, oh. I done fo'got the rest of the Coronas back there."

"I told you to leave them, remember?"

"I'm thirsty. Ain't nuttin' but a shuck. Dang, it's hot. Glad I jumped into dat lady's pool this morning. Got me clean and freshed up some."

"You went and jumped into Lilith's pool?" asked Jude all surprised at the idea. "What did you wear?"

"Just my undershorts. Which I done throws away when I gots out of da pool."

"I threw my underwear away, too."

"So we both be goin' Malibu, eh?"

"Guess so. I had a hot shower. It was niiice. Was the pool water cold?"

"Yez. An' my junk be like a scared turtle. Yo snapper!" Hector shook his crotch.

When the men came to the end of the beach and the surf, they stepped onto Captiva Drive to walk the Gold Coast towards Sanibel. Afternoon was turning slowly to night and the darkness was coming fast. The moon above the two men looked like it was cut right out of the night sky once again.

Jude picked up a confused turtle and ran it across to the other side of the road away from the traffic. "I hope there are no gators around here.

Hector jumped. "Gators?! There are gators around here?! Say it ain't so!"

"If there are turtles around, there are gators. Big ones on these islands."

Hector swore he wanted to give up walking right then and there where they were, which was nowhere. But his suggestion to go banging on the door of some rich jackoff's house looking for shelter was not an option. Jude pushed him onward. There was no place out of sight for them to sleep, even after now passing over the bridge along the Roosevelt Strait. Jude was just afraid of what would happen to Hector if the police came around and started asking questions to Lilith. *What if Lilith went to the police herself? Man, that could be trouble for us both!*

"Hec-tor?" Jude breathed heavily.

"Yeah, boss," he replied hurting.

"Did you ever think... Here we are on this road with no shoulder and no streetlights... We can barely see anything... It's like... Half the world at any given moment is in total darkness... Did you ever realize that?"

"Maybe we should lives in the North Pole parts o' da year when its full daylight all day and at the South Pole da other parts o' da year. Then we gots no darkness."

"I'm not sure I could stand the weather."

"Me none, neither... Call me Money. I'm cashed," Hector heaved.

"Just a bit further, brother. I don't want to be on the road when the sun comes up tomorrow. Cops may see us. You'd be in a lick of trouble I can't get you out of. Keep going with me. We'll make it."

The two men plodded mile after mile after long mile on the edge of Sanibel-Captiva Drive in the dark. Hector moaned about giving up several times. Jude pushed him onwards with promises of better times in Puerto Rico. Fortunately they finally came upon a set of buildings – a church - the only Catholic Church on the islands.

"There's a church over there! Sees da Cross on it?" said Hector pointing to the right. "The lights be on. Less go crash in it for de night. If it be open. Get me away from these island gators."

By this time, Jude had had enough of the walking, and thought Hector may have had a good idea. Why not crash in the pews of the Catholic Church for the night? It might be air conditioned. In the morning they could just pick up and leave quickly before anyone from the Rectory noticed that there were two uninvited 'parishioners' inside the Chapel. The two men walked into the church through the wide unlocked wooden doors. Jude slid into the back pew. Immediately he had an uncomfortable feeling. He was recalling the sins he was so guilty of from earlier in the day and being in a church shocked him back to the reality of being a cheating married man with a daughter. He had indeed cheated on his good wife, Margarita. With this nothing-woman Lilith who went and disappeared on him, leaving him only with clean clothes and a stain on his soul. *How could I do this to my Margarita, my true love?* He repeatedly mumbled to himself with his head down and eyes tearing up. Suddenly, something inside him snapped and he looked up.

"Hector! You can't drink that! That's Holy Water!"

"I don' care what it is. It be water, and I be thirstin' badly here. You don' see a bafroom nowheres does ya?"

"No. But there has to be one here. We can look for it in the morning."

"Can't wait fo' dat. I'ma going oussside to tap a kidney."

Jude was thirsty as well but decided to sleep off his thirst rather than desecrate the Holy Water that Hector had scooped up with his dirty hands out of the Baptismal Font. *I shoulda stole some bottles of water or orange juice from Lilith's refrigerator. That would have been some help I could offer Hector. How I got him – and me - in this situation, I still don't understand.*

Hector was the first to lay himself flat down in the pew, using his gym bag atop two hymnal books as a pillow. "Set your alarm clock fo' early so we don' get awoke by anyone comin' in."

"Can't," said Jude. "My alarm clock was on my phone. Wherever it is. We'll just have to get lucky and hopefully get ourselves out of here and out of sight as the dawn breaks through the stained-glass windows."

"Suits me fine," said Hector, and within minutes he was snoozing away.

Jude stayed awake a while longer. He didn't feel comfortable at all being there in the church. He wasn't a particularly religious man, he knew well, but he felt sore and guilty for what he had done that day. Would he tell Margarita about it? Should he tell her? His mind reeled. With the bright lights on in the church, it would be a few more stiff hours of deep darkness outdoors before Jude let himself relax in the pew. The church's lights were on all night, but that didn't bother the two miscreants. Jude for the first time in his life said an honest but humble sinner's prayer to God asking for forgiveness. His despair suddenly eased, and he fell firmly asleep. For the first time in days, the wanderers slept comfortably well that night.

~~~

A phone rang.

"Hello," said Lilith in a sweet voice.

"Hello?" said the woman on the other end of the line frantically. *"Who is this I am talking to? Is Jude there?"*

"Ohhh… Juuude," Lilith spoke devilishly. "You know, he was around here earlier today. I picked up this phone off the sand while he was sleeping in front of my house on the beach. He left before I could give it back to him. The poor guy." She winked at the young tanned twenty-something buck sitting across from her at the solid-wood booth in the famous Lazy Flamingo restaurant in San-tiva. "Who may I ask is calling for him now?"

"This is his wife, Margarita. Who are you, if I may ask in return?"

"You don't need to know who I am, sweets. Divorce him, I advise you. Take everything he loves. Then take the rest. Bwahaha! But I will tell you something you already know, sugar." Lilith's foot crawled up the young man's muscular leg to his crotch.

"What's that?"

"Your husband—"

"Yes?"

"Your husband is a heckuva good lay."
~~~

8 Touched, and Go

"Sir!" boomed a voice above Jude's head.

No movement from Jude.

"Sir!" said the portly man in the grey apron holding a broom and dustpan. He nudged Jude with the top of the broomstick. "Sir, I say again a third time!"

"Oh, for the love of-. Uh, hello. Sorry. We—"

"Sir, if you are here for Confession, then I should tell you that is has been relocated to the Rectory today so that we may clean the church top to bottom for the jubilee wedding this upcoming weekend." Two other stout men with red faces and bulbous noses stood behind this man, each one holding cleaning supplies.

"Ohhh, Confession," Jude's head cleared. "Yes, well, then. We are indeed here for Confession. We were just napping as we awoke early to pray in the church first thing this morning, and we fell asleep. Hector! Wake up, my boy!"

Hector rubbed his eyes and sat up. He looked straight at the three cleaning men. "Jude, we's in trouble now."

"Not at all. We just have to go to the Rectory for the Confession we are here to do, as this nice man has told me."

"Confession? What the heck fo'? I ain't got nuttin' to confess. 'Cept me followin' yo' sorry ass all these hot days no knowin' where we is. What a mistake I done made. Geez. My head hurts."

"Sir! May I remind you that you are in the House of God!" said the man with the broom stamping a foot down. "Please watch your language!"

"Oh, she-yit. Sorry," Hector said without thinking.

"The Rectory will open in twenty minutes for Confessions. Can I please ask you both to leave and wait there as we are about to start the cleaning?"

"No probs," said Jude. "Hey, what's the name of the priest by the way?"

"Father Dyer is holding Confessions today. If you hurry, you could be the first in line."

"Let's hustle, Hector," said Jude nervously.

"Okay. But like I said. I ain't got nuttin' to confess."

"It's okay," said Jude. "I do. Thank you, kind sir, for directing us to this Confession, um, place. Have a nice day cleaning."

"I needs a bafroom," Hector whispered.

"Relieve yourself outside then," Jude whispered back.

The man in the grey apron tipped his grimy Florida Marlins baseball hat. Jude and Hector picked up their gym bags and scuttled quickly outside from the air-conditioned church into the overwhelming heat.

"Dang," said Hector. "Another dang hot day. How far we gotta walk still to get to town?"

"No idea. First, I'm going to try this Confession stuff. I've never done it, but my mother told me all about it when I was little. I saw myself in a dream last night with Margarita and Chloe by my side. I was bawling my eyes out. I haven't cried in years. C'mon. The Rectory is right over there in that building as the sign above the door says."

"What's with those men in dere?" asked Hector. "Buncha mute losers, dey looked like."

"Dontcha see? Even clueless losers can get a job in America. Is this a great country or what?"

Jude and Hector walked over to the Rectory and rang the bell.

"Yes? May I help you?" a lady's voice came over the intercom.

"We're here for the Confession… thing."

"Do you have an appointment?"

"No. Do we need one?"

"Fine. I'll buzz you in."

Hector and Jude were let into a lobby waiting area where there were two blue and grey velvet-covered bench seats. On one side of the room on a bench sat a rather homely woman – whose age was hard to determine - with two plastic grocery bags filled with assorted non-perishable foods at her feet. She smiled at Jude but frowned at Hector. There was no one else in the waiting area. The woman who buzzed them in was in an adjacent room behind a smoked glass window that Jude could not see into, though he went up close. On the wall was a picture of Pope Francis, and next to it a picture of the local Diocese's Bishop. In one corner was a medium-sized carved-stone statue of the Blessed Virgin Mary kneeling with her head bent over a Crucified Christ in her arms. In another corner was a dripping fountain that made a soothing sound - the only sound in the room.

"What we be doin' here?" asked Hector fearfully.

"I guess we wait here for the priest," said Jude. "I would imagine he will come get us. I don't really know what will happen next."

"I said I ain't got nuttin' to confess," repeated Hector as he folded his arms and leaned them on his knees.

"Do you have anything to confess?" asked the woman, politely, pointing a petite finger at Jude.

"Yeah. Too much in fact."

"Then you can go before me. You know what my problem is?" asked the woman nonchalantly.

"Shoot."

"I'm fighting the stigma that society has placed on me as a single mother. That I must have done something wrong to be in the position of being an only parent. There are people who assume that I could foresee the future. They suggest that I was just too stupid for having a kid with him in the first place. Or that I must have done something to drive my man away. Or yet other people who decide that there is really no way the father doesn't want to see his kid. I must be keeping him from her. Or any of the other excuses that people choose to believe because it's easier to blame the parent that stayed than to accept the horrific truth that some parents just don't love their children like they should. Aand sometimes those parents leave. I've been chasing him down for child support for eleven years now. I never seen a nickel from him. Do you still think the system is stacked against the men? Do you? That the courts are all about bankrupting the men in favor of gold-digging women? I can tell that's what you think. Well, you think wrong."

"Wow," said Hector. "Dat's a load."

"I wish I knew how to help you, ma'am," said Jude. "But I'll confess this here to you that you sum up what I think pretty well. And yes, I am starting to think I am wrong. I am not a good father myself. I am failing miserably at being a father to my Chloe. My mother was a single mother. So I get where you are coming from. No judgment coming from me at ya'."

"My muthah was a single muthah, too," added Hector.

"What day of the year is your birthday?" the woman's face lit up in front of Jude.

"October fourth."

"That's the Feast Day of Saint Francis of Assisi! You are blessed! Now, how did I know to ask you that?" she said slyly.

"Someone did tell me that once. I'd forgotten about it. Not that it matters to me any. Just any other ordinary day for me."

"And what's more," her eyes narrowed as she leaned forward. "Listen to this. Jesus Christ was born on the fifteenth day of Tishri. The seventh month in the Hebrew calendar. In the year 3758 in the Jewish calendar. This equates to the Fourth of October in the year four B.C., according to the Gregorian calendar that we use today. The fifteenth of Tishri is the first day of the Feast of Tabernacles each year. This is when the Jews celebrate the journeying of the Israelites through the wilderness from Egypt to Canaan, the land 'flowing with milk and honey'. Even today, Jewish families build huts made of branches and such. Families live in these backyard huts, day and night, for the whole of the eight days of the Feast. It was in one of these small huts that Jesus was born."

"Why there?"

"Aaaah! Because there was no room for Mary and Joseph at the inn at Bethlehem! Because the little inn was full with travelling pilgrims visiting Jerusalem a few miles up the road for the Feast. So yes, in this respect anyway, the good and holy Pope Francis is right: there were no animals inside to greet the new-born King. No animals in The Lord's hut! The evidence for the date of Jesus' birth is in the Bible, despite what the learned professors with their seminary doctorates think. It is based on Luke 1:5, 1 Chronicles 24:10, Luke 1:23-24 and 36. Aaand!... Here is where it gets interesting! If the Fourth of October is right for the birth, Mary's Conception by the Holy Spirit at forty weeks prior to this would have been in late December. The twenty-fifth maybe?"

"Wowza, woman," said Hector. "How does ya knows all dat?"

The woman shifted in her seat and smiled a toothless grin. "I'm just like you two men. No different, really. We three are Pilgrim wanderers. Making the way slow-step by slow-step through this cold, dark, evil world we live in. But have no fear. You are in the right place. You can't be where God doesn't want you to be. Confession is a Holy Sacrament."

"She's right," said Hector gruffly. "We done been wanderin' fo' days now like a lost pilgrim. I done 'bout had enough of it. It's a shuck."

"Whatever," said Jude, totally uninterested in the whole conversation. "I wonder what Jesus would think about how we celebrate His Birthday today. He'd probably be ticked that we took what was once a great idea and have since built a commercial-filled calamity around it. I'm really just here to get some advice on the next steps to move my life's journey forward. Not confess anything," Jude added.

"Move your life's journey forward! I love it! That is such a Western thought to see life as steps of a journey. Yet it's just the way we think so narrowly in Western Civilization. I suppose you are having problems with your other half?" asked the woman as she leaned over and placed her chin on a hand.

"We got our problems. Like all marriages, I guess. Mostly my own dang fault."

"Your own grievous fault, surely. Love isn't about finding the right person to live with. It's about finding that person you can't live without. There are more than the two options of an unhappy marriage and divorce. But it takes a special effort. You know what Abraham Lincoln said during the crux of the Civil War?"

"That his wife's dress made her look fat? How the heck do I know?"

"He said that he was driven to his knees because he had nowhere else to go," the woman corrected him. "If you don't know what else to do, if your knees wobble and fail you, fall on them. Pray to the good Lord Our God. He forgives all. And saves all who come to Him humbly."

"Yeah, well, that may be, still I am not totally convinced that God is interested in men's lives anyway. My time now in the world as a man is so much different than it was for other men in the past. The whole universe is against me, lady."

"Yes, the universe is against you. Your generation as a man is no different than any other ever in history. It is true that the younger generations usually start out by refusing to believe that God exists. It is also equally true that God will not cease to exist just to please them. You, quiet-one, which of the four S's is important to you: salary, success, sex, or status?"

"Me?" answered Hector taken aback. "Never really done thought about it." He rubbed his forehead. "I dunno. Maybe sex, since I never done had a good salary or been successful at nuttin'. And my status changes with each and every trip through de prison systems. Why ya askin'?"

"There is only one S that is significant, questioning-one. Service. The most beautiful and succinct phrase in the whole Bible is "God is love". For if God is love, then it also means that "Love is God". To serve another person – someone who may even spit on you as you help them - in the spirit of love is as near to the perfect and holy God as you can ever be. Take that thought everywhere everyday as you go about your short time here on earth," she nodded.

"Are you the priest we are supposedly sitting here waiting for?" Jude asked sarcastically. "I thought women couldn't be Catholic priests."

"No," said the woman dryly. "I am not the priest. I'm just a friend. Just a good friend. There are, however, signs everywhere. Every one of us has a burr under our saddle. A pea under the mattress. A thorn in the side. It's just that some people have been dealt a harder hand than others. It's good to alleviate one another's sufferings with our service when we can."

"Look, I already said, ma'am, that I don't know how to help you. Maybe the priest can. Though I am not even sure he can help me. It's probably too late. In any case, I don't even think I should be here myself right now."

"You should be here right now and you are. God brought you here. You've got rough hands; I can see that."

"I'm a mechanic. I make cars go faster than the devil can catch them."

"You work with your hands! Then you are in good company. Saint Paul wrote that men should work with their hands. Knowledge of mechanic skills, that's all you need for service," the woman threw her hands in the air gaily.

"Anything else I need?" Jude asked totally uninterested.

"A good wife, a strong faith, and an occasional brush with death. You are doing well in life, yes very well, despite your heavy conscience at the moment. Don't get down on yourself. Consider all the Cardinals of the Vatican. They neither toil nor spin. Yet Gianni Versace – may he rest in peace - in all his glory in the glamorous parties of Miami was never dressed in such expensive clothing as they are. Are so called men of God any better than you? Is there really a difference between famous men and infamous men? *Great men are usually bad men,* as Lord Acton said."

"I ain't religious," Jude crossed his legs at the ankles, absentmindedly looking out the window and focusing his eyes on the cross on top of the church.

"She said she isn't content, right? That's what she says."

Jude turned his face towards the woman and got wide-eyed. "What the—?"

"Your significant other. She tells you that she's not content, I gather," said the woman with a radiant face like the sun outside.

"No, never. Not her. But... but... I mean... I—"

"Oh, never mind," the woman waved a hand curtly. "Here comes Cheryl to let you in. I implore you to at least enjoy the rest of your stay on Sanibel. It's a lovely place to recreate, if you obey God's Laws." She made a sign of the cross in front of the two men. "In the Name of the Father, the Son, and the Holy Spirit. Hail Mary full of grace, the Lord is with thee. Pray for and bless these two men now and in the hour of their death. Amen."

"Amen," repeated Hector instinctively.

The smoked glass slid open wide and the Rectory secretary called out to Jude and Hector to walk through the heavy wooden door into the main atrium hallway. There, they could sit again and wait for the priest to come get them one at a time for confession. The hallway was long, and there was a solitary marble bench set up against a plain colored wall. White candles burned along the windowsills, dripping wax into saucers.

"Dat woman was da ballz," said Hector.

"She's either lost in life, or we are," said Jude. "Right now, I'm really not sure which way is up. Maybe she's just homeless and needs some help. She said she's a wanderer like us. On the way out I'll give her some money. Maybe that will help her out some. She's either cracked, or I am." He shook his head.

"How does she know so much den? She was strange. And bootiful. Both at da same time. I never done met a woman like her afore. Why would she be a single mother? I take it the church's food pantry done given her da food she had with her in them grocery bags."

"Search me," Jude demurred.

The two men waited for about five minutes. Jude stood up to leave, but without thinking Hector put his hand on his knee to hold him down. Jude shook his head and retook his seat on the marble bench.

"I gots a feelin'," said Hector.

"And do your feelings do you any credit, fool? When did that start for you, pray tell?"

"May I help you gentlemen? One should never call another person a fool, son." There a few feet away stood Father Dyer, a tall trim man with a face that had seen too much sun, deeply wrinkled and leathery, like the southern end of a north-bound elephant in the desert of India. He looked up and down at the two men with utmost seriousness.

Hector whispered, "Dat man's face could sand wood clean."

"Shut up," Jude whispered back.

"Gentlemen, you must be here for a reason, and I haven't got all day. Are you hear for Confession hours?"

"Yes," Jude stood up boldly. Then he thought again. "But…"

"But what? I am the one here today to hear the Confessions of your sins. Please follow me into the Confessional. This must be your first time here at Confession, I figure by your hesitations. No one else will hear what you have to say, if that worries you. You, you can stay here and wait your turn." He pointed a boney finger at Hector. Hector nodded solemnly.

"No," said Jude shaking. "Sorry to bother you, Father. I have to leave now. I have an appointment to go to and it can't wait."

"I see. An appointment that cannot wait. And you, good fella," said the priest pointing at Hector. "Why are you here?"

"I just came for the refreshments," said Hector plainly. "Gots anythin' to drink?"

"Nothing you would want."

"Explains da world fo' me, then."

The priest raised his palms up smiling. "Ah! God is All-Powerful. Man is responsible. Seek ye first His Kingdom and His Righteousness."

"Then explains fo' me what be the Kingdom of God?"

"Wherever the King goes, there's His Kingdom."

"How do we find His Kingdom?" Hector became interested.

"From the Fall of Adam, men looked forward towards the Cross. Now we all look back at the Cross."

"I've always wondered. When Jesus wuz on earth, what was His Spirit covered with?"

"The flesh, as like us. It was meant to be good. I find it amusing, however, all these people at the gym trying to perfect the flesh. They're working with defective material."

"Why does we suffer in da flesh?" continued Hector, now focused intently on the elderly priest.

"The question is not 'Why do we suffer?' but rather 'Given the way we live, why do we not suffer more?'. Jesus suffered in the flesh; why shouldn't you? Suffering is redemptive."

"So suffering is good?" predicted Jude softly.

"Suffering is a lack, not a good. It is a result of sin being on the earth, though not necessarily a direct result of any of your particular sins. Suffering happens even as you take on the life Christ asks you to follow in Him. It's your individual cross to bear. Jesus came to His Cross in complete anticipation of the joy it would eventually bring to men. In the same way, you cannot fulfill God's calling for you without suffering in life. Suffering doesn't only mean no cold water on a hot day such as today. Suffering means giving of your whole self to the service of God and all men. Mother Teresa said to her patients as they lay dying and in agony that Jesus was so close to them and their pain, He was kissing them. Suffering brings Jesus closer. Even then you are attacked by—"

"But I don't gets why we is always bein' attacked!" demanded Hector.

"It's simple," the priest looked above their heads. "You're in Enemy territory. God the Father said to Satan '*You want to play god? I've made this ball, called earth. Go down there and play god.*' And thus the Archangel Michael tossed Lucifer out of Heaven and down to earth like lightning. What that means for you is that the war is waged in the mind. Keep your mind clear of the world's trash and you will be better off. Even when you are attacked, and you will be."

"Why aren't priests married," asked Jude out of nowhere.

"Jesus doesn't care whether we humans get married or not. He doesn't care what job we do. He just wants a chance to cleanse us. If you don't let Him clean you, you will have no part in Him."

"I jus don't gets it no hows," Hector shook his head. "I be too simple a man to understand. Boss, less gets us out. The priest has a busy day ahead of him with confessions and all dat."

"Mmmm, hmmm," sighed the old priest. "Then if you must go in such a hurried state, first let me bless each of you quickly before you head out."

The priest put his frail boney hands on the foreheads of the two men. "In the Name of the Father, the Son, and the Holy Spirit. Hail Mary full of Grace, the Lord is with thee. Pray for and bless these two men now and in the hour of their death. Amen."

"What the-?! That's exactly what that woman in the lobby said to us earlier!" Jude spoke out trembling.

"It's not good to mix liquor and meds, young man. Just a heads up if you are taking anything. It can make you see and hear things that aren't really there. If you need help with substance abuse, there is lots of available help out there for you in Ft. Myers. Believe me, I've seen and heard it all from many island locals and visitors in my twenty-nine years as a priest on Sanibel. I see many a cocaine addict and pedophile and wife-beater who are convinced that their behavior is innate and that they have no choice but to follow these leanings. Nothing could be further from the truth."

Jude and Hector looked at each other with blank faces.

"We aren't addicts, Father," said Jude shaking. "And we aren't violent."

"It's okay. I can see the words are not getting through to you," said the priest, stroking his chin thoughtfully. "How about this. I meet some incredible, delightful, lovable men here on Sanibel who have resigned themselves to being gay because our society today has told them that this tragic aberration is to be embraced as normal. Since they won't come to me for the Lord's help to get straight, they will resign themselves to some secular psychiatrist who will tell them they are okay, that nothing is wrong with them.

The medical professionals along with the greater society will tell them that it's the Christians who are wrong on the issue. The Catholic Church doesn't see it that way. God's Grace is also God's Law. It doesn't matter how high you are on drugs and believe you can fly. If you jump off a tall building, you will go splat on the cement below. The Law of God is The Law you must follow. You make the choices for yourselves. Both of you standing here in front of my presence right now seem to—"

"Uhhh, for real, sir, we are not gay," said Jude looking at the ground and blinking back tears.

"Then do you look at women you are not married to with lust in your hearts?"

Jude started to tear up more. "Don't all men?"

"Actually, no, not all men look at women with lust. They may get lustful thoughts, but remember what Job said, *'I have made a covenant with my eyes not to look at another woman with lust in my heart'.*"

Tear after tear rolled down Jude's cheeks.

"I don't mean to banter with you, son," he said with concern in his voice. "That's not me or my ways. You know yourselves. Whatever your proclivities are." The old priest waved a hand. "I suggest you get some help from the sacraments. Let me demonstrate something for you." The priest pulled a twenty-dollar bill from his pocket. "See this bill? How much is it worth? Twenty dollars, right? Let's say it represents a man. So we dump some cocaine and marijuana on it. How much is it worth now? Still twenty dollars, right? Then we pour some Jack Daniels and Budweiser on it. How much is it worth now? Still twenty dollars, right? But what if," the priest took the twenty-dollar bill over to a large candle setting by the window, set the money ablaze, and left it dangling in a saucer. "We burn this twenty-dollar bill in the fires of Gehenna. How much is it worth now?" Dark ashes fell onto the carpet.

Jude and Hector silently looked at each other with open facial expressions.

The priest let out a breathless laugh from his belly. "Come back to my church anytime, gentlemen. You will always be welcomed openly. Our Good Lord Jesus Christ and I are always here waiting to meet with you. It was a pleasure," the courtly priest smiled curiously as he turned and walked slowly back to his chambers.

Jude stood there without speaking, showing a pained look on his face, with his eyes starting to water again. For a moment he was frozen in his step.

"C'mon, boss. Less go," said Hector pulling on Jude's arm brashly.

"My right knee hurts all of sudden now. Like it has a bulge in it. Yes, yes, sure. Let's go. I want to give that lovely woman we met some money before we leave. I can't imagine what it's like being a single mother with no child support. And right now that is what my lovely wife Margarita is – a single mother. I'm being so very unfair to her. Forgive me, my dearest Margarita, please."

"She'll forgive you, boss."

Jude and Hector walked through the heavy wooden door into the lobby. No one was there. Jude looked vigorously out the window. No one was in sight. He walked up to the tinted glass and rapped his hand lightly on it. It slid open a few inches. "'Scuse me, ma'am, but that nice lady who was here earlier, did she need help with anything? I'd like to give a financial donation to help her, if I can. Just something to help her out some. If I can."

"God loves a cheerful giver. I can see that you are cheerful," said Cheryl with meekness. "But what lady? There was no lady here earlier. I have been here all day since six a.m. You and your friend there are the only ones who showed up for Confession so far today. If there had been anyone else here waiting, man or woman, I would know about it. Have a blessed day." She put both a gentle smile up and her oversized glasses back on and slid the counter's tinted glass window closed abruptly.

Jude and Hector looked at one another in shocked amazement.

"There was no woman here?! What the—?!... I... I...," Jude stammered.

"A CBS episode of Touched by an Angel?" laughed Hector leaning back and holding his stomach. "Even I have trouble believin' in dat!"

"I… I don't know," Jude was flustered. "I just don't know. What can it be? What can it mean? I… I… I just don't know! It can't be! Or can it?... Can it?"

Hector laughed again and shook his head. "C'mon, boss. Less go. We done seen it all now. I'm not even high. This be Florida trippin' us out big time, mon! F'real, mon!"

9 Movers and Shakers and Ill-Playing Players

A *bad day at fishing was better than a good day at work.* That was Peter Collins's motto. A philosophy he had posted on the door of *The Sandy Beach Bum Company,* his private hedge-fund investment vehicle on Sanibel Island – in Florida, with no state income taxes. "Better than New York City, Greenwich Connecticut, and Jersey!" he always remarked when asked. The painted sign with his motto was made by an ex-sea captain who had retired his cap at sea and started up *The Salty Sea Dog Sign Company* in Bonita Springs. A company which for him was a no-brainer as insurance rates for a sign company were a lot less than manning a commercial fishing charter.

Peter, wearing his signature aviator sunglasses, grey golf shorts, yellow *Margaritaville* t-shirt and Timberland boat-shoes without socks, entered the fading blue on gray building gazing up at the sign as he did every day. The funny thing was, Peter didn't do much fishing. He never really liked fishing. Yet he was known to take out a client every now and then onto the Gulf of Mexico from his small powerboat on a slip on Captiva at the Naani Li'i resort and throw in a hook himself. If a client wants to fish while discussing business and finance and money issues, then so be it. Fishing was fun and clients came first, but fishing for the sake of fishing? That wasn't Peter's forte.

The office consisted of only four rooms, one of which was the lobby. Then a bathroom with a stand-up pulsating-all-around shower in it, a small yet orderly kitchen containing a variety of Nature's Valley granola bars and small bags of Nacho Cheese Doritoes (his favorite), and his own private office complete with a fully stocked wet-bar and ice making machine. As he entered the lobby, Peter was greeted gaily by his secretary, Emmannuela Pinedo, who preferred that Peter just call her Emmy.

"Good morning, Peter. How are you feeling today?" asked Emmy.

"G'day, Emmy. Not so bad, really. At least nothing that my gal, Lilith, couldn't soothe over."

Emmy was a gorgeous young maiden. Raven black hair. Shoulder length with bangs. And the most beautiful emerald green eyes that she often times used to her advantage.

Ah, what mysteries lie behind those jewels! thought Peter. After eight years of working with each other, he still caught himself puzzling over such beauty. Peter stopped at her desk and picked up his messages. Looking at Emmy, he asked her to call Jeremy's Florals and order a big bouquet of flowers for Lilith. It was their relational anniversary this weekend, and he wanted to be sure that the flowers would be delivered on time with the appropriate love note.

Peter then bee-lined to the little kitchen where he opened the refrigerator, looking at his watch in order to decide if it was too early to knock down a Dos Equis, his Mexican beer of choice. *Yep. Still too early,* he said to himself. He decided to grab an Arizona Watermelon Iced-Tea, although the Diet Coke next to it was screaming his name. Peter was trying to cut down on the Diet Cokes, per doctor's orders to lay off the caffeine affecting his heart. For the most part it was a losing battle. He toiled a second and put the iced-tea back in and grabbed a Diet Coke.

"Emmy, please be sure to restock the fridge sometime this week, will ya?" telling her more than asking her, but in a kind sort of way.

"Yes, Peter. Anything else while I'm at Jerry's? More Doritoes or granola bars?"

"No, nothing else I can think of, at least for the moment. Thank you. Oh, wait, some packs of sugarless Juicyfruit gum, please. Thank you."

With that said, Peter strode into his office and closed the door. Sitting down in his leather swivel-chair, he popped open his cold

Diet Coke and took a big swig. Turning around in his chair he looked out onto the Gulf to gather his thoughts and get his mind together. Big events were happening in his life, and he wasn't too sure how it would all end up, good or bad. After about ten minutes, his solitude was disturbed by a ring on his phone.

"Sandy Beach Bum Company, Peter here."

"Hey Peter! It's Grimm! What's up?"

"Not much. Please tell me you're not lost at sea again."

"Haha. Funny guy. It's always good to know you are spirited," Grimm replied.

"Well, nobody's had the chance to pee on my Wheaties yet this morning. The market opened up triple digits. I'm waiting on a call from Paco. Do you think you can finally get over him insulting your height the last time you two met?"

"Maybe. What else you got goin' on today?"

"Just the one-year anniversary of me meeting Lilith. Whassup?"

"If ya ain't busy, how 'bout coming on down to the marina for the afternoon? We can go out on the water and drink a few Dos Equis. Whaddya say?"

Peter liked Grimm. Not only was he his boat's mechanic, he was a close friend. Peter had helped him set up the Marina when Grimm left the military, and Peter had finished with his MBA from Wharton. The two had been friends since high school. Grimm had gone on to be a pilot in the Navy, flying F-22's, the Navy's 'Lightening Flyer'. He didn't mind the flying in the Navy, though it did rupture his left ear drum. He much preferred boats now.

"Not a bad idea. But if I do come, I can't get drunk bec—"

"No problem," said Grimm interrupting Peter.

"We'll just take one six-pack with us and some Diet Cokes. You still suck down Diet Coke all day, right?"

"I have to be back by five o'clock to take Lilith out for dinner."

"Lilith. The name on the back of your boat. Only it's not a boat. It's a fifty-three-foot Tyannis Yacht. Look, it's ten-fifteen a.m. now. I'll have you back by four o'clock. Plenty of time to shower and shave and get ready for your date. Besides, I want to show you something that I think you're gonna like."

"You got her done, don't you?" Peter said with a world of excitement in his voice.

"Don't know what yer talking about," Grimm said mischievously, while giving off a bit of a laugh.

"As soon as I hear from Paco, I'll be right over."

"Paco. I can't stomach that guy. Beta male. I'll put my manhood up against his any day. Nothing triggers me more than an effeminate liberal."

"How about someone who also disdains your pride in America?" Peter stated.

"A real man could take his girl, and he knows it. He has chronic limp-wrist. The military would never take him."

Peter knew Paco woke up late every day, and that Paco did not like to be called – he did the calling. At precisely ten-thirty, Paco rang up Peter and asked him about the 'deal' going through as planned. Peter confirmed. Emmy tried to listen in, but the muffled sound through the door wasn't easily discernible. A five-minute call with Paco was like eternity for Peter. Paco wanted to know every detail twice, then repeated again a third time.

"The Energizer Bunny badgers you for advice, doesn't he, Paco?"

Finally Peter had enough and told Paco he would call him later on. Paco wouldn't have it. He was coming to see Peter right away, but still he wouldn't get off the phone.

"So you are on Sanibel already. I'm headed to see what I think is my newest boat. Why don't you come along?" Peter asked cheerfully but reluctantly.

"I just read an NYT commentary on my iPad in the bathroom that said Obama should push the USA to be more like Europe: free healthcare and free higher education. Free healthcare so there is incentive to cure you and use preventative care rather than treating you forever. With free education so a university professor isn't afraid to fail your sorry behind because there is no tuition-profit to lose. Sounds reasonable to me."

"The USA would never go that route. Money is king in the USA. Century notes speak volumes. Billionaires like Trump and Bezos and Zuckerberg are big celebrities plastered all over magazines and the internet. Stick to the tabloids in the grocery check-out aisles. You'll be less confused."

"You know what else I read," said Paco. "The U.S. government is trying to end printing of the century-note. No more hundred-dollar bills for transactions in this country. Trying to snuff out cash transactions while at the same time calling for negative interest rates. I guess that's why in some parts of the world hundred-dollar bills are known as the Bin Laden. We'll have to move to prepaids soon to keep our soon-to-take-off 'business' going."

"That'll bite our 'business' in the behind," said Peter. "The oligarchs need to mind their own business instead of making it their business to mind mine. Bank debit cards and prepaids don't incur fees because people still use cash. End cash and see how long that lasts. Cash may be the last vestige of freedom for the 99%. Of course, when the whole system eventually collapses from all this government debt we are accumulating, the real things to barter with will be items like ammunition, canned foods, alcohol, anti-biotics, nubile Asian teenage girls. Good useful stuff like that."

"Should we blame the state of America on Obama?" asked Paco. "I guess handing out leaflets in Chicago in the nineties wasn't good enough experience to lead the world's biggest economy."

"Obama... At his very best he has lowered the tides, like he promised. Now I can't get my dingy to the docks. Maybe I should have asked Obama if I needed to install floating docks."

"The deal still is going down right?" asked Paco again. "Right? I have no fears if you don't. I have the car. The driver. Although he is unknowingly the key part of it. This is just the first trial run. If it goes smoothly, it can be done again and again, and we are set for good. White collar crime I've done for years now is high return for low risk. It's like cheating on your taxes. Done that since forever. Slim risk you'll get caught before living a long life high on the hog. If caught, slim risk you'll be charged. If charged, slim risk you won't be free on bail. If free on bail, slim risk trial won't be delayed for years. If on trial, slim risk of being convicted. If convicted, slim risk it won't be delayed for years on appeal. If appeals end, slim risk it isn't just a fine. If not a fine but jail time, slim risk it'll be more than a few months. If a few months, slim risk it won't be in Club Fed like Bernie Madoff. If in Club Fed, slim risk the whole time will be served. If whole time served, slim risk you won't be out with all the money you stole waiting for you. So, worst case scenario, a few months in Club Fed in return for years and years of extreme wealth before and after. It's a no brainer. But this deal—"

"Slim risk. I hear ya. I have no fears," Peter wanted off the phone.

"But this deal," Paco repeated, "we're getting ourselves into isn't simple white-collar crime, Peter. It's a whole different ballgame we are playing now. The risks are much, much higher. We could be looking at some serious Federal Prison time if we're caught. And we'd all go down. All of us. None would be spared. I know though; don't I know. We're all going to be damn rich in just a few months if this system works again and again. Richer than a Clinton. Being rich is better than being poor, if only for financial reasons."

"You're already rich. And so am I. I'm just doing this for fun. An affair with money. The pastime of great Americans of all generations. Speaking of the Clintons," said Peter. "I thought we'd try to sell some Russian uranium ore with my new contacts in Moscow, but I hear Hillary has that market all tied up. Haha! As for me, this year I am gonna buy a big condo in the Sixteenth *Arrondisement* in Paris. I have always wanted a nice dig to play in close to the *Arc de Triomphe* and *Champs d'Elysees*."

"Paris, Paris, oh Paris!" Paco exclaimed. "Where your dog is allowed to go with you into the finest restaurants, but your kids aren't. If you ask me, The City of Lights is growing dimmer. It's gay heaven."

"Nice. Speaking of gays, Antoine isn't with you, is he? I'd rather he didn't come along today. Grimm is pretty hard core and won't take a liking to him because he's a fag."

"No," replied Paco. "I think he is at a Barbie doll convention here in Miami."

"Sheesh! What rot. Tell me, can a guy be gay to such an extreme that it all cancels out and makes him straight?"

"L-O-L! Good one. I'll meet you at Grimm's marina in a few shakes. Later, clinker."

Peter wasn't happy at that moment post-conversation with Paco, but he summoned the goodwill to ring up Grimm to tell him, with reluctance, that Paco would be joining them at the marina. Grimm wasn't happy about this either, but Paco was the moneyman and lead deal-creator, and he always had his say in the end. Peter was the one who was going to make the deal arrangements finalized up north, starting a path to making all three men wealthy beyond anything they could imagine.

"Antoine isn't coming, is he?" mumbled Grimm depressingly.

"No, don't worry about him," said Peter. "He's at a Barbie convention in Miami."

"A Barbie doll convention? O.M.G. *Hi, I'm Chris Hanson with MSNBC's 'To Catch a Predator'. Here, have a seat.*"

"Haha! Niiice! You must be psychic."

"No, I'm not psychic," Grimm spoke louder into the phone. "But I did date one once. It didn't work out. She dumped me before we even met. See you soon, pal."

Turning his eyes and thoughts outward towards the Gulf, Peter couldn't contain the feeling within. He felt like a young boy at Christmas. Actually even better, if what Grimm had to show him was what he expected. If so, then it was going to be one heck of a good day, indeed. Peter put on his yellow windbreaker and fishing hat, told Emmy to forward his calls to his cell phone which may or may not be in range and that she could leave after lunch. He climbed into his Porsche Cayman, stopping off at Jerry's on his way off Sanibel Island to pick up a six-pack of Dos Equis and some Diet Cokes. There were no Key Limes at Jerry's, unfortunately, much to his dismay.

Grimm stood on the edge of the dock at his marina in the bay. Looking at the *Princess Lilith,* Peter's yacht, was there even a way to describe her beauty and magnificence? The only word he could come up with was *sublime.* Two years ago when Peter bought the Tyannis it was in sad disrepair. That is what really brought Peter and the yacht together. That and a sixty-five thousand dollars cash exchange. Not a lot of money to Peter. But for a boat that could barely float? That was a lot, so thought Grimm at the time. Not to Peter. He wanted a yacht that was personal and that was customized to his own satisfaction. This luxurious craft was perfect for what he wanted done. Looking at her now, you would never guess that the *Princess Lilith* was over thirty years old - that which wasn't replaced, meaning the frame and the hull only. For the last six months Grimm wouldn't even let Peter see what changes were being made to the Tyannis. *An artist never displays his work until completion,* he often told Peter. For the most part, Peter respected that. So he let Grimm have at it, with an unlimited budget to do what he thought would make her the best sailing vessel in South-West Florida.

The appeal of a Tyannis is its sea worthiness. It can be sailed by one individual who has the skills and knowledge of how to sail a fine yacht. Inside the Tyannis, Grimm put in Philippine teak wood, the largest cost of the reparations outside the motor. The yacht had an old Ford Lehman diesel engine, which, although it was a good engine for a sailboat, Grimm decided on replacing it with a modified two hundred and fifty horsepower twin-diesel Cummins. This served two purposes: one extra power for times when there was no wind, and the second extra weight.

The salon was finished with the teak and mahogany, and so were the decking and the tables, which were covered in prime leather from Istanbul. The counters were done in solid Moroccan marble. A large head with a push-flow shower was installed in the main cabin, using a state-of-the-art vacu-flush. The yacht also sported a large settee and full galley. A fishing cockpit was fitted aft, with a Pan-Panette fighting chair. The bridge was also redone with new vinyls which could be used as flotillas. A water-proof Bose sound system with speakers fore and aft and in both cockpits completed the luxury. A new fifty-five-gallon Watermaker with hot water heater was also included for comfort.

"Obama," thought Peter as he was driving over to Grimm's Marina when he saw a bumper sticker on the back of a minivan supporting the president. *"A jihad terrorist blows up civilians, and Obama goes to Twitter with his outrage. As if a hashtag and feelings will solve the world's problems. We need the Greatest Generation back. My father and men like him. The ones that used to kick ass for America, and knew the difference between a boy and a girl. Obama... He's ended poverty, like he said. Good for him on that. He's stopped the rising of the tides. If only he had a son that looked like him, then it would all be perfect. I'm a nationalist, a protectionist, a Christian, a white male, a heterosexual, and a patriot. Pretty soon all of that will send me to prison."*

Grimm climbed aboard the *Princess Lilith* to set about making final preparations before Peter would arrive, making sure all was in order: sounding off horns, channeling on the radios, checking pumps and lifts, and just about everything else that needed to be toggled. Grimm went back into his marina shop quickly to get some dry staples for the trip he would be taking Peter and Paco on out on the boat. Dried fruits, Lay's potato chips, and just in case anyone was daring, some margarita mix and a bottle of blue agave Amigos tequila. He also brought out a bottle of Dom Perignon champagne which he would hand to Peter to christen the fine boat. Grimm's phone rang.

"Grimm here. Speak to me."

"Yes? Mr. Grimm? Dana Gramling from the Gasparilla Waterline here. I am writing a story for a blog and just wanted to verify a rumor that you recently caught a thirty-one inch snook and a twenty-one inch grouper in Pirate Harbor. Is all that correct?"

"Yes. And a crap-load of fun it was getting them in the boat on a ten-pound line."

"Can you tell me the boat you caught them on?"

"It was a forty-foot Wellcraft. A little big for Pirate Harbor, I will admit, but just giving her a test run after working on her for the past four months. So I dropped anchor and spent the afternoon fishing. Anything else you need to know?"

"Can you tell me what you caught the fish with?"

"The snook I used a mini-spinner rig. The grouper was with live bait. Shrimp to be exact."

"Do you have any pics?"

"I can send them if you text me your email address. Does that work?"

"Yes. That will work fine. Thank you for your time, Mr. Grimm."

"Just please mention my marina in the story. I need all the publicity I can get in this economy."

"Done! Thank you so much! Happy fishing, sir!"

A few moments of rest on the bench on the dock, and Grimm spotted Peter's Porsche pull up. Peter was on the phone.

"Make it a seven-thirty p.m. reservation then. It's a special evening," he spoke rather bluntly into the phone.

"That is fine, Mr. Collins. The Green Flash Restaurant is pleased to make a reservation for you and your girlfriend. We'll reserve a window table looking out over the water."

"And chill some Pommerol champagne for me before I get there. It's our one year dating anniversary. Sound okay?"

"Yes, sir. I will personally make sure it gets done. You and a Ms. Lilith. Seven-thirty p.m. With Pommerol champagne. Thank you again, sir."

>Click<

"Hey Grimm. What's up? What's shaking?"

"You are still dating that Lilith gal?"

"Yes, I is. Someday you will have a woman of your own," said Peter.

"Nope. No anchors for me. Other than ones tethered to my boats."

"You just wait then. You're one day gonna be a salted-dog like me, and then it will be too late for ya."

"Fine by me," smiled Grimm.

"You ever watch *Married at First Sight*?"

"Never seen it. Why not *married before birth*? Makes just as much sense."

Peter grinned. "Paco gotten here yet?"

"Not yet. I'm not excited to see him," grimaced Grimm.

"That goes without saying—"

"Well, I am gonna say it anyway."

"But, big guy, we need him. So don't teeter him off today, please."

"I like his sweet-tart, Vanité. She's a hot ticket."

"She is for sure. But I am tethered to my Lilith."

Grimm got up off the bench and committed to a gentlemen's hug and a pat on the back for his good friend. "I see you brought Dos Equis for all. How 'bout we pop one open to start this affair? No pun intended."

"Keep right on, Grimm. I'll have you back out in the Navy yet again. How's she sittin'?"

"She's sittin' and waiting for you as we speak. We just moved her from dry-docks. When that jerk-off Paco gets here, we can christen her with this bottle of Dom and head off for a day's fill of the harbor and beyond."

"Well, you gonna just stand there? Or are you, Grimm, the Grand Mariner, gonna show her to me finally?"

Grimm popped open two cold beers from Peter's mini-cooler. "No limes? Well, a toast." The two men clinked the tops of their bottles. "To the best friend a guy could ever have."

"*Salud!*" said Peter.

In his most eloquent speech, Grimm continued, "Your Princess awaits. The beautiful, one of a kind, the lady herself, the *Princess Lilith*."

A walk around to the other side of the marina, and Peter was completely dumbfounded and awestruck by what he saw. The fine yacht resembled nothing like the junk he bought and had hauled to Grimm's marina. "Wow! What a lady she is!"

Grimm smiled and thumped his chest.

Peter continued. "You have truly resurrected her from the decays of time and decrepitude. She's absolutely beautiful! Just like my own gal, Lilith!"

Grimm handed Peter the bottle of champagne, which was summarily smashed on the stern of the Tyannis. Glass chips flew everywhere. "I'll have my marina-captain, Nazar, do the clean-up," said Grimm. The two men climbed aboard, with Peter scampering around, amazed at the changes done to the boat's majesty.

Grimm took the cigar stub from his mouth and chucked it overboard. "You know, Peter, I gave up cigars ten years ago. I just bought this one to celebrate. Now I know why I gave them up. They are pretty foul. So no love lost there."

"Grimm, I tell ya, you really outdid yourself with my boat. It's worth every penny I put into it. Well done. I say again, my good man, well done!"

"It's all a part of the natural order of the universe. Makes me wish we knew more about the origins of the universe," said Grimm.

"Why are we always trying to learn about the origins of the universe? Why expend so much effort and resources on this? Are we planning on starting a new universe?" Peter asked rhetorically.

"I'd like to walk onto Florida Gulf Coast University campus into an astrophysics class and say, 'All those in favor of starting a new universe say 'aye'. All those opposed?'" Grimm chuckled.

"And then, 'If you're sure you're in favor of starting a new universe and all that entails with regards to matter and anti-matter allocations, please sign your name on the sign-up sheet while leaving the classroom'," Peter added with a grin. "Now, where is Paco so we can get moving?"

Just at that moment of Peter's question, Grimm's handset radio vibrated. "Grimm here… Mmhmm. Oh, fine, Nazar, send them down to the green south side of the marina. That's where we are. With the *Princess Lilith*. We are ready and waiting. Thanks, Nazar. Take the rest of the day off if you'd like as we will be out on the water until sunset. I don't expect anyone else to show up today. You and I - we'll meet tomorrow morning to discuss the Stewart boat's Cummins repairs. Fine. Fine. Thanks. Have a good day at the studio training… Nice. Out."

"That was my new marina captain, Nazar Mazurkevych. He is from Ukraine and is training to go pro in cage fighting. A mountain of a man. He floats like a cloud but destroys like a Godzilla. Hard as a rock. Nothing soft or safe about him. Tough as a Spanish fighting bull without the malice. He's got a darkness residing in his soul that is deep and primordial. No living by fear or faith in anything but himself. You can see it on his broken face and in his bloodshot eyes. Made but for life in the octagon. And yet one of the finest gentlemen you will ever meet. Completely reliable with all my affairs."

"Maybe he can train us to get tough? I know I could use some toughness."

"You shoulda been in the military like me."

"Military?" Peter laughed. "I got beat up bad or ran away from every fight I had as a kid. The military would have chewed me up."

"Maybe. Paco is here with Vanité. I told Nazar to tell them to walk around and join us here," said Grimm.

"Fine timing. I'm ready to take the *Princess* out and see how she does."

Paco and Vanité slinked down the docks towards Peter and Grimm. Paco had on a navy blue and white seersucker suit, to which Peter hollered out, "Hey, it's The Great Gatsby!" while he clapped his hands together. Vanité was wearing a black, sparkly disco dress with an open shoulder, and carrying a Kate Spade bag over the other shoulder. She was well-tanned and glowing and made a huge impression on both Peter and Grimm instantly.

"Ahoy, mateys!" yelled Paco.

"Swell to see you, Paco," Peter said. "Ready for some fun on my new boat?"

"Let's get shaking!" said Paco, as he led Vanité by the arm across the plank onto the yacht. Once aboard, Vanité took off her sunglasses and went below deck to lounge. Paco and Peter took to placing the Adirondack deck chairs and a small wicker and wood-top table in the aft. Then Peter went below quickly to fire up some icy-cold margaritas to share all around.

Grimm started the engines – which roared to life - and weighed anchor, returning then to the main helm to steer the large vessel out of the harbor and into the expansive bay.

Peter came back upstairs with a pitcher of margaritas, three cocktail glasses and a bucket full of ice chips. He poured one margarita for Paco and then one for himself. "Vanité says she isn't drinking today. She says she wants to lose three kilograms. I just had to laugh."

Grimm waved Peter off, saying he was going to play captain of the main and that meant no alcohol for the time out to sea. Peter walked up to Grimm anyway and whispered, "Play along with Paco." Grimm frowned. Peter continued, "We need him. Just pretend his brain is skipping like a scratched vinyl LP record." Grimm let out a bellowing laugh.

"You predicting anything from him?" whispered Grimm.

"Never predict anything, unless you are a meteorologist. Even then they only get it right less than fifty percent of the time. Don't mind him at all."

"I'm guessing his mind is like concrete: all mixed up and permanently set."

"That's pretty much exactly what I was thinking this morning, too," Peter scratched his head.

The *Princess Lilith* pulled out of the marina and set out onto the bay. It was a beautiful time of day, with the sun rising high and the strong bay breeze cooling the passengers. Grimm continued as captain while Peter and Paco set themselves down aft on the two deckchairs.

"Bernard Shaw claimed that capitalism will always exist because every one of the poor believe someday they will win the lottery," said Peter.

"Where did you hear that?" asked Paco. "CNN?"

"CNN is for people who are stranded in airports or stuck in a doctor's office. Or for people eating a cheap hamburger at

McDonald's. I think I heard it on PBS. Soros also said recently it's hard to give away a billion."

"Soros?" laughed Paco. "Where is a fine suicide bomber when you really need one? Just give a map leading to Soros' estate to Jihadi-John and let him make history."

"Yo! Putin! A little bit of polonium over here for Soros, will ya?" The two men smacked hands high laughing.

"Isn't Vanité a little young for you, Paco?" asked Grimm.

"You are young as the woman you feel," Paco entertained.

"You feel like a woman? How so?"

Vanité came up from down below with her sunglasses back on. "Can someone please help me watch the Brazil-Argentina football game? There is TV in here, no?"

"Are you praying for a soccer win for your country?" Grimm asked gayly.

"I pray all the time," replied Vanité, smiling a bright-white smile with ruby-red lips. "For many reasons."

"I was just joking. You can't tell me you really believe in prayer? Do you think talking to yourself really works?"

Peter joined in, "Well, you are sure to get the answers you want. Jesus did say the Kingdom of God is within you. So when you pray, you are talking to yourself and God at the same time."

"It brings me happiness when I pray," said Vanité as she strolled lightly by the edge of the yacht.

"Happiness can't buy me money," joked Grimm.

"Money is the root to younger women," said Peter. "Why have a forty-eight-year-old when you can have two twenty-four year olds?

"That's so disgusting. Why do men talk about women to be sex objects? I have faith in Jesus," said Vanité as she turned slowly towards the standing men.

"Why do women talk about men as success objects?" Peter countered cunningly. "That's so disgusting. My faith—"

"Explain away with the unfounded theories on faith," Grimm started off. "Because the faithless and the faithful are asking two different questions. Faith answers the question 'why?' showing intentions. The faithless ones ask 'how?' wondering about the machinations. But I ask you, are they mutually exclusive?"

"Machinations? God gave man a brain to be a chemical engineer," Peter sat back down. "Not a Unabomber."

"I don't pray," said Paco. "As for faith, I try to have faith in governments doing the right thing. Usually I am wrong."

"John F. Kennedy put a man on the moon. Barack Hussein Obama put a man in the woman's room. There is your government for you today," said Grimm dryly.

"This president believes people are misdirected but essentially good. '*The people just need knowledge*', he says. I fully disagree. '*Sorrow is knowledge. Those that know the most must mourn the deepest. The tree of knowledge is not the tree of life*'. Byron wrote that. Smart man, that Byron," said Paco.

"At least you have your Vanité," whispered Peter to Paco. "She's a real Brazilian treasure. A cutie. Why you have her, I have no clue. Don't ever lose her because you'll never get lucky enough to find another one like her."

"Oh, I won't lose her," said Paco proudly. "That's for sure. We have our fun. I take LSD and she takes birth control, so we have a trip without the kids"

All three men watched as Vanité walked lithely around the fore of the magnificent yacht twirling her sunglasses.

"Oh, I do say," commented Paco. "When I first saw this extremely gorgeous and sexy Brazilian girl there in New York City's *Spice*, and… Oh!... Just the way she moved in her tight-fitting Armani jeans and white Calvin Klein t-shirt. It boiled my hormones and made me believe there is a God… Ohhh, Vanité! Come back here to us, honey! If you can!"

The tall, slender model slowly stepped up back to the men gaping at her, adjusted her yellow hat and sat gently on Paco's lap. She took a drink from his margarita and kissed him on the lips.

"Vanité, my love. If I lost all my money, would you still love me, *ma cherie amour*? Would you?"

"Ohhh, Paaaacooo," she purred in her sweet Brazilian accent. "You know so well that I will always love you," she continued with a sweet kiss on his cheek. "And I would miss you, too."

10 You Can't Make It on Your Own

The walking in the sun and guilt wore on Jude like a fisherman's heavy lobster net. He was inconsolable and hung his head low in shame even after meeting with the priest. *Nothing came of it.* He thought to himself. *Absolutely nothing. What good is religion if it doesn't make you feel better?*

Nothing Hector was saying to him made him feel any better about himself, and his right knee still hurt. The two souls were continuing on their seemingly hopeless long walk to the center of Sanibel where they hoped to God to find someone who knew Paco or Antoine. The road was long, the sun was hot, and Jude muttered under his breath his discontent of this big mistake of being down in Florida away from Margarita and Chloe. With miles to go before they would be near the commercial center of Sanibel, the two of them argued over and over whose fault it was losing Jude's cell phone. Hector wouldn't have it. He placed the whole blame on Jude. Jude said Hector shouldn't have been sleeping all morning when he was inside Lilith's house, saying someone on the beach probably walked off with the phone.

"You shouldn't oughta been getting' down and doin' the nasty either," said Hector derisively. "Thinkin' about that are ya?"

"Oh, shut the heck up before I pop you one. I don't need that right now, understand? We're both in this mess together."

"Ma-a-an, I need to get the heck outta here and aways from you. Afore I does some serious damage to yo ass," Hector stepped into a fight stance with his fists up. He checked and weaved a few slow steps, following his shadow. "Master Chon and all would tell me to be a gentleman. Walk away. And keep from hurtin' ya. But I ain't so sure of m'self."

"Fine with me. Run. Go on. Run on ahead," Jude waved. "Let me know when you make it back to Miami on foot. With no cash for a way to Puerto Rico,"

"Suck," he bopped to this side once and put his fists down and relaxed. "You gonna go pay for my boat ride to Puerto Rico soon? They are gonna be lookin' fo' me back in Baltimore in a day or two. I best be off the mainland and headed to P.R. or they will so sure locks my butt up for a long, long time. A boat captain headed to P.R. won't ask me for no I.D. I can't take a plane cuz I needs I.D."

"Yeah, no probs," Jude stopped a second. He put his right hand on his knee and wiped his brow. "I'm sorry. Bear with me a while longer. I'll cover your rides to Miami and Puerto Rico. Once we get the registration from Catty and locate the Bel Air and get that all straightened out with Paco. Hopefully today. Then I will send you on a bus back to Miami with some cash to buy a boat ticket to P.R. And then me. I can finally head back to Baltimore. Margarita must be royally ripped at me by now, even though I wired her the money. What an effing nightmare. Sorry, brother, that this trip has been such a bad shuck for you."

"Awww, it's okay, bro," Hector patted Jude on the back. "It's been an adventure. I'm just playin' wit' ya. Just get me to P.R. afore my butt gets locked up by the po-po fo' good. You knows well I'm AWOL from my parole back in Baltimore big time."

"Maybe we should have stayed at the church until the priest said Mass. That would have made me feel better, wouldn't it?"

"I wents to a Catholic Mess once!" said Hector excitedly.

"You did?"

"Yeah! It was great! Me and an old girlfriend. First, they had some prayers. Which I didn't really know. Then they gave us a snack. But it was only a small cracker and a quick drink of some lousy wine. The only good part is they passed around a basket with cash in it! I didn't want to bees greedy sos I only took a couple hunnerd out of it. Dat wuz really a great time in a church Mass!"

"Dude?! You took money OUT of the collection basket?! You are supposed to put money INTO the collection basket, not take it out. It's for the church and its ministries!"

"Well, nobody done told me nuttin', and Julia was in da bafroom. I jes thought it was for the takin', you know, like they bees wantin' to help me out and such. Seein' as I was poor and all. I only took a couple hunnerd."

"It isn't like the Catholic Church needs the money anyway."

"They doesn't?" Hector questioned.

"Look at all the Cardinals of the Vatican. They neither toil nor spin. Yet neither Yves Saint Laurent nor Gucci in all their splendor was ever dressed such as these. That's what the nice angelic woman back at the Rectory told us. Or something like that."

The two loners plodded onward for endless more long miles in the heat of the day. On past the elementary school. Past side streets leading to expansive beach homes. Past the J.N. Ding Darling wildlife refuge and preserve. They had no water, no food, but still Jude had plenty of money on him. Thousands upon thousands even, left over from what Paco gave to him back at Lummus Park in South Beach. Jude promised Hector that at the first restaurant they came to, he would buy Hector whatever meal he wanted, so long as he promised not to eat too much and toss his groceries all over the sidewalk as he had done the night before on Captiva Beach. Hector just gave Jude a sour look.

The two men finally arrived at the wide intersection of Gulf Drive. Jude remembered that the young Uber driver had driven them around a corner by a general store called Bailey's the day before. He was pretty sure he could find the general store just by turning right and heading straight ahead. Past the post office on the right, and even past a few restaurants that Hector impatiently pointed out, Jude kept the pace on and made his way to Bailey's, where he was sure they could find a phone and get some much-needed fluids at a minimum. Hector so wanted to stop at the restaurants, but decided to keep up with Jude because he was out of smokes and surely Bailey's sold cigarettes, right? When they got to the general store, Jude gave Hector two twenties. He told him to go in and buy some bottles of water or Gatorade, and see if they had any sandwiches and chips or anything else they could munch on.

"Can I buys some butts?" asked Hector pleadingly.

"You need some more of those ragweeds? Yeah, go ahead. Whatever, Money."

Hector went inside while Jude sat on a bench outside the store with the sun in his eyes. He was fiddling with his wallet when he noticed inside that he had a business card from Paco that he had forgotten about. *Cool!* He thought. *All I need is a phone now! Why didn't I notice this card earlier? It would have saved us a crap-load of trouble!*

Jude looked across the parking lot. There was a young Latino guy with a weed-whacker trimming the edges of the lot. Jude walked quickly over to him and asked to use his phone. The Latino kid took off his noise-blocking headphones and said, "I don't can."

Jude looked at the kid a moment. Then he spoke slowly and loudly, "I need to use your *telephono*," pointing at his head with his hand like a phone.

"I don't can Ingish," said the Latino kid.

"Great. Busted," said Jude as he sulked away, hoping Hector would come outside soon so he could ask the Latino kid in Spanish for his phone and they could then call Paco to rescue them and get everything settled on Sanibel. Paco, he figured, by now had to be on the island with the registration for the Bel Air in his possession.

Just then, Hector came outside yapping and being pushed by a rather furious man who was as round as he was tall. "Hey man! Don't be such a butt-head!" said Hector.

"I told you to git out of the store. Now git!" said the fat man with the Dolphins ball-cap.

"Man, you so fat, when you sat on an iPod it became an iPad!" yelled Hector at the man.

"Git!"

"Yo momma's so fat that she has free internet because she already be world-wide!"

The fat man flipped off Hector and waddled back into Bailey's.

"What the heck did you do now, Hector?" Jude said exasperatedly.

"I only wanted a package of menthols, but they wasn't gonna sell them to me because I don't gots no I.D. So I told the pretty blonde cashier to kiss me to knows I'm of age. That's when this fat dude grabbed me and pushed me out the slidin'-glass door."

"Fantastic. So you have nothing for us to eat or drink because—"

"Because, the fat dude wouldn't let me settle up at the register. He had me out the door afore I could buy nothin'."

Jude shook his head followed by a face-palm. "Go over to that kid there with the weed-eater. He speaks Spanish. Ask him for his phone so you can call Paco. Here. I found his business card in my wallet, thanks be to God. I'm gonna go inside quick and get us some drinks and munchies. Try not to blow it, 'kay?"

Hector walked straight over to the landscaper and asked to use his phone. He rang up Paco who was surprised to hear from him. Paco impatiently told him that he was just then finishing up sailing for the day with some friends, but he would ring up Antoine, who, too, was on Sanibel, to come pick the two men up at Bailey's immediately.

"Good. Cuz we be hot here."

I got the Bel Air this morning!" said Paco excitedly. *"The car show is tomorrow so we got it just in time."*

"Fine. You gots de car. Jude will be happy wit' dat. Just tell the homo to come get us now. I means it. We be needin' food and drank and showers. I be done sweatin' on this island fo' ya, Paco, mon. No mo'! Ya hear me?"

Paco hung up without responding to Hector. Jude came walking up with a six-pack of orange Gatorade and some small bags of pistachio nuts and smoke-house almonds. He asked Hector to go up to the kid with the phone again and ask if he could make one more call. When Hector did, the landscaper rubbed his thumb and finger together and said, "*Dinero*".

"He wants money," said Hector. "I don' be wantin' to give him no cash, but we needs his phone, say?"

"I'm all for amnesty for these people, but this joker and others like him need to learn some English if they want to live in my country," Jude popped with a mean look on his face. He pulled a twenty spot from his envelope and gave it to the kid who returned a mean look on his face. Jude then yanked the phone out of the boy's hand and dialed up Margarita. He let the phone ring eight times when he was about to hang up-

"*Hello?*" said a sugary voice on the other end.

"Margarita baby?"

"Yes? Jude?"

"Yes, honey, it's me. How are you? How is Chloe? I miss you both so much, my love!"

"Forget Chloe. We have a problem, you and me. You cheated on me with another woman."

"What?" Jude dropped to the ground. "How... do you know... that?"

Margarita screamed into her phone. *"The woman you cheated on with me has your phone! Why did you give her your phone? Why? Was she a good lay, like she said about you? Huh? Was she good in the sack? She said YOU were!"*

"Ohhh... Margaritaaaa..." Jude hung his head low and fell face down onto the grass. "I am soooo veryyy sorryyy, honeyyy. I am sooo veryyy sorryyy. I don't know why it happened. I don't. It will never happen again. I promi—"

"No! Stop it! You can't promise anything! Ever!"

"But, honey, please listen," Jude tried to calm her down. "I can explain it. It was all a mist—"

>CLICK<

"Ooooh! Uuungh... She hung up on me," Jude lamented. "What am I gonna do now, Hect? Ohhh! My heart aches!"

"Jude, bro, she loves ya. She'll get over it. C'mon, get up. Paco has the Bel Air. Antoine will be here in a minute. We will go gets cleaned up. We gotta keep movin' fo'ward. I cans shower and shaves and gets cleaned up afore I takes da bus to Miami. Then I will gets me on a boat to Puerto Rico, and you can head on home to your Margarita and Chloe in a couple o' days. It ain't all that bad, homie. She'll get over it. I knows her good. She will. She loves ya. She a good woman and all."

Hector grabbed a bag of almonds and an orange Gatorade and started to gorge himself. Jude just sat there cross-legged on the grass with his head in his hands, weeping and sobbing at the thought of how he had hurt the love of his life, Margarita.

The fat guy from Bailey's came outside again and wobbled across the parking lot to Hector and Jude. "You pay for dat stuff there, man?" he said angrily pointing at the Gatorade and nuts.

"Yesh," said Hector with a mouthful of almonds. "He did pay fo' it all. By de way, yo papa's so fat, it took Google-Earth to take his high school picture."

The fat guy opened his mouth wide but didn't say anything. Hector grinned widely and shoved another handful of nuts in his mouth. The fat guy shrugged and walked back across the parking lot to the inside of the Bailey's store.

"You pay for this stuff here?" asked Hector.

"Nope. Just took it and walked out the door," said Jude as he sat on the grass with his head in his hands, crying his eyes out. "They set me off angry with how they treated you, my buddy, my friend, my very good pal."

The landscape boy asked for his phone back. Hector lowered a hand and asked Jude softly to get up, saying that Antoine was on his way to get them at any moment. Jude, for himself, was still inconsolable and wept bitterly as he sat.

Hector sat himself down on the grass next to Jude. Right then and there he felt sorry for his boss, a feeling he had never had felt before for anyone since his own mother died. Hector had always had it rough in life, and both men knew it, so when Hector rubbed Jude's back to soothe him, it meant something to both of them.

Minutes passed by and still Antoine didn't show.

"Where is dat homo?" asked Hector with some desperation.

The landscape boy came back over and handed the phone to Hector. "Alguien."

"*Quien*?" Hector was confused.

"No se."

"Hello?" said Hector into the phone.

"Hello, Hector? It's Filiberto. Margarita just called me with this phone number. I need to talk to Jude immediately. It's really important. Is he there?"

"Jude, it's Berto. He needs to talk wit' ya now, he says."

"Hello?" said Jude with bloodshot eyes and a spinning mind.

"Jude, dangit, I been tryin' to find you for days. What lady has got your stupid phone anyway?"

"It's a long story. A long and sad and bitter story. An effing mistake—"

"I'm sorry to say that it's about to get worse for ya. Mr. Wright from the bank came by two days ago with some guy with a high-end camera and took photos both inside and outside the garage. I asked him what he was doing, but he wouldn't tell me nothing. I figured he just needed the pics for insurance purposes. The next day I came back, the locks on the garage bays had been cut off, and all the cars' been hauled away. There was an eviction notice from the sheriff on the door and above that a notice of foreclosure with Mr. Wright's signature on it. Jude, man, we lost the shop. All the cars are gone. All of them. Even the customers' cars, they took away. The tools, the equipment, the desk and chair, the safe. It's all gone. Nothing is left. I called Mr. Wright and he said he wants a hundred-twenty thousand by the end of the month or it all goes up for local auction. I told him he took away the customers' cars, but he said that was my problem. I called the police department, then the sheriff. They all said there was nothing they could do. We'd have to go to court, they said. We gotta get the money or we are totally screwed, Jude. Did Paco settle with you yet? And just now some young weird pimply guy with curly hair and a scraggly beard came back demanding some three hundred dollars cash. I didn't have it, I told him."

Jude said nothing to answer Filiberto. He just started wailing out loud, holding his head in his arms.

"Jude, man, get a hold of yourself! We gotta get it together,

homeslice. I need to know. Did Paco give you the money yet? Did he?... Well?"

"No," mumbled Jude into the phone. "He didn't. I don't even know where he or the Bel Air are right now."

"Paco gots de car," said Hector.

Jude looked up at Hector.

"Let me call Paco. I'll get it straightened out. You sound pretty messed up. I will handle Paco."

"Berto, brother. I totally effed up my relationship with Margarita. It's over. I done messed it up bad."

"Yeah, she sounded really angry when she gave me this number. You shouldn'ta given your phone away to some woman. That was stupid. I know her well, and you know what? Margarita will be okay. She said you sent her and Chloe some money and she was happy about that. Let's focus on settling with Paco now. We can't lose the whole garage, and the Italians and the customer's cars, especially. We've put too much into it to lose it all now. The customers are gonna be rippin' angry, Jude. We gotta get those cars back from Mr. Wright. Pronto. I'll call Paco. You can relax. Take it easy on yourself. You sound awful. I'll take care of everything from here. I promise."

"Promise. That's like a four-letter word." Jude hung up without saying goodbye. He put his head back into his arms and continued to sob. "Oh, what the heck have I done? I've lost everything? How did this happen? Where did I go so wrong? So, so very wrong? I ask you. Oh, Lord, I need you now."

The landscape kid took his phone back, "I speaky de Ingish, you knows. I study in Birginia. In REEP. In Arlington. You knows REEP? Very good Ingish program. Last years. In Birginia. In Arlington."

Hector asked the kid in Spanish where he was from.

The boy raised his eyebrows and smiled. "My from is Venezuela. I nineteen. You no like my Ingish?"

At that moment, Antoine pulled up in a yellow Volkswagen convertible and honked. "Hey funny dust-bunnies, do you want me to drive you to Paco's lair or what?"

"Figures a poof would be driving a fag-bucket," remarked Hector. "C'mon, Jude, get up. Less go."

Jude struggled to get on his feet and ambled over to Antoine's car.

"He looks terrible. What's his problem?" Antoine asked Hector.

"Nunya bidness!"

Antoine rolled his eyes as the two men climbed into the soft backseat of the yellow VW.

"Do you think you could be mistaken for—"

"Enough talk! I'm not messin' 'round! Take us to Paco's now, Anto!" Hector yelled, then softened up. "I'm glad I ain't be walkin' no more."

"Yessir! Why I am doing all this for you derelicts, I don't know. Paco owes me big time for this. My pay is certainly not commensurate with all that I do for him."

"Git goin', I said!"

Antoine rolled his eyes again at Hector. As the VW was driving away from Bailey's, a motorcycle cop pulled into the parking lot up to the store's entrance. "Oh daaang," said Hector, partially scared by what had just gone down moments before. "We knows dat cop. We mets afore. He the one that done took the Bel Air. And fo' sure he be there lookin' fo' us now. The fat man done called the po-po on us."

"You prob'ly deserved it," said Antoine. "What did you do now? Let me guess. You stole something, right?"

"Anto. You poof. Yo' lived exper'ence doesn't means you gots unlimited wisdom."

The officer took off his helmet, dismounted his bike, and went inside the store. A minute or so later, the fat guy came outside with the cop and looked all around, but it was too late for him and the cop - everyone was long gone.

The way to Paco's estate took the men through some winding roads on Sanibel that unsettled Hector's stomach, even as Antoine drove good and straight and well below the speed limit.

"Anto, I needs a ride tomorrow to the bus station. I'm takin' a bus to Miami and then hoppin' a boat to Puerto Rico as soon as I can. Can you takes me early morn, homie?"

"If you apologize for calling me a poof and yelling at me, then yes."

"Sorry for callin' you a poof, my good brutha. I only yells at peoples I like. Take it as a compliment."

"Oooooh, what the heck have I done," moaned Jude curled up in a ball in the backseat. "I've lost everything. This is an absolute nightmare come true. What have I done? Hector tell me I am still okay. Tell me, please. I'm losin' my mind."

"Yer okay, boss," he patted Jude on the head. "I'm with ya. Anto here is with ya. Paco will settle it up. It will all works itself out. Berto will be takin' care of everything wit' da garage. He's been wit' ya for years; you can trust him. Margarita ain't goin' nowheres. Knows what I means?"

Paco's home was massive – three levels and decks - and sat right on the bayside of Sanibel. A long boat-dock extended out into the bay that had a few dinghies and a forty-two-foot Azimut motor-yacht tied onto the end of it. Hector let out a resounding, "Holy tokes! What a spread Paco be enjoyin'!" when he saw Paco's manse. "The spread" was complete with a guesthouse, three lane lap swimming pool and an eight-person in-ground hot tub.

All three men climbed up the stairs to an outside deck and went inside the house, where they met up with Paco's houseboy, who showed Hector and Jude to the guest bedrooms and bathrooms on the top level. Jude immediately went in to one room, stripped bare-naked, and set himself into an ice-cold shower in the adjacent bathroom. He stayed in there for a long while, letting the cold water cool his parched skin and aching soul. The pain in his knee subsided a little. When he got out of the shower, he shaved clean without looking at his eyes in the mirror. Though it was only just past four in the afternoon, he crawled into the guest bed and moaned himself right to sleep.

"Let 'im sleep," said Hector to Antoine and the houseboy as they all peeked into the bedroom. "He's had a rough coupla days. As for me, I needs a drank. Any alcohol in dis place? And any good food that I can eats?"

"You need a shower to clean yourself up first, Hector, friend. You smell awful. Like rotten lobsters. I'm going to take a nap, too," said Antoine with his heavy eyelids as he sauntered away towards another guest bedroom. "It was a long night for me last night in Hialeah and then the drive here today. I'm tuckered."

Hector shrugged and went into a different guest bathroom for a shower. After he got himself dressed with some news duds the houseboy had left for him, he went back downstairs looking for the houseboy. "Alcohol? Food? Does ya talk at all, kid?"

The houseboy clapped once and led Hector into the bar area where there was top-shelf liquor bottles lined up behind the rail, lit up by back lighting against a mirrored-wall. The houseboy politely showed Hector where the clean cocktail glasses were and where he could get ice if he wanted it. He then opened the small refrigerator for Hector to find whatever mixers he desired to use for making himself a stiff drink or two.

"Wowza," said Hector. "This is one nice layout of booze Paco be sportin'. Any food, mon?"

The houseboy clapped once and bowed and left Hector at the bar to mix his own drink. The young man returned a few minutes later with a silver platter of chilled, peeled shrimp and cocktail sauce in one hand, and in the other hand a large plate of a variety of cheeses, crackers, different flavors of hummus and toasted pita bread. "Here are the china plates and silver utensils, suh," he opened a cabinet door. "Napkins under the counter. Would you care for anything else, suh?" asked the houseboy.

"No, kid. I'ma all set fer now. Thanks."

The houseboy clapped once and bowed again, and left Hector alone at the bar. All Hector could think about as he mixed up some Captain Morgan spiced rum with pineapple juice now was how could he catch a boat from the Port of Miami headed to his homeland of Puerto Rico? Surely he would need some serious cash to bribe a ship captain headed that way. Enough cash so that the captain asked no questions. That meant hitting up Jude for a wad of benjamins. Hector knew his time was up in the mainland. It was serious now. The police in Baltimore would put out a national BOLO bulletin - if they hadn't already - for him for missing his pick-up date to go back to jail. He was sure the Florida police wouldn't mess around if they picked him up for any reason and found out he was a wanted felon from Baltimore.

"This been one heckuva trip," Hector murmured to himself as he stirred the cocktail. "I still be trippin'. Shake mah dang head. If I smells like a lobster, then I'm gonna get me boiled like a lobster. I might as well takes advantage o' it. This could be mah last hurrah here at Paco's crib."

Jude slept all afternoon, into the evening, and on through the night. Like he hadn't slept in years. Hector proceeded to get tanked on the free-flowing alcohol, and then chose to go to the game room with a cocktail in hand to play some billiards by himself. Antoine came downstairs from his nap a little while later and sat in the corner of the game room as Hector continued to play on the table.

"You is sure you gonna be able to drives me to the bus station tomorrow, ain'tcha, Anto?"

"Yes, it's a done deal. We will leave first thing in the morning after breakfast and have you at the bus station right away. I'll be sad to see you go. Not really, but in a nice way."

"Thanks, bro. Ya know, you ain't such a bad guy after all. Being gay and all even. I gots respect for ya anyways. Eight ball corner pocket."

"I knew that. But thank you. I'm going to mix myself a cocktail. Can I get you another?"

"Rum and pineapple. Captain Morgan spiced rum, please. Plenty o' ice."

Hector and Antoine continued drinking on into the evening. The houseboy repeatedly brought different plates of foods for all three of them to munch on. While the three guys were engrossed with the billiards game in the central part of the house until nightfall, a small sedan yacht pulled up to the dock-slip in the darkness. The lights on the Sedan were off, and it made no sound as it came swishing into the slip. None of the three men were near a window to notice its arrival.

About an hour and a half later, Paco and Vanité arrived home in his Alfa Romero Spider Veloce, which he left parked in the semi-circle driveway. Vanité went on inside, but before Paco joined her, he took a quick curious look out back of the manse. There it was. The lightless sedan sat quietly, bobbing in the water next to the dock. It was the yacht he had been eagerly expecting. Paco smiled widely to himself and thumped his chest. He hesitated for the present moment to go out and meet whoever was on board, and instead went inside to check on everyone in the house.

"Paco," said Hector. "I bees waitin' for ya. Tanks for the stay and all. Not enough 'O's in 'smooth' for how dis Captain Morgan is goin' down. Yer houseboy homeboy here is a fine billiards player and food-maker. Even tho' he don' talk much. I never done had my own servant. Or sh'd I call him da slave?"

"Good to see you, Hector. You're looking well. For once. It's getting late gentlemen. I suggest we all go upstairs and retire to our rooms for the evening. The Fort Myers car show is tomorrow, and we will have some righteous fun and reveling to do then, will we not? How's your time on Sanibel? The Isle of Fun?"

"It ain't been good, fo' sure. Where's da Bel Air?" asked Hector.

"Where's Jude?"

"He bees sleepin'. I asked you where da Bel Air is."

"Why, it's in the garage underneath you, of course!" Paco pointed at Hector's dirty shoes.

"How'd you gets it from da po-po without I.D.?"

"Nothing for you to worry about. The Bel Air is all shined up and ready for the show tomorrow. Yes, she is. Now, hurry along upstairs. We are getting up at the crack of dawn for exercises and stretching to start our day."

"Exercises? Stretching?" said Hector and Antoine at the same time.

"I don' knows 'bout dat," said Hector.

Everyone filed out of the billiards game room. The houseboy took all the empty plates and glasses and dirty utensils on a big tray and went the distance to the kitchen. Paco led Antoine and Hector to their bedrooms and shut the door behind each of them curtly. He checked on Vanité, who was fast asleep, naked herself like a Playboy Bunny in the master bedroom underneath the silk sheets. Then Paco quietly stepped back downstairs to the salon to relax with a passionfruit daiquiri and wait until he was sure everyone in the house was asleep.

It's time. He thought to himself. *Let's see if we can pull this off.*

The mysterious sedan's lights were still off. Paco slipped out of the house quietly and down to the dock to climb aboard the Sedan. Inside the poorly lit cabin were two scraggly, wiry men in dirty clothes, poorly shaven, who looked as if they hadn't slept in days.

"Man, you dudes are as thin as a heathen promise. Phew. You reek bad. Don't just stand there," whispered Paco in the darkness. "Let's get the digs unloaded."

The two gaunt men carried out multiple plastic crates from the sedan down the dock and around to the garage where Paco had opened the automatic door. There the Bel Air was exposed, with the metal linings of its doors and hood and floorboards and trunk already taken off. The two men cracked opened the large plastic crates, which made a slight noise.

"Shhh," whispered Paco angrily. "We can't wake anyone up in the house."

The men continued with their work, diligently and well-calculated, emptying the contents of the plastic crates into the sidewalls welded with little sills and down into the underboards of the Bel Air. Paco ran his hand across the inside of one of the plastic crates and touched his finger to his tongue. "Delicious. Like money."

Thirty-five or forty minutes passed, and the contents of the plastic crates were packed into every crevice and opened area of the car's skeleton. There wasn't an inch of free space inside the skeleton of the car. Then the two men took a couple of short phillips screwdrivers and attached back on the sidewalls of the doors and hood, and recovered up the floorboards beneath the seats and in the trunk. When they finished the work, Paco placed a thick envelope of cash into each of their sweaty hands. "Don't fill up your diesel tanks tonight. Wait until late morning. Go to Grimm's Marina to get the diesel. He'll be waiting for ya, but don't cause any suspicion getting there. There's some Subway cold-cut subs, bottles of water, a fifth of Jack Daniels, and bags of Fritos in a sack by the Jacuzzi."

The scragglers scurried by the Jacuzzi for the pickup of the full sack of nourishments, then made their way back to the Sedan, and set off from the dock as silently as the diesel engines allowed them to in the dark.

"Excellent work, men," said Paco under his breath. He pulled his iPhone out from his pants pocket.

"It's set and ready," Paco whispered into his cell phone while leaning against the shiny Bel Air. "It's allll set and done."

"Perfect," said Peter. *"Excellent. Job well done, my friend. We're gonna be richer than God. Rich-er… than… God."*

11 Upright Falling Down

The priest extended a hand to Jude's limp arm.

"So. You've decided to come back to see me. Good to see you again, handsome young man. You'll have to forgive me, though, as I have forgotten your name. It's called Irish Alzheimer's - you forget everything, except the grudges," the priest winked. He had a dignified demeanor, a quietness of self-respect that showed on his worn face. He gave a heavy, serious look at Jude all over, as if he were looking at himself in a mirror forty or so years earlier. "Here, have a seat next to me on the bench. Can I get you a juice or a muffin or something? You look bone-exhausted."

"My name is Jude. Is it too early for Communion?" Jude asked wearily. "Yes, I am back to see you. Though I am not sure why, sir. Maybe what I really need is to see a psychiatrist."

"That may be. But I sincerely doubt it. You seem mentally stable to me. Perfectly fine in your communication and stance. Doctors could do nothing for Lady Macbeth's guilt. If you didn't have that look of guilt on your face and were instead stoic, then I'd be a tad worried about your mental state. Psychiatrists have taken the place of priests in our modern era, and with that all the added problems it creates in our society. Is it really possible to diagnose greed as a mental disorder? How about sexual idolatry? Why not call sin something to be solved with allopathic medicine and forget God altogether? That's where society is headed."

Jude shrugged. "Do I need to make a donation here before we talk?"

"No, thank you. Your donation is of no use to us."

Jude showed a confused look on his face.

"In some bad parts of Miami, an addict will stab you to death for the two dollars in your pocket. That's how much your very life and money itself are worth to some lost souls. I take money out of the equation, and then changes can happen. But you and me," continued the priest, "we can start here by getting to know one another. As for Communion, are you Catholic?"

"Not really. I don't know. I was as a kid. I think I am an atheist. Is it really wrong to be atheist in Judeo-Christian America?" Jude shifted nervously in his seat.

The priest shook his head. "I can't answer that; only Jesus can. I am suspect about your being atheist. If you weren't a Christian, you probably wouldn't be here right now. Believing in Jesus and obeying Jesus are two very different qualities, mind you."

Jude looked around. "Is there a real problem with atheism in America? I wonder about that sometimes. The separation of church and state. Like in my daughter Cloe's school."

"People claim that Atheism is absence of religion. It isn't. Atheism is absence of God. It's still a form of religion called Humanism. So why do they allow the religion Secular Humanism in schools, but not... God? For us Christians, we must love the atheists. That's what Jesus calls us to do. To love others as He loves us. We shouldn't make negative commentary or jokes about atheists. Or any other beliefs for that matter. Only Jesus can judge."

"So the announcers on Christian radio stations say."

"Better that commentary than the talk radio shows. It's all negative talk on the conservative news radio stations. Not that I am a big Obama fan, but why be so shrill about America's problems? I can only give you Communion if you are Catholic."

"My mother was Catholic and took me to church when I was a child. I took Communion then. I kind of left the church as I got older."

"*Rien n'est parfait, dit le renard.*"

"Um, excuse you?"

"Nothing is perfect, said the fox." The priest put his hand on Jude's knee. "It's from the book *The Little Prince*. My favorite book. Besides the Bible."

"I like that book, too. Though I don't know it in French."

"So, do you have any questions for me, son?"

"Yes. Perhaps. Maybe. Don't you have any profound questions in life?"

"Yes, I do," replied the priest. "Take John 11:35, the shortest and most perfect verse in the Bible: 'Jesus wept'. There is no 'Jesus laughed' anywhere in the New Testament. And why did Jesus say to the thief on the cross, 'Today you will be with me in Paradise', but after the Resurrection, Jesus said to the women, 'Don't touch Me as I have not yet ascended to My Father'. Off the record, that sounds inconsistent to me."

"Oh. I—"

"You didn't bring your friend with you today."

"No," Jude didn't want to tell the priest that Hector was on a bus headed to Miami at that very moment. "I feel bad about it, but I think he's lost faith in me, father. Really. He worked for me in the past and was faithful and all, but now he's moved on and away. I hope he stays safe. I'm kinda worried about him. He's lost faith in me. I've lost faith in me. I fear—"

"Don't fear men. They have but the breath in their nostrils—"

"I'm not afraid of men!" Jude was taken aback.

The priest pointed a bony finger at Jude. "If not now, you will be. You will be. If that fear hasn't happened to you, yet, it will. Dark forces reside in the hearts of men. As for your friend losing faith in you, not to worry. Even Jesus' best friend John the Baptist lost faith in Him when he was in prison before he was beheaded. He sent a note to the Holy One Jesus asking Him if He was truly The One everyone was waiting for. And Peter, too, let's not forget him. He was the leader of the disciples. He was called the Rock. And he denied Christ three times at the salient point when Jesus needed him the most. So don't take it personally if your friend no longer has faith in you. The bible says have faith in no man but Christ."

"I'll have to remember that the next time I'm in Vegas."

"What's your favorite beer, son?"

"Um, Corona bottles."

"Do you put a nipple on the bottles?"

"What?!" Jude leaned away from the priest.

The priest smiled with a curl at the ends of his mouth. "What's the matter? You can joke, but you have never seen a pastor with a sense of humor? Tell me, please, then, why you are here to see me."

Jude started to speak but stuttered and put his hands on his head. "I cheated on my wife," he forced out a reply, then took a deep breath. "I had an affair, and she knows about it. I had never, ever done that before. I was always loyal to my wife and daughter. And I had planned to be for life. It just happened. It just did. And my phone is still at the home of the woman on Captiva whom I cheated with."

"And she called your wife on your phone, right? That's how your wife knows?"

"Something like that. Now I want to get back at her. At least get my phone back from her. Not that I want to see her for any goodly amount of time, just to get my phone back."

"Bad idea. It's better for you to stay away from her. She stabbed you in the back, but you still have the knife. That can lead to all kinds of problems. Not that we should be discussing names, but I'm guessing this is Lilith. Again."

Jude's jaw dropped. "How did you know?"

"Yes. Yes. Yes," the priest shook his head and breathed out. "She's always that woman at the party every man in confession wishes he hadn't started a conversation with. Her ruby lips speak words that drip like sweet honey and draw him into her web. In the end he has to pay for it with his soul. It's timeless. It's all over the Bible."

"I feel awful about it, father."

"Do you believe God loves you and forgives you?"

"I- I'm not so- sure."

"God's love is sometimes kind and soothingly gentle. And sometimes God's love is real discipline. Unbearable discipline that almost breaks us. But all the time God's love is righteous and true."

"I am going to try to stop sinning now," Jude rubbed the back of his arm.

"Be not mistaken. You can't stop sinning. That is Satan deceiving you with Scripture. We are not sinners because we sin. We sin because we are sinners. Do you complain about the life you live and your circumstances?"

"No. Not really. Why?" Jude could not understand where the priest was leading him.

"Do you know why the Jews wandered the desert for forty years looking for The Promised Land with Moses?"

Jude tilted his head to the side, "Someone lost a nickel?"

The priest scowled, "For murmuring. Simply complaining about their circumstances. You need to establish a healthy relationship with Christ. He is calling you. His Father is drawing you to Him. That is why you came here to see me today: to start to mend your relationship with God. Whether you see it or not."

"That's a relationship I know nothing about, father," Jude said sadly.

"Tell me about your childhood relationships. How you grew up. Anything come to mind?"

"I never had a stable home. My parents separated when I was eight years old. My father committed suicide when I was ten. Like Peter Pan, maybe I never grew up."

"Was there anything in your father's life at the time that caused him trauma for which he decided to end his life?"

"WHY YES! There was this dead gerbil that he buried for me in a formal gerbil funeral ceremony. But the neighbor's happy dog, Tucker, dug up poor Fred and paraded him around the neighborhood in his mouth. It ruined my weekend. >sniff< Thanks for asking."

The priest frowned. "What's the worst thing you can think of? Be honest."

"I coulda been your father, but the guy in front of me had the correct change."

The priest pounded his fist into his hand and spoke angrily, "That's not quite what I meant!"

"I thought that's what you asked, father."

"Be serious and let me simplify it for you. Which do you choose, young man, Heaven or Hell?"

"You want me to choose between Heaven and Hell? I break a sweat with a free coupon in front of a 7-11 soda cooler."

"I'm sorry son, but all joking aside, if you can't face your past seriously head on, your future is doomed. It explains clearly how you fall into sin so easily. Do you have a pornography addiction?" The priest leaned to one side and put a finger to his own temple.

"No. No porn. But I do, uh, have a problem sometimes with sexual self-abuse."

The priest sighed and nodded. "I wish I had a dollar for every adult who confessed to me their sexual self-abuse in the Confessional. I could rebuild that firetrap of a church over there. Sexual self-abuse is rampant in this sin-filled world. It's nothing I haven't heard before a thousand times from teenagers and adults. Mostly adult men and teenage boys, but women, too. All the same for everyone. I have an easier time understanding why the teens have their bad habits. The adults are the worst for it."

"Adults. I think being an adult is overrated. They should give trophies for just getting up in the morning and taking a shower. I mean, think about it: as adults we go to bed when we are not tired, and get up when we are. When will this madness stop?"

"Responsibility is not overrated. Jesus had the responsibility at a young age to care for his mother as a widow."

"Didn't Jesus leave His parents once when they were travelling, and they had to go find Him in the temple? That's pretty irresponsible and immature. Or was that a sin?"

"It certainly was no sin. It's what His Father in Heaven called Him to do. Just as He went willingly to the Cross. We humans cannot comprehend that kind of obedience. Our minds are too small and weak to—"

"I try to be responsible," Jude interrupted, "but my wife tells me that a pop-tart is not an appropriate breakfast before school for our daughter. And she says that, no, I can't have one, either. Even though my own father ate chocolate pop-tarts when I was a kid every morning for breakfast as he headed to the hospital where he worked. When I asked her 'when can I have a pop-tart?' she said when my daughter is in college. But I said I'll be dead by then! I never knew my father much other than his daily chocolate pop-tarts."

"Fatherlessness is the most serious social issue of our time in America. It's a crisis of immense proportions, and quite confusingly it goes on for generations. Like a vicious cycle. God's Holy Grace can wipe the slate clean between you and your father if you allow Him to do that for you. That will help you begin anew. Do you miss your father still today?"

"Not as much as I miss being a young boy. Even with the shattered dreams and endless taunting of other boys. I want to be a boy again. I don't know why because I hated being a kid and couldn't wait to grow up. Now that I am a man, I want to start over. I can't even explain boyhood or manhood to my wife. She doesn't get it. When I was in elementary school, we played a messed-up game called Smear the Queer where you and the other boys who weren't fairies beat the heck out of the boy who was holding a ball until he dropped it. Makes you wonder why we even picked up the ball in the first place. Of course today boys can't even play tag at recess without signing a legal waiver or else getting sued."

"So you had good relationships with friends when you were a young boy?"

"Not really. My mother didn't give me a birthday cake to take to school. We were poor and on food stamps after dad died. She made sugarless pop-up biscuits for my birthday. The other kids in my class threw them at me in the cafeteria. I wasn't very popular as a child."

"I see. You must have had it very hard. But what about your relationships now? Do you do anything loving for your wife?" inquired the lively priest. "You can't be open to God's Grace unless you are a giver. If you want to be a real man, your wife and daughter have to come first in your life. What do you give to your wife that no one else does?"

"Sometimes when my wife is lying on the couch after a hard day's work I will come over and lay on top of her just because I can and I find it hilarious that she can't move. And then my daughter will come lie on top of me. My wife usually hates everyone in the world anyway, so I don't care that she yells at us and tells us to get off. She would yell at anyone to get off. And that is only the start of it."

"Here's an idea for you: avoid worthless arguments which only lead to strife."

"She makes me so damn angry, father!"

"Take it easy, son. You have to understand that you can't have intimacy without conflict. What I am actually asking is this: do you provide well enough for your wife and daughter? Here you are on Sanibel, and they are… where?"

"Baltimore. Because I am the man of the house and the husband and the father, I am supposed to be the provider, right?"

"Yes. That's the way it's always been in this world. Since Adam was condemned for his sins to hoe the fields outside of Eden by the sweat of his brow. As King Solomon says in Ecclesiastes, it's a heavy burden God has laid on men. It still happens, just as night follows the day."

"Somehow that never works out for me anyway like I want it to. I barely make ends meet with my garage. At least the household bills get paid. Though mostly late. And what's worse is now I may lose the garage to foreclosure. It had such great potential. It's gone now."

"More importantly, right at this moment now your daughter is growing up fatherless just as you did. Do you see a pattern here like I do?" the priest addressed Jude with sincerity.

"It's not at all the same. I will be home soon. My father won't because he didn't care enough to send the very best. I'm not sure when I'll be back home to Baltimore. But soon. I'm waiting to pick up a car. Or sell it. I'm no longer sure which way is up with that. It hasn't been all that long that I've been gone from them. Just a couple weeks now."

"It's been long enough for a young girl not to have her daddy. Despite what Hillary Clinton suggests, a village can't take care of her. Only you can. Do you like our ways in American society, our government?"

"I hate it. The admin is the worst. It's taken this admin only six years to undo what over two hundred and thirty years of good leadership did to build up this country to the greatness it once was. And President Obama did it all while playing golf. The libs are happy at the same time by using a hemp rope on America – more 'greener' that way. A true leader takes responsibility for his actions at work. When I make a mistake at my garage, I admit it to the customer and take my lumps and make it right again. Or at least I did when I had the garage. Obama doesn't seem to want to do that."

The priest leaned into Jude and spoke directly eye to eye. "You have to understand: Obama's problem is that he is a fatherless man like you. He was once a very empty and scared little boy like you were. Both of you with no father to love and protect you. No child, especially a boy, can rightly survive well being raised by his mother only. It's a modern-day lie that single mothers can make up a complete family. And right you are about men needing to be good leaders and fathers. Obama is showing himself to be an excellent leader for this country, an exemplary husband to Michelle, and a very good father to his two daughters. Despite being fatherless himself. That is what a true Godly man does. Most people in the U.S.A. today no longer care about Godly leadership. All they want is the president to say 'hip-hip-hooray for you' and endorse their weird little perversions. I hear it every day from all sorts of people here on this fantasy island. Do you need or receive government help?"

"No," Jude shuffled on the bench. "But my mother and grandmother both did. I just never thought it was worth the hassles. I probably wouldn't qualify anyway."

"So even though you say you barely make ends meet, you make a good enough salary in your garage to provide for your wife and daughter?"

"Yes. I'd say I do. The household bills seem to get paid. Always."

"Blessed be God the Father for that."

"There was even potential for greater things for us. I had some good investment jobbies that would have been taken care of just as soon as I get back to Baltimore and get grease under my nails again. Those are probably gone for good now, unfortunately. I don't know. Maybe I will get them back from the bank before they are auctioned off. Do you know a wealthy man here on Sanibel who wants a rebuilt Ferrari classic for a good price?"

The priest smiled and raised a hand. "You're into classic cars at your garage. I owned an early model racing-green Jaguar E-type. I eventually sold it and bought an MGB hippie buzz hoopie. I guess you could say marijuana made me do stupid things back then."

Jude almost choked. "You smoked ganja, father?"

"I did a lot of stupid things in life," the priest spread his palms wide. "I onetime got busted by a State Highway Patrol Officer going eighty-nine miles per hour on the Massachusetts Turnpike when I was in high school. I once rode a motorcycle at one hundred fifteen miles per hour while in college. Which is interesting in itself, because when you are riding a motorcycle and you reach one hundred fifteen miles per hour, you suddenly realize just how stupid it is to ride one hundred fifteen miles per hour on a motorcycle."

"Ah! So, you, too, have done stupid things."

"As all men. I've done and probably will still do a bunch of stupid things in life," confessed the priest with a straight eye. "More than I care to admit. So I can't say I've never sinned myself. Clearly, I'm much older than you. I probably have done more stupid things in life than you have, son. None of us has the right to judge another."

"Stupid things. Not like I have done, father. I cheated on my true love, Margarita. I have to be a better husband and father."

The priest leaned into Jude's face again sternly. "Then I suggest you get back to Baltimore and do just that. Be a better husband to your wife. Be a better father to your daughter. You can forget what sins have happened here in Florida if you are ready for Confession and Contrition and want to right the wrongs of the past. Blood makes you related to your daughter. But loyalty makes you, your wife, and daughter a family. There is no book or documentary, none, on learning to be a good – let alone perfect - husband and father. Learning it only comes from experiences."

"Um, is there an app for that I can download?"

The priest was not interested in continuing on that bent and didn't show any change on his face but tilted his head slightly and slowly. "What do you do for an outlet? All men need an outlet."

"I train for mixed martial arts. I've been doing it for years around the world.

"Hmm. I see that deep and primitive intensity in you. Jesus was a fighter. Antifragile. I enjoyed learning the sweet science dance as extracurricular at Princeton. Ever hurt anyone?"

"Never outside the studio. I mean. I want to often. Especially men. Or the boys they were, when we were kids. Some of them I would really love to do a ground and pound and—"

"Better to seek Jesus before you make that decision. Most men wait until they are in the courtroom defending themselves to start praying. Are you still fearful of the world like you were as a boy?"

"I'm afraid of getting my penis caught in my zipper like I did in elementary school. Almost pee'd all over myself as I ripped the zipper down again. It hurt like heck. But now I'm in a different state of fear. I don't even know if my Margarita will take me back, father. Right now she doesn't want to talk to me."

"Oh, she will take you back. If you show true contrition. Just like Jesus accepts you unconditionally under His Grace, a good woman will almost always infallibly accept you after you sin if you are contrite and honest with her. Women can be very forgiving. I've seen it many times in my career as a priest. For a good worldly example, Hillary stayed with Bill. Trust in Jesus to help you get through this setback with your wife. But make no mistake: there is no hope but in the Grace of Jesus Our Lord and Savior. Jesus paid the price. You get to keep the change."

"Jesus paid the price. I get to keep the change. I like that. It gives me something to live for."

"Mmmhmm... I am sensing you have other sins to confess. Am I right?" the priest looked at Jude with consternation and a nod.

"Nothing I can think of. I lie a lot. Too much lying. Oh, wait a minute... I stole food and drinks from Bailey's store yesterday." Jude's heart was in his throat.

With a sharp eye, the determined priest pushed, "Have you ever helped a woman to have an abortion?"

Jude stiffened, shuddered, and fell to the ground crying, "YES! YES! OH, YES! My girlfriend from Spain! Paloma!... She had an abortion when she got pregnant and I said I wasn't ready to get married! She left me soon after that! Ooooh! MY HEART IS BREAKING!... I am not a man! I am a worm!" Jude lay there on the carpet rolling around with his body scrunched up and crying his eyes out. Sharp stretching pains around the corners of his mouth caused more tears to well up pouring out of his eyes.

"I'm so sorry," the good priest whispered, handing Jude a few tissues. And again a soft whisper, "I'm so sorry."

Jude cried and balled and wailed hysterically. "OH, I AM NOT A MAN! I AM A WORM!" More pains around the corners of his mouth and along his lips. His throat felt painful pressure in the back near his tonsils that he had never felt before, forcing his mouth open wider.

"I'm so sorry," the priest gently whispered again, offering Jude some more tissues. "The Lord forgives you, son. Believe that. Nothing you have ever done can separate you from His Loving Mercies. Accept Him into your heart and life."

The priest sat silent a moment with his hands out in front of him on his knees as Jude balled on the floor. *It wasn't so long ago,* thought the priest, *that I was this man feeling searing pain like this.*

"Ohhh... SCREW THIS! SCREW THE WHOLE WORLD!" Jude cried. "I EFFING HATE IT ALL!"

"Emotions, son. Emotions. Don't expect them to always feel good."

After a few minutes passed of Jude's wailing and sobbing and rolling around on the carpet, he got up slowly and sat himself again on the bench. With a tissue from the priest, he wiped the last of the tears from his cheeks. For a brief instant, he chuckled uncontrollably.

"It's the love you feel for your wife now."

"Is love an emotion? Just a feeling we have?" Jude rested.

"Not, it's not. Love is not an emotion. Love is the Body of Jesus Christ. Dwelling in you," the priest nodded wisely. "You have to accept your culpability. But you also have to understand that society is engineering itself to make men behave thus. That is the way society is going. I'm talking infanticide. Soon babies will be murdered after they are born, and it will be called 'protecting the health of the mother'. The innocent are condemned while the guilty go free. The only good sense is it means Jesus is coming back soon."

Jude held his head in his hands. "I feel better inside. But I still feel worthless as a man. I am not a man."

"Hold on a second," the priest smiled. "Let me read you something that a young man from here on Sanibel wrote to me a few months ago. I think it will mean something to you." The priest got up and pulled a folded piece of paper from a side drawer in his beat-up wooden desk.

"This is how the letter starts off: *Father, I write this story to you humbly as I lay here in my hospital bed with tubes in my arms, not knowing how much longer I have in this world or what to expect in the next. I pass it on to you who will keep it and treasure it. Maybe you can submit it to a local newspaper or national journal once I'm gone? It is one of my best memories in my short-lived life. You always appreciated my writing ever since I was a young boy. You know I always wanted to be a writer. I hope you really like this story here. It's all true, father. Here it is."*

~~~
~~~

"There I sat in the Oruro, Bolivia bus station, worn out from three days of drinking, partying, eating, dancing, and more drinking. Carnaval in Oruro. There is nothing like it. You have to experience it yourself to see how vastly poor people can live and party like no other. For just a few days, it was like living with no tomorrow in mind. If someone had wrung out my smelly shirt right then into a glass, they could have gotten drunk from drinking the sweat. The rickety wooden bench I was sitting on had about fourteen men, but was probably only made for ten at the most. The station was filled with drunk, abusive men who were waiting for buses to go God-knows-where-else in Bolivia and beyond. Not a woman in sight. Carnaval was over, and the angry reality of living again normally for everyone was sinking in. I was falling asleep, exhausted, beat, and could barely keep my head up, but had to hold my bag tightly to my chest or it was sure to be stolen. When would the bus come to take us back to Cochabamba? I sank into a semi-conscious state.

"Hey, *cholo,* he wants to talk to you," said my friend, Javier, as he poked me in the ribs. Bolivia is Javier's home country, and he and I study together at Edison Community College. He invited me to come to Bolivia to meet his family and travel around for five weeks there. One of the best times in my life, though I probably need to go to you for Confession now, father. It wasn't a moral time for me in Oruro, for sure.

"Wha—?" I pulled out of my stupor. "Who?" I sat up straight and looked around and then looked down. At my feet was a rather small skinny boy, about six years old, holding a shoe-shine kit. He was dirty from head to toe, and his shirt and pants were ill-fitting and torn. He pointed at my brown buckskins.

"Your shoes, seignor? Can I clean them for you? They look terrible Too much fun for carnaval, no?" the small fry said to me in Spanish.

"Yeah, go ahead," I smiled. *"Do your best."* The lad grinned from ear to ear and started to break down his shoe-shine kit and attack

my filthy, grimy shoes. God knows what was all over them. Beer. Dirt. Garbage from the streets. Pure crap.

"Isn't it sad," I said to Javier. "That a young boy has to work the bus station shining shoes? I mean, where are his parents? Why isn't he in school? This is no place for a small kid to be by himself. The gruff and violent men here could kill him. The poor kid looks like he lives in the streets."

"Probably does," said Javier. "If he didn't have your shoes to shine today, he probably wouldn't be able to eat. You're a *gringo*. An easy mark to get some good money for himself and possibly his family in need. The kid isn't stupid. He's sharper on the streets than you are."

"He can't be more than six. That breaks my heart," I responded sadly. "Look at him. Look at how sweetly he is smiling. He is so happy to have the fare. I mean, I just want to take him home with me back to America."

"Yeah, *cholo,* I wish we could help all these poor little ones here in the streets of my beloved country. But what can we do? You can't cover the sun with your finger, as my mother always told me and my brother," said Javier.

The boy worked diligently on each shoe. Washing, scrubbing, putting on some shinola and shining away diligently. He spent nearly seven minutes on each shoe, and though my brown bucks were now black (I guess the kid had no brown wax), they did look like new. A job well done by a poverty-stricken six-year-old. The boy tapped me on the knee to let me know he was finished.

"*How much do I owe you, son*?" I asked with elation. The boy looked at me with puppy-dog eyes and one finger raised.

"Un Boliviano, Maestro, por favor… por favorrr."

One lousy Boliviano. About sixteen cents in U.S. currency. That's all he's asking me for. Sixteen cents. That kid did the better work of a grown man, and all I owed him was sixteen cents? I pulled a ten Boliviano note from my pocket, scrunched it up in one hand, and put both hands behind my back. The boy tapped my left arm. I brought my empty hand forth. We both laughed.

He touched my right arm. I opened my right hand and gave the little guy the ten Bolivianos.

"Gracias, seignor! Muchissimas gracias," he cheered as he ran off while waving a hand. He obviously was in a hurry to get to someplace else. Tears ran down my face. I should have given him more than the ten Boliviano note. I could certainly afford to. I had spent many times that just on beer alone the past three days.

I fell back to my semi-consciousness, and drifted off in my mind to another place, another time where six-year-old boys can be out playing with a ball with their friends and don't have to work for their food. Several minutes passed. Javier nudged me, "Hey, *cholo,* the bus is here. Let's split. I've had enough of this joint."

I got up with my bag in hand, thanking God it was still there and not nicked by some thief. Javier grabbed my arm and led me to the right bus. As we got on, I caught a glimpse of the small boy who shined my shoes. There he sat at the corner of the station under the torn awning, sitting on his shoe-shine kit, eating a good-sized plate of platanos and beans. It seemed he hadn't eaten in days; he was gorging on the food so quickly. We waved to each other. He smiled happily with a mouthful of food. I got on the bus, crashed into a window seat, and the bus pulled away heading back to Cochabamba.

I will never forget the look on that little boy's face as we pulled away. It was like sunshine on a dreary day.

Hold on, small fry. Hold on. Jesus is coming for us.

~~~

"The letter continues. *Father, I know you are a good man of God, and you have always been good to my family, helping us deal with the pain and sadness when my mother died. I don't know why my mother had lymphoblast leukemia first and why, now for me, myself, why I have it. The doctors say it is not something contagious, but it could be hereditary. All I really want to know, father, is it true that Jesus really*
~~~

loves me unconditionally? Sitting in this hospital bed with nothing but my thoughts, I am not sure my body's strength will keep my soul on this planet much longer. Any commentary you can give me to help me know Jesus better would be greatly appreciated. Sincerely,"

The priest folder the worn paper and put it back in his desk. He had a slightly depressed look on his visage. Jude could tell that the story meant a lot to the old man.

"That story was written by a young man I had known since his birth here on Sanibel. I baptized him and confirmed him. I knew him his entire life."

"He was born on Sanibel? A true local?" Jude was inquisitive.

"Well, I wouldn't go that far. His father and mother were relocated to Florida from Vermont like me. As we said in Vermont, if kittens are born in an oven you don't call them muffins, do ya? My point is, I baptized him, I gave him his first Communion, and I even kept him with me in the church through Confirmation. He came to church every Sunday and Confession regularly with his father, who is a motorcycle police officer on the island—"

"And his younger brother in high school drives for Uber on the island, right?"

The priest grinned and nodded knowingly. "His mother predeceased him from leukemia six years earlier when he was a teenager. Then it was his turn. The young man was only twenty-two years old when he died of leukemia about seven or so months ago now. I performed the funeral and Last Rites. I tell you this letter and story he wrote for me shortly before he died because I want to show you that our time is short here on this planet, and we should not take each breath for granted. Life is a gift of Almighty God the Father. None of us knows when the Lord Jesus will call us home. God's Grace is a free gift for you if you choose to accept it, but it was costly to Him. It cost Jesus His short-lived earthly life with extreme suffering and a painful death. My suggestion to you, son, is that you rejoin the Catholic Church faithfully. Get right with Jesus and God the Father joyfully through the Power of the Holy Spirit, and get right with your wife and daughter honorably. Sanctify your marriage. Make it a Sacrament. Renew your vows again in front of a Catholic priest."

"How do I do that? After all that's happened?" Jude was a bit shaken.

The priest paused a long moment with his heavy-set eyes and put one hand to his chin and the other on Jude's knee before taking a deep breath. "If you do your part, son, God will do His. Together you and He can make it happen. With God nothing is impossible. That is His Unconditional Promise of Love to us. The Cross proves it. Let's pray. *Our Father, who art in Heaven, hallowed be Thy Name. Thy Kingdom Come. Thy Will be done, on earth as it is in Heaven. Give us this day our daily bread. And forgive us our trespasses, as we forgive those who trespass against us. And lead us not into temptation, but deliver us from evil. For Thine is the Kingdom, and the Power, and The Glory, forever and ever. Amen.*"

Jude looked at the ground. "Amen," fell from his lips lightly. The carpet was dirty and worn, like it hadn't been replaced in years, which he hadn't noticed earlier. There was a long silence and Jude didn't move; he was frozen in his seat.

"So?" the priest lightened up with a sigh. "How are you feeling now?"

"I started this day on a downer. Now this conversation and my confession with a prayer was an upper. So in truth I am feeling pretty sideways."

The old man curled the edges of his lips up. "Off-center. You need to get copacetic. Plans, plans, plans are what you need now. What are you going to do for the rest of today? Lunch somewhere to calm yourself down then call your wife?"

"I hate to say it, father, but I will probably eat a six-pack for lunch. My head is swimming right now. I have a long walk to go back to where I am staying on the island."

"You need a ride back into town. I can call the young man you know who drives for Uber. You can tell him you met his older brother vicariously through his writing."

"No, thanks," said Jude, still looking at the ground. "I need to walk. I need to think deeply about what I've done, where I have been, and what I am going to do about it. Time for a serious change. Time for contrition. A long walk in the Florida sun. Wouldn't you call that penance?"

"If that be so, then I think our Sacrament of Reconciliation time together is over for now," the holy man smiled clasping his hands on his lap before making the Sign of the Cross in front of Jude. "In the Name of the Father, the Son, and the Holy Spirit, by your own Confession and Contrition, I absolve you. Your sins are forgiven. Go in peace."

"Thank you, father," Jude said wiping his brow, with a hint of relief. "But you can see that my faith is not that strong."

"I understand. Let your soul be at ease. The remaining eleven of the disciples hadn't much faith until Jesus appeared to them in Person after the Resurrection. Remember Doubting Thomas? I say there were the eleven who didn't have faith because, again off the record, I believe the only disciple who believed before the Resurrection that Jesus was God's Only Son was Judas. Unfortunately by the time he came to that revelation, it was too late for him. He had already betrayed The Holy One, 'The Innocent Man' he called Him. In his guilt he ended his own life before contrition. Before Jesus rose again."

"Suicide. As I told you, I'm too familiar with that."

"Yes, and I am so sorry for that for you. Have you forgiven your father for taking his own life?"

"I don't think I have, now that you mention it," Jude said reflectively, his lips quivering.

"Forgiveness is a key issue in life. If you don't forgive people when they sin against you, Your Heavenly Father won't forgive you your sins. It's good to remember that always."

"Do people who commit suicide go to hell, father? That's what I've been told so many aching times."

"What would heaven be like if the people we loved on earth aren't there? That's not the kind of heaven I want to be in. Do you have a good relationship with your mother?"

"No. Not really. She's always angry for some reason. No matter what I do for her."

"So she vents on you," the priest alighted.

"Yes. Very much so."

"When you were younger, she called you her prince, right?"

"Actually, that is correct, father. How do you know that?"

"What greater position is there in this world than to be the mother of a king? Is there anything you would like for me to pray daily for you?"

"My marriage first. And then I have always wanted a son. My own son to love and cherish. Like I cherish my daughter, Chloe."

"Your marriage and a son of your own. Easy enough," the priest acknowledged. "Just remember everything what I've told you here today. This is true also: no one has even gotten through this life alone without Jesus. You're not going to be the first."

"Christ is with me."

"Yes. Walk with Him. Talk with Him like you talked with me today. He is going to be Your Best Friend from now on. There are Signs everywhere, but don't be a Sign-watcher."

Jesus. My Best Friend. Jude thought about Filiberto for a flash second.

The priest was suddenly stricken with a heavy coughing attack.

"That sounds serious, father. Have you seen a doctor?"

"Yes, I have. Quite often of recent. No one knows when it is our time to leave earth. I am old and I ready to go. But I'll tell you. I kind of like it here. I am not sure I want to sing for all eternity."

Jude laughed.

"Remember well that you will find Jesus when you seek Him with all of your heart. He promises you that. Just be careful. Putting on the uniform means you will be shot at by the Enemy. Now more than before."

"I understand, father."

"It's a hot one out there, little brother. You sure you don't want a ride with some cool air conditioning?" offered the good pastor. "You are already red from the walk here this morning. I'll have Cheryl write you up a church voucher for a taxi so it won't cost you anything."

"No, thank you, father. I appreciate it. I need to walk in the blistering hot sun. It's the pain of penance."

The priest nodded slowly. "Did you know that Saint Francis of Assisi put rocks in his shoes?"

Jude shook his head.

"Walking long and hard is good for the soul. I recommend it to everyone. To make it even better, put a small rock in each of your shoes under your feet. Like Saint Francis of Assisi did. Not a large rock. Choose one just big enough to cause discomfort as you walk. I do it all the time." The priest nodded knowingly. "Old age has seen me change. God doesn't. When I was younger, I ran. Then later I could only walk. Now I can only shuffle my feet forward."

"A small rock in each of my shoes. I can do that. I will walk step by step. Christ will be with me," Jude showed a hint of joy in his words. "Thank you for everything, father. I will take leave now. Thank you so very much. I will walk back to town in the Florida sun. Getting a good Florida sunburn."

12 When All Else Fails, Do Nothing

The classics car show was well under way in the early afternoon at the Fort Myers fairgrounds when Jude, after walking from the good priest back to the center of Sanibel in the hot sun, took an Uber to join Antoine, Vanité and Paco who had already arrived at the Bel Air's side. All Jude could think about at that moment was Hector, questioning Antoine about his ride to the bus station, and hoping Hector made it by bus okay to Miami and was able to hitch a boat ride off to Puerto Rico safely. He had given Hector two thousand five hundred dollars cash to help him. Yet he feared that may not have been enough for a sufficient bribe of a salty sea-captain. But too late now. Antoine confirmed he had taken Hector that morning early to the Fort Myers Greyhound bus station, and speculated that no word was sure to be heard from him until he was either in Puerto Rico. Or back in prison.

The Bel Air sat among the other older classic cars in its own staging area, gleaming in the sunshine. Jude could only remark at how beautiful that forged metal looked. His heart fell at the thought that he would soon part with this heirloom of his family's history, something that meant so much to his own father and grandfather both. But he knew that he and his family needed Paco's money desperately more than he needed the car. Still, he wasn't quite ready in his soul to give her up just yet.

"Let's walk around and look at the new hyper-cars," said Paco. "I'm feeling like I'm going to be buying something new, fast and exotic again in the near future in addition to the Bel Air. Hehehe!"

They came upon a show area where there was a low metal fencing around three models of McLaren machines. Jude walked over to the sales representative and inquired about the specs of each of the cars. Just to get his mind off the Bel Air, he asked if he could sit in one of the McLarens.

"Sure," said the rep, winking and opening the metal gate to let Jude in. "Anything for an ace mechanic. This one here will do zero to sixty in under three seconds. If you need it faster than that to get to the bank, get out of bed two seconds earlier."

"That's what I've often said about super-cars!" laughed Jude.

"For three hundred seventy-five thousand dollars plus tax, I'd need a little more information," Antoine gaped.

"Are you kidding me?" said Jude with disdain in his voice from the driver's seat leaving the scissor door open. "You think Paco here needs more info before buying one of these? Laugh my tail off, dude! You really think some rich millionaire or billionaire dropping close to half a million clams is telling this McLaren salesman, 'I need more information'? This car sold out the minute McLaren announced its production. There's no test drive, kicking the tires, asking for a fold-out brochure."

"For Paco, it's his money, and he can do what he wants with it. I don't begrudge him or any other wealthy man a bit. But to me it seems more like vanity of self and egomania to spend hundreds of thousands of dollars on a car because of the mere reason it is something few can own or even lay their eyes on. I personally think it's a waste. It's nothing more than a piece of metal with rubber getting me from point A to point B. Life's too short to waste on material possessions."

Jude looked over at the confused rep. "You'll have to excuse him. As your prototypical, garden variety, bed-wetting gay man, he is desperately trying to come off as condescendingly contemplative. Stick to breast feeding till your next diaper change, Anto. Perhaps you'd do better with a Ford – Fix Or Repair Daily… Or, backwards - Driver Returns On Foot."

Antoine sniffed, "I'm parched and going for some lemonade. Care to join me, Vanité?" He held out his arm to lock with hers as they walked off.

"I'm always looking for something new and exotic," Paco proudly stated. "Today is no different. Let me have your business card, and I will be in touch with you soon."

The sales rep smiled and gave Paco his business card, which showed that the McLaren dealership was in Ft. Lauderdale off Commercial Boulevard.

"I'm certain to be in touch to make an appointment," Paco continued. "I like what I see here."

The sales rep winked again at Jude as he and Paco walked away.

"You really gonna buy another exotic, Paco?" inquired Jude.

"Might. Maybe. I may be coming into some serious money soon. What good is serious money if you don't use it foolishly?"

"We still need to settle on the Bel Air. You have flip-flopped over it since I got to Florida. I need to know what the final answer is. I need to get back to Baltimore ASAP."

"Hmmm, I think I have an answer for you. But not one you're expecting. Here's an envelope with another twenty-thousand dollars in it. I want you to drive the Bel Air after the show up to my cousin in Brooklyn. His name is Carlito. He is interested in the car, too. If he likes it, I will pay the rest of the money by wire to your account. If he doesn't like it, you can keep the forty grand I have given to you already. Deal?"

"BROOKLYN? W.T.F, dude?!" Jude pushed Paco a few steps back off his stance. "That was never part of the deal! I need to get back to Baltimore, man, like, as soon as yesterday! I haven't got time for Brooklyn! What the heck's up with that?!"

"*Carajo.* Easy, lucky. Carlito has been asking me for a cool classic for some time now. I really owe him. I think he will like the Bel Air. It's his kind of car more than mine. What with his oily hair and silk suits and open-necked shirts over his hairy chest. If you take the car to him, I will add another ten grand to the price we agreed on in South Beach. Tell me, will you pass that up?"

Jude hopped, and it looked as if he had steam coming off the top of his head. "How soon can I leave? I will never come back to this horrid State of Florida. I may even sue you to get back the nine days I lost here."

"You can leave today if you want. But why don't you want to come back to Florida? I was kinda hopin' you would come back in February to join with me and some friends for the annual python hunt."

"What in blazes is a python hunt?"

"The Everglades are overrun with Burmese Pythons which are eating up the rest of the mammal population. Florida Game and Fishing organizes python hunts to cut down the number of the predators. They compensate men who find them and bring them back, dead or alive. It's great sport for real men."

"I have a simpler solution. Tell the Asian men that python meat is good to grow their wankers, and the pythons will disappear in a week. Problem solved. I'm outta here today and never coming back."

"So be it. Here are the keys."

"I left my bag at your house."

Paco reached into his seersucker jacket and flipped open his wallet. "Mmm. Here's three hundred more. Cash. Go buy yourself some new clothes whenever and fill up your stomach as needed on the way to Brooklyn. Here's Carlito's business card. Call him before you get to Brooklyn so he can arrange to meet you pronto. I'm sure he will love the Bel Air. The deal is almost done. Have some faith. Trust me."

"Trust me. Screw me. That's what you said before."

Jude grabbed the keys and the cash with force from Paco and walked away towards the Bel Air. When he got into the driver's seat, one of the car-show's officials came over and asked him what he was doing.

"I'm blowin' out of here. Now. Done had it with Florida".

"But the show isn't over, sir. Wouldn't you like to wait for the prize for best classic car?" asked the official.

"No, I wouldn't. Now stand out of my way so I can drive this beauty out of here. I don't care where I'm headed off this playground as long as it's North-bound."

Just as Jude fired the ignition, a sultry, tanned, red-haired woman with long black fingernails and a wide-brimmed white lady's hat came up to him next to the Bel Air. "I heard you are going to Brooklyn," she breathed in Jude's ear. "Can I go with you? I don't have any money, and I need to be in New York City tomorrow."

"Swell," said Jude with his eyes fixed straight ahead. "I'm outta here."

"But wait!" the vixen exclaimed. "I'm willing to give you all the pleasure you could ever want all the way there! We can be together, you and me. Don't you want to get lucky?"

"Get lucky? I'd rather BE lucky than smart most any day. But right now I gotta be smart."

The woman let out a low growl.

Jude didn't turn his face to look at the woman and instead let off the emergency brake and drove the car off the grassy area and onto a main road in the direction of I-75 North. He stopped off at a gas station to fill up the tank, check the oil, and get a Monster energy drink as he knew he would be driving a very long time until he reached Brooklyn. He debated whether he could even do it straight without sleep. He had just finished filling the Bel Air's tanks and paying with Berto's credit card when out of nowhere sirens blared. The Bel Air and Jude were surrounded by FBI and DEA marked and unmarked cars and SUV's with flashing red and blue lights.

"FREEZE!" shouted a muscular DEA agent as he jumped out of a black SUV. "Don't make a move! Put your hands on the hood of your car!"

"What the heck is going on?" asked Jude, scared that maybe he had hit someone with the Bel Air and that a hit-and-run accident report was called in.

"SHUT THE EFF UP!" The DEA agent went into the Bel Air's glove compartment and pulled out the car's registration. "Yep. Jude Layden. We've found it."

An FBI agent stepped out of another car and came and opened the doors and hood and trunk of the Bel Air. Jude stood back.

Other men in various uniforms appeared and surrounded the scene. The muscly agent gave a brief shout to another agent, who came with two angry canines and a heavy crowbar. The dogs sniffed around the car's doors and trunk and bayed loudly. The muscly agent began wildly to rip open the door panels with the crowbar, while the other agent with the canines pulled out the floorboards. Out fell hundreds, if not thousands, of small packets of white powder, which had been neatly stacked on tiny shelves welded into the car's frame.

"What the fu—?!" Jude cried out, not knowingly what the heck was going on. "Catty! Paco!"

"SHUT UP!... Well, well, well… What do we have here?" asked the lead DEA agent with a smirk while picking up a packet off the ground.

"Umm, powdered sugar?" commented Jude with a hint of fear in his voice. "I like pancakes in the morning."

"SHUT UP, I SAID! YOU WANT AN ANAL CAVITY SEARCH RIGHT HERE, RIGHT NOW!?" The DEA agent pulled a buck-knife from his belt and stabbed one of the powder packets. He touched the tip of the knife to his tongue. "Powdered sugar. Your powdered sugar tastes very much like cocaine, Mister Jude Layden. You're in a whole big heap of trouble, man."

"But I—"

"SHUT UP, I SAID! And don't move an inch. I'll tighten you up till your wrists bleed out!"

Other officers came out of the big cars wearing plastic gloves to collect the small packets just as more DEA and FBI cars pulled up to the gas station. The station manager came outside to see what all the noise and commotion was, but quickly ran back inside. The Bel Air – the car that belonged to Jude's father and grandfather before him - was systematically ripped apart to pieces right there at the station lot next to the gas pumps in front of Jude. Many, many more small packets of cocaine fell to the ground or were pulled from the car's skeleton. A Lee County police cruiser came into the station, and an officer hopped out to talk to the lead DEA agent.

In a few head-spinning minutes, Jude was tightened in handcuffs by the Lee County Officer as he watched his car still being shredded to metal scraps. Tears were streaming down his red face. *How the eff did THIS happen? This Florida nightmare is never-ending! I'm so screwed! W.T.F.?!*

Jude was placed in the backseat of the police cruiser and hauled off to the Lee County Jail. He was motionless and expressionless in the backseat, and could only think about his wife, Margarita and his daughter, Chloe. This didn't look good for him. He could be put away in prison for a long, long time. He understood that good and well. What would become of his wife and daughter? The garage, he no longer cared about it. It was long gone. But what about his wife and daughter? Who would be their provider, as the old priest had asked him just that morning?

Taken to the Lee County Jail, Jude was briefly interviewed in a room with a video-camera, alone and afraid, not having been advised that he could have asked for a lawyer to be present. He signed a few statements with a shaky hand, and then was led away to be placed in a holding cell with six other angry men. The only objects in the holding cell were a steel bench that could sit three men and a steel toilet in the corner with no toilet paper. Jude sat in the corner of the cell, holding his arm and pinching himself sharply to keep from weeping so as to not look weak in front of the other inmates. Still, he kept his head down as he sat cross-legged. Jude sat that way without moving for hours until one of the jail's officers came and called his name.

"You don't look good, Mister Layden."

Jude looked up slowly with a tear-stained face.

"With that distraught look on your face, the captain is worried yer a suicide risk."

Other inmates started to snicker. Jude hid his face again.

"Get up and come with me," the uniformed guard snapped his finger. He then led Jude to a new open-viewed cell across from the officers' station. At least there Jude would be alone and in privacy without any safety risk from other inmates, and with only his own desperate thoughts to keep him company.

Inside the solitary cell was a low cold-steel bed with no mattress or blanket that Jude curled up on. There were no outside windows letting in any light, but the place was noisy. Jude managed to fall asleep on the steel bed from his emotional tiredness of the bad events of the day. Before he fell asleep, he last looked out of the cell and into the eyes of a correctional guard who was focused on him. Jude thought nothing of it, and quickly passed out from mental exhaustion.

Night arrived heavily, and a female jail officer came by with a tray of food. Jude opened his eyes briefly at her yelling his name above the din. With little effort, he waved her away without saying a word. She left the tray outside on a cart, telling Jude that she would bring it in if he called out to her and asked for it. Jude turned his back.

Though he had to lay on a cold steel bed with no sheets or pillow, Jude slept deeply. He was solidly into REM sleep and had no dreams. The sounds of the jail cells clanking shut all night and the loud inmates nearby did nothing to wake Jude from his much-needed sleep.

Very early the next morning, Jude was awakened by a tall, thin Lee County Detective with bespoke spectacles. The detective was wearing a navy-blue suit, red-striped tie, and shiny wingtips, and came into the prison cell holding a metal stool in one hand and a brown calfskin briefcase in the other. A uniformed female Lee County officer stood behind the detective with her arms folded showing a foul face.

"Mister Layden?" said the detective sitting himself down on the stool. "I am Detective Sullivan, and I am handling this investigation. I am going to ask you a few questions. Is that okay with you?"

Jude forced himself to sit up on the steel bed and looked at the detective silently. He rocked himself back and forth slowly on the bed to keep his fear from showing.

"By your sworn statement yesterday, you say you had no idea there was the cocaine in the car, that you were completely unaware. Is that correct?"

Jude nodded slowly with bloodshot eyes.

"I need a verbal answer, Mister Layden."

"Yes."

"Noted." The detective wrote lengthy notes on a yellow pad. "The estimate is that there was over fourteen million dollars in street-level cocaine stuffed in the car. You say you had no idea about it. Recorded, then. Even though this may eventually turn into a Federal Case for crossing state lines, the Florida State's District Attorney has decided not to press charges against you at this time and will grant you full immunity if you will agree to testify in court against Paco Roman and his accomplices. All of whom have yet to be fully identified. The investigation is still ongoing and will take a long while to be completed. We will expect your full cooperation. If you work with us," said the detective as he looked over his spectacles. "We will work with you. Do you agree to do this, Mister Layden? Your decision to do so is not compulsory, I might add, but I highly advise you to take this option, per the D.A.'s pending inquiries of you."

Jude nodded slowly, his head swimming.

"I need a verbal answer, Mister Layden."

Jude looked down at the hard floor. "Yes."

"Just a few more quick questions, and we will be finished. One suspected accomplice is Peter Collins. Have you ever met him, Mister Layden? Do you know anything about him?"

Jude shook his head side to side slowly, looking at his feet slumped on the pale floor. "No."

"Noted. Another is Victor Grimm. Any knowledge of him?"

Jude shook his head again but wouldn't look up, "No, sir, I'm sorry, I don't. I don't know these people. I promise you."

"No need to be sorry, Mister Layden."

Jude choked, "You might want to check into a Catty O'Haro who owns a high-end mechanic's garage in Miami near *Calle Ocho*. He may be involved. I don't really know."

"Heard and very well noted," the detective wrote more on his yellow pad. "Anyone else?"

"Filiberto Bobadilla. He is - or was - my partner at the garage back in Baltimore. He may be involved."

The detective looked over his glasses at Jude, then looked down to shuffle some papers and pour over some notes. "Hmmm… Do you know any-thing more about him?'

"A very dull edge in a drawer full of steak knives."

The detective chuckled. "Thank you for that. That confirms what our inside-man, Antoine Ferri, found for us as well."

Jude looked up quickly, astonished at what he had just heard. "Antoine Fairy? As in Tinkerbell? He's the inside-man?"

"No, Mister Layden. Fairy as in F-A-I-R-Y Tinkerbell is Antoine's street name. His real name is Ferri, as in Ferri, F-E-R-R-I. He has been with us for months on this investigation. He is the one who told us you are completely innocent in this affair. He also mentioned another man with you in Florida. A Mister Hector Genovieva? Do you know where he is so we may speak with him as well?"

"No, sir. I have no idea where he is. He took a bus somewhere. That's the last I saw of him." Jude smiled in his mind but didn't show it on his face. *At least Hector got away. Hopefully he is on his way to Puerto Rico right now. I should have given him some more money before he left. Oh, Lord, please let Hector make it to Puerto Rico safe. It's all I ask of You.*

"Mr. Genovieva is wanted by the police in Maryland, we discovered."

Jude sat silently. He thought it best now to say as little as possible.

The detective handed Jude some white papers on a wooden clipboard and a ballpoint pen. "Sign and date this sworn statement here at the bottom for the D.A., Mister Layden, and you will be released. Officer Mahoney here will sign as your witness. I will make sure you get a copy before you leave. It explains all the details of your arrest and release. By your signature you show your agreement to the full and complete responsibilities you will perform for us in the upcoming investigation of this case and subsequent trials. The D.A., however, demands that you leave the

State of Florida immediately until the first court date we call you down for. You are not to return to the State of Florida under any circumstances. Not even for a vacation. Until we do call you forth. If we need any more information, we will contact you in Maryland. Is that perfectly clear?"

Jude nodded slowly, rubbing his red eyes. *Maryland. It's a million miles away right now. And what do I have there anyway? Most likely nothing.*

"A Lee County officer will be taking you to the bus station later this morning to send you back to Baltimore. Your wallet and its contents will be returned to you before you leave the station. We are keeping the two envelopes full of cash as evidence. Also your car will be kept as evidence. The cash and the car will not be returned to you; they belong—" the detective looked quickly back to the female officer standing behind him, "-to the State of Florida. I'm not sure you would want the car anyway as it is in many pieces now," the detective glanced back again at the woman officer who was smiling. "This you have no choice herein in this matter. The forfeiture of the cash and car is compulsory on your part as you will now sign. You will not be reimbursed, nor will you be allowed to sue for reimbursement, for the car or the cash."

Jude's face fell. *My grandfather's Bel Air. My father's Bel Air. Ruined and seized.*

"Do you understand everything I have explained to you, Mister Layden?"

Jude nodded slowly in agreement, eyeing the officer standing in the door and the gun at her waist.

"I need a verbal acknowledgement, Mister Layden."

"Yes," Jude forced out.

"Then sign and date here for the D.A. We will have you discharged within the hour and then taken in an officer's car directly to the bus station. A bus ticket will be provided for you. You are to go straight back to Baltimore and stay there until you hear from us again, or you will be cited for contempt of court and be jailed again indefinitely. We will pay for all your expenses and incidentals to come back to the State of Florida for the trials. Did you understand everything I have explained to you, Mister Layden?"

Jude sat motionless. *Maryland. Margarita. Chloe.* His heart was beating fast.

"Do you understand, Mister Layden, or am I speaking too fast and confusing you with my questions, sir? Do you find this all mentally challenging? Or do you think that I am being unreasonable with you in any manner?"

"No, no," Jude mumbled. "A matter of consequence, only. I understand everything fine, sir. Everything." Jude crossed his arms and his legs.

"You look pale and faint. The night officers said you haven't eaten anything in the past day. Can I get you something to eat, Mister Layden?"

"Some water, please, sir," Jude replied weakly.

The detective took off his glasses and turned around in his stool for a moment. "Get him some water, please."

The female officer left quickly and came back immediately with two half-liter bottles of cold Polar Springs water. Jude downed them both as if he were in a hot desert and this was the last water on earth. He signed and dated the papers on the clipboard where the detective pointed out the signature lines without taking the time to read what was written. He thought it better to just move the situation along since he was promised by the detective to be released upon signing.

"Very well. I think our time here together is finished until further notice. We will have you out of here within the hour with your wallet and its contents, Mister Layden. We have also called your wife for you to explain to her the full situation and your release, and that you will be back in Baltimore soon."

Jude groaned and put his head in his arms. *Oooh, Margarita!*

"You don't look so well, Mister Layden." The detective looked back at the officer leaning in the doorway. "Can we get him a shower and some toiletries before discharge? Maybe some clean clothes?"

The officer said yes, that she would have one of the male guards take Jude to an empty shower stall where he could clean himself up with some soap and shampoo and a toothbrush, but the jail had no other clothes for Jude.

"Thank you," Jude mustered up, hanging his head low.

"So, in the end, have you learned anything from this matter, Mister Layden?" asked the detective as he put the clipboard with signed papers into his briefcase and snapped it closed.

"Yes, sir. Never trust anyone ever again. Never, ever."

"No. That's not what I meant," he said as he stood up and brushed his sleeve with his hand. "Go with your gut. It's the better way."

"Mmm," Jude demurred, with his head still hung low.

The detective halted himself a moment. "Do you know the type of men Jesus used to start His Spiritual Revolution?"

"No, sir, I don't."

"Fishermen. The toughest men of that time. Jesus was a meek and gentle Man. Yet, the tough fishermen followed Him. Rough and hard men, they were. Kind of like the car mechanics of our time with grease under their nails."

Jude perked and looked up incredulously.

The detective smiled. There was a glare off his spectacles. "Do you known what Peter did after Jesus was crucified? He sulked and went back to being a fisherman. His Lord was dead, and he knew he had failed His Lord. But Jesus soon showed up again on the beach and served the fishermen a cooked meal. 'Come back to Me' Jesus said to Peter. 'I forgive you. I will make you a fisher of men.' Peter willingly obeyed until he suffered his own crucifixion."

Jude was as alert as a judge now.

"Thank you for your voluntary agreement to the D.A.'s terms. You are not in any trouble anymore, Mister Layden, for you are doing the right thing. You can thank the D.A. for that offer. I'm not so sure I would have been as lenient with you, but the D.A. is a good man. Do what he tells you to do, and you will be able to walk away from all this. Good luck to you and your family in the future." The detective held out his hand with a straight smile on his face. Jude briefly looked into the detective's bright golden eyes and shook his hand calmly. "You are smiling, Mr. Layden, whether you know it or not. Behind every smile there is a story. Go and tell yours."

"Yessir."

Jude didn't move again on the steel bed until everyone had left the cell and the lock was set with a loud metal clack. He looked around the room to take in everything that just happened, breathed a sigh of relief at the thought of his release, and even let a simple chuckle come forth. Things were bad, really bad. However, as it now appeared, things had just gotten slightly better.

Jude thought about the Catholic priest. What would he tell Jude if he were next to him here? *He would tell me to thank Jesus with all my heart.* Jude pondered a moment, took a deep breath, then with his eyes closed, head bowed, and hands gently folded, spoke aloud, "Thank you, my Lord and my God. For once again You have provided a way out for me."

~~~

>BAM BAM BAM!<

No response.

>BAM BAM BAM!<

A loud shout, "Mister Bobadilla?!"

No response.

"Screw this. Do you want to bash it in?" said a voice.

"Hold for Kelly and Dugan," there was a second voice.

>BAM BAM BAM!<

"Mister Bobadilla?!"

(From the other side of the door) "For eff's sake! It's effing six a.m.! Crissakes, people! Can you come back at a reasonable hour?"

>BAM!< "Mister Bobadilla!"
~~~

"Ye-e-s! Who is this? It's too damn early to be selling Girl Scout cookies, lady!"
"FBI!" shouted one voice.
"DEA!" followed another.
"… Um, is this a spelling bee?"
"Screw you! Okay, Kelly, Dugan. Bash it in—"
>BAM!< >CRASH!<
"Yow, people! You broke my damn toes! What the hell?!"
"Mister Bobadilla. We have a warrant for your arrest."
Filiberto put a hand to his chin, "… What took you so long?"

13 Can a Man Go Home Again?

A Lee County police officer came and got Jude from his cell after Jude had showered and cleaned up, and brought him outside into the glaring sun to lead him towards the patrol car. The officer could see that Jude was not prepared for the harsh sunlight after being in the dimly lit jail for so long and gave him a pair of cheap sunglasses. Jude looked confused. "Complements of the department's lost and found," said the officer.

Jude was placed unrestrained in the back of the police vehicle and driven to the Fort Myers Greyhound bus station. He looked out the window the whole way, not saying a word to the officer driving him. All Jude had on him was his wallet, which he hadn't looked in yet. He recalled that the detective had said his bus ticket would be taken care of. He wasn't sure he had any money for food for the long bus ride back to Baltimore, however.

Standing in line to buy a ticket at the Fort Myers Greyhound bus depot, Jude fingered in his wallet. There was no cash. Not a single dollar bill. *Damnit… Oh! Forgive me my words, Lord.*

The officer was standing off to the side, leaning against a post. Jude glanced at him, then looked at the ticket clerks behind the counter. It was now obvious to Jude that he was the one who was to be responsible for paying for the bus ticket. He saw that he still had Paco's business card, which he promptly ripped up angrily and threw away. But, in addition to his driver's license, he still had Filiberto's credit card. Since he had no way to pay, he prayed a quick Hail Mary the priest had taught him that the *G. Alber* credit card would work for the one hundred thirty-nine-dollar bus ticket.

The prayer went unanswered, as the credit card was rejected, and Jude stood there stunned at the counter with a dead blank stare. The police officer, who was still there to make sure Jude got on the bus to get out of Florida and head back to Baltimore, walked up and exchanged a few words with the ticket clerk. The officer winced and said to Jude that he hadn't been told to do so by his superiors, but he would now see to it that the Lee County Police Department would pay for the bus ticket as well as give Jude a few extra dollars to get some food on the twenty-six hour ride back to Baltimore, not including the time waiting for the change in buses in Atlanta, Richmond, and Washington, D.C. Jude thanked him with a pained expression, looking at the cement floor. The officer took the bus ticket receipt from the clerk and sighed, thinking to himself that he hoped the sergeant would understand and the department would reimburse him thus. He foisted a twenty-dollar bill into Jude's sweaty hands. "Food on your trip."

Both Jude and the officer milled around the station silently, not saying a word to each other for the next hour and a half until Jude's bus came into the depot. When Jude went to the restroom, the officer followed him in. The air conditioning in the bus station was blaring artic cold. When Jude walked outside into the sun for a moment to warm up, the officer was only a step behind him.

Walking around the bus station pushing a stroller was a young mother with a curious tattoo on her right arm. From one angle, the tattoo looked like the head of a lion. From another angle, the tattoo looked like the face of Jesus. Jude couldn't help but stare at this tattoo as the woman pushed the stroller around the station humming songs to keep her little boy child calm. At one point, the mother turned to Jude and smiled with a courteous wave. The boy in the stroller cooed and gurgled. *Such a delightful little boy*, thought Jude. *I would love so much to have a son like him. If it be the Lord wills.*

The bus finally came to the depot, and Jude was last in line to get on the bus. Waiting in the line to board, he finally summoned the courage to speak to the officer, "I don't know you, sir, but if you are a praying man, please pray for my marriage."

The officer, walking along next to Jude in the line, promised solemnly to do so, saying he was a devout Christian who went to church every Sunday morning, prayed every morning and every evening, and that is why he became a cop, to help people in need such as Jude. "Prayer can do amazing things, Mister Layden, if we will let God handle the details. No man knows the time or day when Jesus will return, but until then we will have our trials and tribulations and temptations. That much is guaranteed in life. Leave your marriage completely and fully in God's Hands. God can mend a shattered heart, if we give Him all the pieces."

It was at that moment that Jude realized the officer was a much older man than he had earlier recognized, and that the officer had a slight limp in his left leg.

"I read your file before they brought you out for me to drive you here," said the officer. "You have had quite the rough time these past few weeks in Florida. I certainly hope things look brighter for you in the future in Baltimore."

Jude smiled weakly and his face fell, "Please pray for my marriage. It's all I'll ask of anyone ever again."

"You need to read the bible and get into God's Holy Word. Do it daily in addition to prayer. It will help you and your marriage. Pray with your wife. It sounds cliché, but a family that prays together, stays together."

"I get confused by the bible, sir. I would guess you don't?"

"Actually, there is a short piece of Scripture that confounds me. The night of His Betrayal, the disciples said to Jesus, 'Look, Lord, here are two swords'. To which Jesus replied, 'That is enough'. I can in no way fathom what the significance of those verses is to anything else that is said in the Gospels. Two swords. For what purpose? I don't know the answer to that. I also have another question. Again on the night of His Betrayal, Jesus did not stop Peter until after he drew his sword and cut off Malchus' ear. I wonder: would Jesus have defended Peter if Malchus had struck first? Or would Jesus have let Peter be injured or possibly killed? I think our whole Second Amendment in America rides on that issue. Here, take this." The officer pulled a small, worn card from his shirt pocket. "I carry it with me wherever I go. It helps me when I am down on myself. Take it. I can get another one at my church."

On the card, it said in large blue letters, *"For all have sinned and fallen short of the Glory of God – Romans 3:23. Remember: You are no better or worse than any other person who has ever lived. The exception being Christ Himself, who gave His Life up for you because He loves you!"*

Jude read it, paused a moment to marvel at the wonder and simplicity of the verse and its meaning. With relish, he thanked the officer profusely. The officer shook Jude's hand firmly. And then Jude boarded the big bus. He took an empty seat next to a window near the back of the bus, where fortunately no one else took the seat next to him. As the bus pulled away from the depot, he waved a warm goodbye to the officer who had helped him. The officer only nodded curtly and turned on his heel to head back to his patrol car.

The bus ride to Atlanta would be long and drawn out, then a change to another long bus ride to Richmond, then to Washington D.C. Union Station, where he would catch the final bus to Baltimore. Through this twenty-six-hour trip, Jude had all the time he needed to plan out what he would say to Margarita. He also wondered if Filiberto was in on Paco's cocaine deal gone bad. Should he have mentioned Berto to the detective? Berto might only be the patsy. Jude decided to put that idea to rest. Filiberto was in God's Hands. There was nothing he could do about his guilt if Berto was involved. Jude knew he needed to focus on his marriage. The garage was now in foreclosure and probably lost, and there was nothing he could do about that, either. *How can I provide for my family now*? He pondered it over until his mind ached. Perhaps he could get a job at another custom garage, or a gig working at some store like Advanced Auto Parts or Pep Boys as a salesclerk. Perhaps drive a gig for Uber. Or maybe he could just change flat tires on the sides of highways. Jude had so much to think about and figure out, and as the miles passed by, his mind worked on.

A thought popped clearly into Jude's head. *Don't worry about a job, Jude. Follow Me. (But what about Chloe and Margarita?* Jude argued back. *Who will provide for them?) I will. Come and follow Me. I will bring you home. I am yours and you are Mine.*

Jude leaned against the bus window and wept bitterly.

The miles did pass by quickly through Florida and on into Georgia. At the Atlanta bus station there was a forty-five-minute wait. Jude bought himself a turkey and cheese sandwich, some stale potato chips that had expired, and a small carton of orange drink with the money the kind officer gave him. *God bless that good man,* Jude said to himself as he ate, thankful to God as well for the little food and drink he had in his hands. He did wish he had had more money to buy some gift for Chloe on his way back. *Imagine if I had those thousands from Paco. I could buy Chloe an iPod.*

"Do you trust in theee Lo-o-ord Your Go-o-od?"

Jude heard this but did not look up from the torn newspaper he was reading. It didn't matter that the newspaper was weeks old and merely screed from the local Jehovah's Witnesses.

"Excu-u-use me. Do you trust in theee Lo-o-ord Your Go-o-od?" Jude felt a warm hand on his shoulder.

Jude looked up from his seat and uncrossed his ankles. Standing in front of him was a thin African man of uncertain age. The poor chap had deep wrinkles on his hands and face that belied a hard suffering in life. He reached a hand out to Jude.

"I noticed you ah reading my newspaper." The man tilted his head and smiled.

"Oh! I am so sorry, my friend. I didn't know it was yours. It was on the chair here and—"

"It's okay, bruddah. I am ha-a-appy to see you enjoying it. God bless you."

"God bless you, too," Jude shook his new friend's hand firmly.

"Can I ax you yor name?"

"Jude. But some people call me The Space Cowboy."

"Okayyy. Nice to me-e-et you Mr. Space Couwboyyy," he held his other wrinkled palm out to Jude who withdrew the handshake. "Would you like to go to church with me this evening?"

"Thanks. I appreciate the offer highly. But I am about to get on a bus to head home."

"Ah! Home! Where is home?"

"Um. Baltimore."

"Sometimes it seems like the world is a mighty fine pla-a-ace, don't it? If just to meet a long-lost friend. Did you know Go-o-od has a name for each stah in the sky?"

Jude paused a second and crossed his ankles again. "I actually did not know that. But thanks for telling me. I will have to pass that info onto my daughter when I see her. If I see her. Where are you from?"

"Ghana. Accra. 'Ave you heard of it," the man asked.

"Yes," Jude rubbed his eyes. "How did you get here? To Atlanta, Georgia?"

"Ohhh! That is a very lo-o-ong sto-o-ory. I have had my share of struggles. But like we say in Africa. Go-o-od is good all da time. And all da time Go-o-od is good. Nietsche said Go-o-od is dead. Not that Go-o-od died. He said Go-o-od is dead because He is no longer necessary in our lives. Do you believe that?"

Jude shook his head slowly. He was entranced by this man's deep dark eyes softly acknowledging Jude's presence. He wanted to look away, to see if his bus was in the port yet, but the man's being transcended any understanding Jude had at that moment.

A rather large African American woman in her late twenties with tight cornrows and bright white Adidas high-tops stepped between the two men and looked the African man square in the eye. "Why do you people always gotta talk about God? God this. And God that." She flung her hands and hips around. "You are always bringing Him into the equation! Leave God alone!" she showed her teeth.

"I am sooo so-o-orry, Miss. I was just inviting mah friend here to church. You—"

"I quit church! People are angry with guys like you coming 'round and spoutin' off about your God. Like your religion is better than any other. You're the ones creating division, choosing one religion over another!" She pinched the thin man on his shoulder.

The African man held his tongue and smiled nervously while taking a short step back.

Jude hesitated a moment but then intervened to help his new friend, "That doesn't sound very tolerant and inclusive. You've heard it before. Without love we are nothing."

"So what! Who axed you?!"

"So are you a strong and proud empowered African-American woman? Or are you a victim? Obviously it's not possible to be both," Jude folded his arms.

"Racist! I came over here to tell you that all your prophets were Muslims! Including Jesus!"

"Racist? My wife is Latina. Please seek professional help before your ill feelings turn into a disorder of dangerous extremism. God forbid your feelings now follow your behavior."

"I said, who axed you?!"

"You did. By jumping all over my friend here. This isn't a counter-protest to a Black Lives Matter event. He was only asking me to church. Which I can't do, because I have to get on a bus soon. Can you just try and see that we mean you no harm? Yes, Western Civilization is in decline. And, no, Obama is no longer on his world apology tour. But that isn't our fault. Or yours."

The young woman mumbled a few curse words with her upper lip raised exposing bright white teeth. She turned her heavy waist around and walked away knock-kneed while cocking her head repeatedly.

Jude turned unconsciously to watch her waddle away. The African man standing behind Jude's back put his hands lightly on his shoulder blades and whispered. "Goood man you are. When Jesus spo-o-oke to the ignorant, He spo-o-oke with love. Jesus did not respond to hate with hate. Don't worry. The answers you are looking for are: your lady will take you back and God is immutable. Look in your wallet for $20."

Jude heard the whisper, and absentmindedly spoke, "Yeah. I folded like a cheap lawn chair."

Then Jude realized someone was touching his back, only to have the touching feeling stop when he became conscious of it. He turned around quickly. The nice African man was gone. *Who was that man?* Jude thought to himself. A soft voice spoke to him in his heart *just a friend, just a good friend*. He continued his interior conversation. *You lady will take you back? Wow. Such emotional thoughts. Should I cry? No. Of course not. My mascara would run.* He chuckled.

A few moments later and Jude was removed from his trance. He opened up his wallet as instructed. In the corner behind a leather flap was a crisp folded twenty-dollar bill. Jude perked up.

Some random passerby stepped on Jude's foot. When he turned aside, a mangy old man with a salt and pepper scruffy beard asked him for some spare change.

Jude held out the newfound twenty-spot. "I can change the channel. If my wife lets me. I can't change the world. Maybe soon I can change my Brita filter."

"Change the world!" the old man heaved a laugh as Jude dropped the twenty-spot in his hands. "I can't even change political parties! Blame the government! It needs to help me!"

"The world is full of morons, nuts, and liberals. My apologies if that is redundant. I don't want to fail this test."

A scratchy man's voice blasted over the bus terminal loudspeaker, "Last call! Bus to Richmond, Virginia, Washington, D.C. leaving in five! Bus to Richmond and D.C. leaving in five!"

No one sat next to Jude on the bus again. He wondered if he smelled as bad as Hector. *What I would do to have my pal here with me now. Lord, please keep him safe. Amen.*

A dark blue minivan passed the bus on Jude's side. On it was a *Hillary 2016* bumper sticker. *Hillary Clinton,* Jude posed to himself. *Who will run against her in the election? Not anyone that can win. That's for dang sure. She has it locked. It's not going to be an election. It's going to be a coronation. I can think of a thousand things to be outraged about in America. President Hillary Clinton is not one. I once heard Bill say he was gonna make America great again. Can Hillary do that? It's her turn now.*

The buses droned on and on. The miles passed by. Jude could not sleep a wink all through the dark night. He racked his mind as to what his future with Margarita would portend, coming up with no solid conclusions. There was nothing else to distract him from these thoughts.

Jude sang quietly to himself a song he had learned at summer camp many years before when he was a young boy. *Day by day, oh Dear Lord, these things I pray, day by day. To see Thee more clearly, day by day. To love Thee more dearly, day by day. To have Thee more nearly, day by day. Day by day by day by dayyyy.*

Jude closed his eyes and whispered, "Oh, dear Lord, I am so sorry for the way I have been living my life. Forgive me my many sins. Right now I make the change to honor You and what You have done for me all my life. Even when I was not with You, You were there for me. From now on I trust in You alone, and no longer in myself. I choose to follow You. In Your Son Jesus' Holy Name I pray. Amen." He said nothing more to himself on this leg of his long ride.

The stop in Richmond wasn't long enough to let Jude step off and stretch. The bus headed north to Washington, D.C. Union Station. The miles had passed quickly through Florida and Georgia, then South Carolina, then North Carolina. The heaviest traffic was on I-95 between Richmond and Washington, D.C. Jude laughed to himself as this was the same kind of heavy traffic he had had to deal with in the Bel Air with Hector and him going the other direction.

Finally the bus came to Washington, D.C.'s Union Station in the cool and crisp early morning air. The soonest bus for Baltimore left in two minutes, not giving Jude enough time to get anything to munch on or drink. No matter. He would get to Baltimore soon enough, and then he could take care of his thirst and hunger.

The bus to Baltimore was not air conditioned and had Jude in a full, heavy perspiration. Soon he would be meeting up with his lovely Margarita, and he was still unsure what exactly it was he would or should say to her. His mind raced from bad thought to bad thought. What if Margarita had moved to her mother's house to get away from him? Or worse, taken the money he sent to her and moved out to somewhere else unknown with Chloe and he wouldn't be able to find them? What then could he do? What if he had lost his family forever? Could he live with himself if that was the situation? Jude sank into a light depression, leaning his tired head against the bus window.

Seated across from Jude was a young, single Latina mother with her toddler daughter, who, while playing with her rag doll, was singing a children's Christian rhyme, "Jesus loves me, this I know, because the Bible tells me so. Little ones to Him belong. They are weak but He is strong." A few tears fell down Jude's face as he thought of his own little Chloe. The little girl repeated this rhyme the whole hour and a half ride to Baltimore, making Jude smile inside.

The arrival in Baltimore's Greyhound station mid-morning was un-ceremonial. Jude got off the bus, knowing he didn't have enough money for cab fare, and knowing for certain he didn't want to call Margarita to come pick him up. He wasn't ready to see her. No, he would have to walk home, all alone in his thoughts, just as he had walked back to Paco's house on Sanibel from meeting with the good priest. Those two walks were much the same: filled with prayer and much second-guessing himself. Jude felt unsure whether he should go home at all. He recalled the old priest telling him about Saint Francis of Assisi walking with rocks in his shoes. Jude found two small pebbles and put one in each shoe.

And walk home he did. He walked the three miles home with his face always looking down at the sidewalk. Step by painful step from the pebbles in his shoes, he occasionally stopped himself to think a moment. Each time he made the decision to trudge on some more.

His MMA studio was closed to the general public, but as he walked by, Jude looked in the large bay window. There was Hector's mentor Nakarmi, training a young boy on the mat. Near to the two was Master Sugi with another young boy. This pint-sized boy had a t-shirt on that read "It's not the size of the dog in the fight. It's the size of the fight in the dog! I'M A FIGHTER!"

I'm a fighter… Antifragile… I'm a goddamn fighter. Jude stopped tight and smacked his head. Lord, forgive me my foul words! I'll get myself right soon!"

A few steps later, he passed by an elderly homeless man, all tattered and torn, sitting on a blue milk crate on a street corner in front of the convenience store where Jude would always buy his lite beer and cheap wine. Jude reached into his pocket, then knelt down and passed all his left over change into the old man's hands. The old man smiled a toothless grin and tipped his worn-out Raven's hat to Jude, who lowered his head and smiled in a small way in return.

"Good to see you again, Jude," said the old man boldly as he reached out a wrinkled hand and grasped Jude's forearm. "It's been a while."

"I'm sorry. Do I know you?" Jude asked.

"Now you do!" said the old man laughing from his belly. "God bless you, Jude!"

Jude stepped away, a bit befuddled. The old man laughed again and smacked his hole-ridden knees. Jude, scared in his soul, ran away not looking back. He halted himself short a moment later and remembered what the good priest had told him: *Jesus! You will find Him when you seek Him with all of your heart!* Jude's heart skipped a beat. He turned around in an instant and saw the empty blue milk crate. The elderly man was gone.

And when Jude finally got to the front door of his row house, breathless, tired and almost delirious from the mental turmoil, he found it was unlocked. *Lord, I need You now more than ever. Be with me, I beg of You.* He slowly opened the creaky door.

"DADDY!" squealed a happy Chloe as she ran towards Jude.

"Hi, sugar. Did you miss daddy?"

"THIS MUCH!" she held her hands out as wide as she could.

"I love you so much, sweetie," he picked her up and gave her a tight hug. "I'm gonna fix your bicycle tomorrow. Okay? I promise." *Unless it was taken with everything else from the garage. Forget you, Mister Wright. I cannot murmur against you, though I wish to.*

"YAY! Thank you, daddy! But what about my iPod?"

Jude sighed. "That will unfortunately have to wait. I'm sorry."

"It's okay, daddy," she hugged Jude again.

"Where's mommy, sugar?" Jude kissed Chloe on the top of her head.

Chloe frowned. "Upstairs in bed. She told me to play down here because she's feeling nawshhh—"

"Nauseous?"

"Yes. That's it. Is that bad, daddy?"

"No. I don't think so." *At least I hope not. Lord, be with me now. I need You, please.*

"Two police officers came by this morning looking for Mister Hector. Mommy told them she didn't know where he is."

"Oh? Really?" Jude began to tremble.

"Yes. But mommy told me when they left that Hector called here last night to find you. She said he told mommy he is with his three brothers in some place called Rincon in porto…porto….

"Puerto Rico? Is that where he is?"

"Yes! He said it is very beautiful there and we should go see him. That's what he told mommy. Did you ever go there, daddy? Can we go there someday? Huh, can we, daddy?"

"Yes, we can," Jude closed his eyes and smiled with relief while hugging and kissing Chloe again. *Thank you, Jesus. Hector made it home. Thank you, Lord. What a blessing.*

Chloe lowered her voice. "Some weird man with brown spots on his face and an ugly beard came by asking mommy for three hundred dollars. He was angry and said you owed it to him. Mommy gave it to him and told him it was the only money she had in the house. He was really scary, daddy. He left on a bicycle and he rode it kind of weird, too. He wobbled around on it. He won't come back, will he, daddy? I don't want him to. He made me scared."

That Mr. Tumnus looking guy from the garage! "No, he won't be coming back. If he does, I will take care of him. Don't be worried, honey."

"Mommy said it was all the money she had. We don't have any more money, daddy?" Chloe sounded fearful.

"You don't need to concern yourself at all with that, baby. You are too young. Be a little girl and let daddy take care of that, okay? Daddy is home now and he isn't leaving. Is mommy sleeping?" he asked Chloe.

"I don't think so. She was just on the phone talking to a doctor."

A doctor? Nauseous? Oh, please, Lord, tell me she is not ill.

"Earlier she said she was talking to some Maryland government man. She said it was important. It will change our lives. What happened, daddy?"

"I… I don't know, sugar," he said with a tremor in his voice. "Let's hope it is not something bad for daddy." *Oh, my dear Lord, I pray. I need you now more than I have ever needed anyone*. Jude kissed Chloe on the cheek and gently put her down. He sighed, took a deep breath, and slowly gathered the courage to step up the stairs. Each deliberate step he could feel his heart pounding harder and harder in his chest and the hard pebbles in his shoes. *At least she is in the house,* he thought. *She hasn't left me. Yet.*

Jude walked carefully into the bedroom. Margarita was lying in bed and sat herself up. They both looked at each other silently. Moments passed that seemed like minutes. Margarita was glowing, but Jude was blinded to it. Jude took a chance and spoke first.

"Margarita, my love and my life, I—"

"Jude, I won the lottery. I have to go to the lottery office downtown tomorrow afternoon to collect the check. It's over fourteen million dollars."

Jude stood there, staring at the wall, completely stiff as a board, scared, and silent.

"Jude. I'm pregnant."

Sometimes you just cannot hold back a flood. Jude collapsed in frailty at Margarita's feet with his head and hands on her knees. He wailed, and he wailed, and he wailed some more, loudly and out of control of himself, which brought Chloe up quickly from downstairs.

"Oh, Jude, my love," said Margarita stroking his hair with her soft hands. "It's okay. It's all okay. All is forgiven. Stop crying. Please. Stop crying, baby. All is forgiven. We are a family again. We always will be."

Chloe climbed onto the bed confused. Jude slowly picked himself up off the floor, still wailing loudly. He rolled onto the bed, hugging his beloved wife and daughter tighter and tighter, promising Jesus and himself he would never, ever leave them again.

Jude had never, ever in his whole life felt so much of God's peace and love fill his heart as he did at that very moment.

(And all the Congregation said…"AMEN!")

THE END

One final diatribe and then the author will clam up…

A "big hefty shout out", "applause", and "a pat on the back" to the fathers/husbands out there who put in 100% percent of their very own lives each and every single day for the good of their wives and children, even despite a society that is stacked against them. The biggest and worst social crisis we have in America today is **FATHERLESSNESS.** A single mother is not equipped to raise her son to be a man. It requires another man, preferably the boy's father, to do that critical job. The camel's back is already broken in America on this issue, but by God's Grace and His Power it is not too late for some real substantive change to happen which will right this moral wrong. *In addition, it is far past the time for our political, economic, and (many) clergy leaders to stop being passive about this horrific and debasing problem destroying young boys and thus America from within.* The clear evidence? America's prisons are full of fatherless young men and women. Who is shooting up schools, playgrounds, and theaters? Not alpha males who were raised by real men.

One has only to turn on the television to see a sit-com or commercial portray what society, advertising agencies, and Hollywood think of fathers: we are stupid, idiotic, bumbling fools who need "a smart woman" to catch us before we fall any further down the rat hole. This is beyond absurd and abysmal - It is a callous detriment to Godly manhood, and places women in a role they were never meant to have.

Men, take a stand! If not for yourselves, then do it for your progeny.

About the Author

Michael William Newman is a car aficionado who lost his prized Racing Green '63 Jaguar E-Type on an all-in failed spade flush. Sadly, he now drives a faded blue '98 Toyota Rav4 with bad brakes and no rearview mirror. But who needs to stop and know the past? Michael's life is now in its third chapter, which includes mixed martial arts training, writing for a purpose, and teaching the younger generations. He lives in Northern Virginia with his beautiful Peruvian wife and their two all-knowing teenage children.

Michael has written three other novels available on Amazon.

Cocktails In Paris
www.amazon.com/dp/B0791M9H52

Following Hemingway to Paris
www.amazon.com/dp/B0791LWJ8W

Captiva Daze
www.amazon.com/dp/B0090PSIEQ

Proceeds from Michael's previous novels support various children's charities. Sales of FLORIDA SUNBURN benefit the non-profit **I Support The Girls**. You can read about the excellent, life-changing work Dana Marlowe and this organization are doing to meet the basic hygiene needs for impoverished women and teenage girls around the world on the website www.ISupportTheGirls.org. Thank you for being a part of this good cause by promoting the organization and reading this book.

Made in the USA
Middletown, DE
22 September 2019